Indi Raye
IS TOTALLY
FAKING IT

HODDER CHILDREN'S BOOKS

First published in Great Britain in 2023 by Hodder & Stoughton

1 3 5 7 9 10 8 6 4 2

A CIP catalogue record for this book
is available from the British Library.

ISBN 978 1 444 95972 7

Typeset in Gothic720 BT by Jouve (UK), Milton Keynes
Printed and bound in Great Britain by Clays Ltd, Elcograf S.p.A.

The paper and board used in this book
are made from wood from responsible sources.

MIX
Paper from
responsible sources
FSC www.fsc.org   FSC® C104740

Hodder Children's Books
An imprint of
Hachette Children's Group
Part of Hodder & Stoughton Limited
Carmelite House
50 Victoria Embankment
London EC4Y 0DZ

An Hachette UK Company
www.hachette.co.uk

www.hachettechildrens.co.uk

For the girls who make me laugh
so hard I require my asthma inhaler.

CHAPTER 1

NO PHONE, NO LOO ROLL AND ZERO BOOBS...

SUNDAY SEPT 6th
7.06 p.m.

Just had a thought. I'm fourteen years old soon, right? Which means I *should* start looking like a model from the front cover of *Vogue* magazine any day now. That's what happens when you hit puberty. One minute you're a puffy little cygnet and the next minute, BANG! You're a sassy swan, with loads of mates and heaps of boyfriends and a menagerie of bras.

The bathroom light flickers – it's on the blink *again* – and the black-and-white vinyl floor is soaked; turns out I did a bit more sloshing about in my bubble bath than previously planned. I use my hand to wipe the condensation off the bathroom mirror to get a good look at my butt-naked body. Door's locked, I checked. Wouldn't want Tubs walking in.

Hmm. Not quite a sassy swan. More like a pudgy pigeon.

1

Quite like my pudge though. It keeps me warm in the winter and would probably help me float if I ever found myself overboard at sea.

My ears are on the large side. Once, a random man in the street said, 'You'd better be careful in this wind – with lugs like that, you might take off!' which was rude but also probably true, sadly.

Flat-chested, obviously. I have not been blessed in that department yet. But my hair is super luscious and long, so although I haven't got boobs (so far), I have been blessed with locks of a goddess to compensate.

I sigh and pull on my PJs (the ones with the rather demonic-looking cartoon pugs all over them) before moseying down the hallway into the living room and perching on the arm of the olive-green sofa.

'Tubs? Can I have a fiver, please?'

'Hmm?' she replies, not even taking her eyes off the TV. She's rewatching an old episode of *Strictly Come Dancing*. She's got about a million of them recorded on the telly. She's been gushing over a man in red spandex all evening. Hideous.

Tubs is my mum, but I don't call her 'Mum', I call her 'Tubs'. It's what my dad always called her and it stuck. It was affectionate. I think? Anyway. Tubs loves *Strictly*. Sometimes I think she loves it more than she loves me.

I'd rather listen to music any day of the week. We're kinda opposites, me and Tubs. She's fair with ruddy cheeks. A bit squat. Scruffy shoulder-length hair, which she says is blonde but let's be honest, she's going grey. Whereas I've got tanned skin, long dark hair and big brown eyes. From my dad's side. I love cheese but she can't stand it. She believes in God, but I believe in horoscopes (I'm a Sagittarius). I'm not very fashionable but she *loves* getting all dressed up.

I mean, she's not dressed up now: she's bundled up in her grey dressing gown, like a big ol' badger, transfixed by the telly.

'I said, "Mummyyyyyy, could I have a fiver, please?"'

'What d'you want it for?' she asks, monotone, still dribbling over the spandex man, who now appears to be shimmying down the camera lens, whilst winking.

'Errr . . . ham?' I lie.

'Indi, there's ham in the fridge,' she says, wafting me away with her hand like I'm a fly.

'OK, listen: I was thinking . . . the loo roll we've got, it's a bit . . . you know . . . scratchy and I thought, "Oooh, do you know what Tubs would love on her bum, she would absolut—"'

'Indiana Raye . . .'

Uh oh. Full name. Time to cut to the chase.

'I'M STARTING MY NEW SCHOOL TOMORROW AND I NEED TO STUFF MY BRA WITH TOILET ROLL SO IT LOOKS LIKE I'VE GOT BIG BOOBS.'

Tubs reaches for the remote on the coffee table and turns the TV up, which is her way of saying the conversation is over.

7.10 p.m.

Urgh, stupid Tubs. Feel proper deflated. Much like my chest. I trudge back along the hallway to my room and flop on to my bed, staring at the cracks in my ceiling. Can hear the people in the flat above arguing over the thudding bassline of some hideous dance music, and there's a car alarm going off outside – neither of which is particularly soothing.

We only moved to Manchester a few weeks back. Tubs's hometown. We had to swap our perfectly decent London house for this tiny little flat, a couple of miles outside the city centre, overlooking a busy road with a big ASDA and a petrol station on it.

It's on the eleventh floor and, at first, I thought it might be fun to live high up but it turns out it gives me full-on vertigo when I look out of my window. The lift up here shudders like a bloody earthquake too, and I CANNOT deal, so I have to climb eleven flights of

4

stairs every day. It's like scaling Mount Everest – I'm bloody knackered!

A woman I've tenderly named 'Hawkeye' lives on the first floor of our block, right next to the stairwell. She watches that staircase like a hawk (hence the nickname) and hangs out of the window questioning the identity of potential intruders into the building. She's a bit like Gandalf in *The Lord of the Rings* when he yells, 'WIZARD, YOU CAN'T COME INNNNNNNNNNN!' or whatever.

Hawkeye has a cat with three legs. He was a victim of a terrible hit-and-run accident so she keeps him inside her flat to keep him safe. But the other day he escaped and I found him hopping around by the bins.

'Hello, Hawkeye . . . I mean . . . erm . . . Mrs Malone. Found your cat!' I beamed, holding out the cat in front of me, on her doorstep. My arms were covered in scratches 'cause it didn't like being picked up . . . 'No need to thank me. Maybe just give me, like, a tenner or something for me troubles and I'll be on my way!'

'Oh my! How on earth did yer get out, Mr Biggles? Oh thank you, Indiana! Now, I haven't got any money for yer, love, but I haaaave gooooot . . .' she said, throwing Mr Biggles inside and reaching for her purse, '. . . this! It's all yours.'

She smiled, showing all her crooked teeth, pressed a chocolate eclair into my hand and closed the door on me. The chocolate eclair had no wrapper and it was sticky, like perhaps Hawky had already sucked on it.

Brilliant. Last time I do a favour for anyone round here.

Anyway, Number 64 is our new abode and I think it's fair to say it's proper hideous. It's full of old carpets, deep crimson red in colour with a gaudy floral design, and ancient curtains that have never been washed. Even the smell is old, like centuries of dust and shed skin.

Why did 'yester-year' smell so bad? I suppose Febreze wasn't invented then, was it?

Everything's shabby and Tubs has been fixing dodgy lights and leaky sinks since we moved in. It's also small. I'm never more than six feet away from Tubs, which . . . actually, isn't that the same thing they say about rats?

My bedroom has thick *peach* wallpaper. It's the type that's so thick, I have this constant urge to run my hand over it to find an edge and peel it off. I've been doing loads of artwork to cover the damp patches on the walls, mainly of my very own cartoon character Disco Girl. She loves music and wears sequin leggings and roller-skates and launches disco balls at her enemies and has lasers that she can shoot out of her fingers. Hoping to turn her into a full comic one day. I'll also need to save some space on the walls for Polaroid photos of me and my new friends from school. If I ever manage to get any, that is. A few fairy lights might be nice too. I'll do a bedroom makeover in the next few weeks and the centrepiece will be Dad's old record player. It's ancient, like, from medieval times or something! You have to lift the lid of the player and slide the record out of its sleeve and slot it on *really gently* so you don't scratch it, and then lower the needle down on it really delicately. To be honest it's a bit of a faff, but it'll do until I can get a phone with Spotify on it.

He's a right laugh, my dad. He's called Paul. I don't think he's ever told me off once in my entire life. Unlike Tubs, who tells me off ALL the time. He's quite handsome too. I'm not saying that in, like, a weird way or anything, it's just a fact: he's tall with brown skin and jet-black floppy hair and a charismatically wonky nose. My dad always wears old vintage jeans and baggy T-shirts, but he makes them look cool.

Once, this old lady on the street said to my Dad, 'Oooh you look just like James Bond' and he replied to say *she* looked like Beyoncé (even though she was about ninety and looked like she'd had about three hip replacements). She almost laughed herself into the grave.

That's the thing, though – Dad could charm the pants off everyone he met . . . and I mean that *literally*. Apparently Tubs caught him with another lady in London a little while back. It's probs just one huge misunderstanding, they'll probs get back together any day now, but for now, Tubs and Dad are officially broken up. If I had a mobile phone, I could just send him a WhatsApp and be like:

> heyyyyyyyyyyy dad you
> coming home soon?

And he'd probably be like:

> ye just dealing with some stuff
> here see you at weekend xx

And it would be all sorted. But Tubs is being sooooo annoying and won't get me a phone. I'm literally the only thirteen-year-old in the world who hasn't got one. Or Nikes. Or the popcorn maker I want for my room OR Marc Jacobs perfume. *No phone, no loo roll and zero boobs. Honestly, what is the bloody point . . .*

Tubs has got an interview for a job tomorrow and they'd better hire her 'cause it's like living in the bloody 1940s at the minute.

10.24 p.m.
Can't sleep.

10.27 p.m.
I'm nervous.

10.33 p.m.
St Catherine's Secondary School's uniform is monstrous: a grey, pleated skirt, white blouse, green jumper, itchy grey blazer and *long grey socks* which are *actually* mandatory. Like, if you forget your long socks and put some short ones on instead, they will ACTUALLY send you home, according to the brochure.

Tubs says it's because if you show off too much knee, the boys will think it's too sexy and it'll put them off their trigonometry, which has got to be the *stupidest* thing I have ever heard. There's no way my knees are putting anyone off anything; in fact, if you look at them closely, my left one looks like it's got the face of Hitler in it. Which, actually, *would help* the boys with their history so it's beneficial if anything.

10.55 p.m.

Oh god, what if everyone hates me tomorrow? What if I don't know what to say!? What do people talk about? TikTokers? Crisps?? How strong the Pound is against the Indian Rupee!? Maybe I should try walking with a cool walk? A bit of swag. Yeah, I can do swag, that'll impress people. URGH, WHAT EVEN IS SWAG? WHAT AM I TALKING ABOUT? OH MY GOD I NEED TO BREATHE.

11.01 p.m.

See, *this* is why people become religious. Tubs is perpetually disappointed that I'm not as Jesus-loving as she is, but from time to time, in moments of great peril, I like to pop my head in.

Dear God,
If you are listening, PLEASE let me make some friends tomorrow.
Just a small group of friends.
OK, just ONE friend, that's all I ask!
If you can do this for me, I swear I'll pray even more 'cause it would prove that you are listening and therefore real.
Oh, and don't forget about my ongoing request for boobs. Can I say 'boobs' in front of you? Nipples? Do

YOU have nipples? . . . no, that's weird.

Sorry if I'm asking for too much, but it's super important.

Many thanks.

Amen.

CHAPTER 2

THE ONLY FRIEND I MADE TODAY HAS SCALES

MONDAY SEPT 7ᵗʰ

8.17 a.m.

'INDIANA! YOU'RE GOING TO BE LAAAAAAATE!'

I sit bolt upright like I've been electrocuted.

'WHAT TIME IS IT?' I call, bleary-eyed and croaky-throated.

'Comin' up to twenty past eight . . .' Tubs hollers back.

BLOODY HELL, TWO HOURS LATER THAN PLANNED!

'THAT IS TWO HOURS LATER THAN PLANNED!' I scream, hurtling out of bed and pulling on my stiff grey uniform, stopping to do a cursory wetwipe of the armpits.

Oh god, the bus will be leaving in twenty-five minutes!

I run to the bathroom. 'Why-di'n'-'ou-gimme-a-shou-!?' I slur, trying to brush my teeth, stuff my left foot into my non-Nike shoe (which is defo too small for me, by the way) and scold Tubs all at the same time.

'Y'what?' she asks from the sofa in the living room, where she is casually eating toast, riffling through the post or some bills or something, without a care in the bloody world!

I spit my toothpaste out in the sink. 'I said, "Why didn't you give me a shout!?"'

'Indi,' she says, 'you really are gonna have to start being more responsible for yerself now that yer father's not here, and—'

I interject immediately and say, 'ERRRRM, there's a funny smell coming up from the bathroom sink, we might need a plumber!' before running off to grab my sandwich from the kitchen counter.

Truth is, there *isn't* a funny smell coming from the bathroom sink. But I've worked out something *phenomenal*. When Tubs starts talking about Dad and I get all awks about it, I whack out a lie.

A small lie.

A big lie.

It doesn't matter. *Anything* to distract her.

She'll be like, *'Blah blah blah, Dad this, Dad that,'* and I'll be like, 'WOAH, TUBS, DID YOU JUST SEE THAT MASSIVE RAT?' or 'OH NO, TUBS,

I THINK MY HAIR'S FALLING OUT!' and she'll immediately stop talking about Dad and tell me to stop being silly. It works! I'm a genius. An evil genius . . .

'Good luck for your interview today!' I call, legging it out for the bus, then heading back in to grab a loo roll, before slamming the door.

8.46 a.m.
This school bus is massively giving me the ick. The body heat and morning breath of its passengers hits the cold of the windows and creates steaming condensation.

Bleurgh, window sweat. Mustn't touch it.

I can see dust and *all-sorts-of-god-knows-what* lurking down the gaps between the seats. It smells like body odour and Lynx Africa.

Sitting right at the front. Didn't want to walk the length of the bus with everyone looking at me wondering *who's the new girl* . . .

And, actually, with everyone seated behind me, I can start to subtly push a few sheets of my stolen toilet paper down my bra.

Gotta be careful, don't wanna get caught.

I stuff away, observing my new schoolmates.

There's a small group of kids behind me chatting about *Minecraft* and *World of Warcraft* to an extreme degree of detail and wearing their school uniform all proper. A bit further back, a few girls are gossiping about their weekends and two of them are sharing headphones: I can hear a tinny rap song bleeding out.

Must listen to more rap. No way these lot will know who Radiohead are . . .

Then I twist round to sneak a peek at the back of the bus: a couple are already necking on with each other, a boy with extra floppy hair is vaping, and one of the hockey girls is showing off a tattoo that – if it's actually real – she's *defo* too young to have. It's all a bit too 18+ back there for a Monday morning. Think I'll pass trying to make friends with that lot.

Just then a pretty brunette girl teeters downstairs from the top deck holding on to the rail with one hand as the bus swerves round the corner, a hockey stick in the other. A group of girls shout, 'Oh my god, Ameliaaaaaaa' and they hug and air kiss like they haven't seen each other in ten years. *She*'s wearing Nikes. Two of the girls are flirting with a boy they call Harry, one of them starts painting his nails neon green and a few older lads have started wrestling.

My heart suddenly starts beating harder in my chest and I have to steady myself with a few low-key deep breaths.

It's fine. It's all gonna be fine. This is all totally normal and you are equally as normal. We're all just a big bunch of normal people. Apart from that one boy over there who appears to be licking the seats. That is abnormal and someone should probs have a word with him about that . . .

I look down at my chest to check the bra-stuffing progress.

OH WELL, THIS IS JUST GREAT.

No matter how much I ball up the bog roll in various different ways, pushing it down, scrunching it up, trying to make it look as boob-like as possible . . . one boob looks all pointy like a Mr Whippy ice cream, and the other looks all sad and droopy, like a golf ball in a sock.

Not my greatest work.

9 a.m.

I ting a little retro brass bell at the school reception desk and I'm greeted by a bespectacled receptionist called Miss McGregor, who signs me in. She has these *massive*, cuddly boobs – I reckon she's at least a 38F from where I'm standing, and in my panicked state, I want to clutch on to them and for her to tell me *It's all gonna be OK*.

'. . . so you'll do form, then art, science, THEN you get your lunchbreak – canteen is just down there, look, on the right – maths this afternoon, then geography, then it's home time!'

I look up to her with pleading eyes that must give away the internal breakdown I'm having.

'You'll be fine, Indiana . . .' she says, in the way you might to someone going for a dip in shark-infested waters or, y'know, going to war or something. I notice she has a pencil peeking out of her top pocket, perched on those 38Fs.

'Hey, Indi!' it seems to say.

'Oh hey, Pencil!' I reply (in my head, obvs. I'm not totally insane).

'Listen, girl, this school situation is soooooooo sad. Why don't you just say you're scared of guys like me? I mean, we're literally everywhere. It would be practically abusive to make you stay in a school full of scary, SHARP HB pencils, wouldn't it?'

'I HAVE A PHOBIA OF PENCILS, MISS!!!' I blurt out.

She looks surprised before peering at me over her glasses and saying, 'Well, Indiana, lucky for you, we mostly use laptops and biros round here and I'd ask that if you *do* happen to come across a pencil, you just refrain from touching it and – oh look, here's your form tutor *and* he's pencil-less, would you believe! Good luck now!'

She toddles off down the hallway, leaving me with Mr Frederick. Mid-forties, *stinks* of stale smoke and has a few rogue black teeth. I can smell his breath from a mile away!

He ushers me into the classroom with a proper over-the-top bow, a flourish of his hand and a greeting of 'Welcome, welcome . . .' which makes me feel proper uneasy 'cause I feel like bloody Othello entering the stage for the first time, when I *really* want to keep my head down.

'Everyone, please can we welcome *INDI-AAAHHHHNA* to our form group.'

Mr Frederick puts way too much (incorrect) emphasis on the last bit of my name and sprays the front three rows of desks with spittle. A few of the girls deep-dive under their blazers for fresher air.

People often pronounce my name wrong 'cause of my dark hair and tan skin; they think I must be from some distant, exotic country. I was born in Croydon, for goodness' sake.

'It's just Indiana, actually.'

'*Indiaaahhhna*,' he tries again, gassing a few more students.

'No, not *Indi-ah-na* . . . just, Indiana.'

'*Indiaaaahna*.'

'INDI. ANNA. Imagine it's like two names.'

'*INDIAAAAAAAAAAAAAAAAAAHNA* . . .'

'Never mind,' I say quickly, before I physically gip all over the classroom. Nobody needs *that* on their first day of school.

1.04 p.m.

Sitting in the proper furthest corner of the noisy canteen, on a table all on my own, eating my cheese sandwiches. No butter. Cheese is the only thing that makes me feel better when life is so ridiculously hideous. Doodling some hearts and stars on the corner of my new school diary to make it look like I'm busy.

Will probs give myself a heart attack from all the cheese I eat, but to be fair, death-by-cheddar doesn't sound all that bad seeing as my life is ruined anyway.

What kind of parent drags their child to a brand-new city and school where I have nil friends? Tubs, that's who. It's an abuse of power. I should report her to the social services for this.

1.07 p.m.

A group of girls sashay in wearing their hockey kits. No scratchy blazers and buttoned-up shirts for them; they look soooooooo on point in tight, green polyester T-shirts pulled across their ample bosoms, socks pulled up high and pleated skirts showing off their long legs. One of the girls has fake-tanned so much, her thighs look like bronzed, basted Christmas turkeys.

'Oh my G, look who's here!' whispers a girl on the table next to me, eating a tuna and cheese toastie. She's got the cutest button nose and pearly blonde hair tied up with a lilac satin scrunchie, and, by the looks of things, the perfect 32C bust. I can see a glimpse of her bright pink bra through a gap in her shirt. *God, am I a pervert!?* Anyway. Her eyes zone in on the hockey girls, analysing the action and she says, 'Do you think they'll come and sit near us?'

'Urgh, I hope not,' quips the second girl, rolling her eyes.

The blonde girl laughs. 'Er, but seriously, shouldn't you be in your kit too, Nisha?'

Nisha is tall and built like a tank and she looks even tougher by the way she wears her school shirt buttoned right up to the collar. Her skin is a deep warm brown and she wears a big plait full of jet-black, shiny hair.

'Er, no? Miss Reynolds is always like, "*Girls! Get changed at lunch, I want you ready for when the Kingston Academy team arrive!*" But it *literally* takes two minutes. *That lot* just uses it as an excuse to parade around in their kit at lunchtime, ennit.'

'If I was on the hockey team, I'd defo be parading around,' the blonde girl replies, biting on her crusts wistfully.

'Yeah, well, no offence, Grace, but you're never gonna *be* on the hockey team because a jellyfish could run on land faster than you.'

Grace pushes her on the arm. 'Aw, shut up! How unreal does Megan look, though . . .?'

I don't know which one Megan is. It could be any of them, because they literally ALL look like Pretty Little Thing models. They're loud and giggly and their eyes scan the canteen to see who's noticed their arrival. Scanning like robotic goddesses sent from another planet. A pack of boys has started to surround them, drooling like golden retrievers.

Ugh. Must be great being the hockey team. A gang of friends handed to you on a plate. Immediate popularity. They're literally winning at life.

Meanwhile things are looking proper bleak for Indi Raye. No one's even said hello to me yet, not even a measly dinner lady! I briefly consider introducing myself to this Nisha and Grace but GOD, UGH, NO that'd be soooooo embarrassing! It'd be like:

'Oh hewwo, I'm Indi. I'm new here. Why yes, I do eat cheese sandwiches. I love cheese. Will you be my fwend?'

I'm not being dramatic, but I think I'd actually rather DIE IN A HOLE.

2.04 p.m.
Oh great. They've put me in the *second set for maths*. I feel like I'm sitting in the same room as Albert Einstein and that lady from *Countdown* right now.

This is the problem with starting new schools: the teachers don't actually *know* how smart you are, so they just guess! What a stupid idea. It's especially difficult when you're a bit, y'know . . . *academically challenged* like me. Did home-schooling for a bit once. Tubs taught me some maths and science and stuff but, it turns out, she's rubbish at it as well. We ended up just doing drawing or, y'know, watched *Loose Women* and when I said we needed to do pi, we actually just baked A PIE. Now I'm faced with a hideous sprawl of numbers and symbols and equations and EVERYONE ELSE seems to know the answers.

The problem in the textbook stares up at me:

Cindy is thinking of a secret number. She tells her brother that it is divisible by 2 and tells her friend that it is divisible by 11. If Cindy is telling the truth to both of them, what is the smallest secret number that Cindy could be thinking of?

Straight away I'm thinking Cindy sounds like a right divhead so I just write down the number 8 and hope for the best . . .

'How are you getting on, Indiana?' asks Mr Basi, in a slightly haunting voice, looming over me like Dracula.

'Ah, yeah, totally fine, thanks. Smashin' it,' I whisper back with fake gusto, covering up my textbook with one hand so he can't see all my wrong answers and giving him a thumbs up with the other.

'I just loooooooove Oasis so much,' I overhear someone say from behind me.

Oh my god. Someone who loves Oasis? I love Oasis!? Mine and Dad's favourite band in the world. Noel and Liam are rock gods. They're brothers, who wrote the best songs in the universe all the way back in the 90s and then they had this massive falling out and the band split up but their music lives on forever.

I turn round and it's that Amelia; you know, the one from the bus, with the hockey stick? TIME TO MAKE SOME FRIENDS.

'I love Oasis too. What's your favourite album, *(What's the Story) Morning Glory* or *Definitely Maybe?*' I ask, grinning ear to ear.

Amelia looks at me blankly and whispers to her friend next to her, 'Jasmine, who is this girl and what's she on about?'

Jasmine sniggers. 'What?' she asks me, chewing on gum.

Why are they looking at me like I'm insane?

'I was saying, what's your favourite Oasis record?'

Jasmine scowls at me, messing up her pretty face, and swivels a plastic drinks bottle round towards me so I can see the label.

Ah. Oasis. The drink. The Summer Fruits one. Should have known.

Amelia waves goodbye at me, her indication for me to turn back around and sink into my chair, my face feeling like it's LITERALLY ON FIRE FROM EMBARRASSMENT.

I think we can all agree it would be best you keep your nerdy little interests to yourself from now on, Indi Raye.

2.51 p.m.

Mrs Ibrahim is going on about tectonic plates when someone on my left taps me on the shoulder. I jump out of my skin, terrified it's Amelia and Jasmine ready to tease me again for my lack of soft beverage knowledge but instead . . .

OH MY GOD, IT'S A BOY.

An ACTUAL boy, a freckly boy!

Oh god, not ready for male interaction!

'Pass it on!' hisses Freckly Boy, handing me a note and pointing at a girl ahead with red hair, near the window.

I unfold the crumpled piece of paper and it reads:

> alice welby has ginger pubes

Immediately feel bad for Alice Welby's pubes. But I guess she *DOES* have red hair and therefore, she probs DOES have ginger pubes. But still, this is a geography lesson – if anything we should be sending notes around about arable farming, not Alice Welby's lady parts.

Nevertheless, I tap the shoulder of a boy who must be called Kwame (that's the name doodled all over his pencil case anyway) who's sitting in front of me. He looks around and reaches his hand behind his back covertly. I lean forward and stuff the note into his palm before Mrs Ibrahim catches me.

Well, I couldn't NOT pass it on, could I!? Freckly Boy would think I was proper basic if I didn't join in!

And, wowzers, what an adrenaline rush! I feel ALIVE! Disobeying school rules on Day One, baby! I am now officially <u>a bad B</u>. Gonna start riding a motorbike and get tattoos of skulls and commit some serious crimes.

2.56 p.m.
(Was just joking about doing crimes. Please don't report me to the police.)

3.41 p.m.
Walking out through the playground and there's something kicking off over near the bike sheds. A gaggle of students gather around looking at something I can't quite see. I'm about to walk past and not get myself involved but I notice that Freckly Boy is at the centre of the commotion. He's got something in his backpack and everyone's craning their necks to see what it is.

'. . . so, basically, make ya offers, ladies and gents, highest bid wins, we'll start at ten pounds. Ten pounds anyone, for this *liddle beaudy*?'

A boy laughs and puts his arm around one of the hockey girls from earlier. 'Charlie, bro, you are havin' a laugh if think I'm payin' a tenner for a freakin' . . . like . . . dinosaur, man.'

'OK . . . nine pounds then. Anyone for nine pounds?' Charlie shouts. He spots me trying to sneak a peek. 'Oi, you, Stupid New Girl . . .'

'That's defo not my name, it's Indi.'

He throws a glance over my shoulder to check there's no teachers coming, tilts the backpack towards me, and inside . . . is a lizard.

'You wan' it, Indi? G'waannnn, take him, I'll give yer a good price!'

'Erm, why have you got a lizard in your bag?' I gasp.

Charlie thrusts his backpack towards me, with a grin. 'Found it!'

'You can't just stick a lizard in a backpack! It's mean!'

'Ten pounds and he's all yours, darlin'!'

'Bleurgh, no, it's gross! AND I just heard you offering it for nine pounds so . . .'

'OK, NINE POUNDS THEN.'

Let me tell you, this thing is mad, right! It's all yellow and black and scaly and it's got, like, eyes on the side of its head! *I can't buy a lizard . . .*

. . . can I?

OK, woah.

Bear with me here a second.

Here's what I'm thinking, right . . .

If everyone around school hears that I rescued a rare lizard, they'll be like, 'Wowzers, is she related to

Attenborough? She is SO cool AND environmentally friendly!' And then everyone will wanna be my mate!

'*Buy me!*' squeaks the lizard. (I told you, things talk to me!)

'Actually,' I say quickly, reaching into my backpack pocket for some cash. 'I've changed my mind. I love lizards. I'll give you a fiver for it.'

'FIVE POUNDS, LADIES AND GENTLEMEN! FIVE POUNDS FROM THE STUPID NEW GIRL. GOING ONCE . . .'

Uh oh . . .

'. . . GOING TWICE . . .'

He took five pounds without even bargaining, what a terrible businessman. Alan Sugar would totally fire Charlie if he was on The Apprentice.

'SOLD! Here you go!' He snatches the fiver from my hand, thrusts the tiny speckled reptile at me and runs off. Now that the spectacle of the auction is over, everyone drifts off home for the evening.

What am I doing? I am alone in the playground with a lizard for company! I stare down at his little scaly face and wonder where the hell to put him.

'Sorry, little guy . . .' I wince, tucking him down my school shirt. It'll be nice and warm for him in my bra – plenty of sweaty toilet roll for him to nestle down into. 'Let's get you back to Number 64.'

TUBS IS GONNA KILL ME!

3.51 p.m.
OMG, DO LIZARDS HAVE TEETH!?

4.14 p.m.
Missed the school bus! Had to wander the streets with a lizard scurrying round my top trying to find the number 201 bus, which I know stops outside the big ASDA near ours. Nightmare. BUT a boy just got on board. He's older, proper unreal and he's staring STRAIGHT AT ME. He looks like Harry Styles, if Harry Styles worked at B&Q. His name badge says 'Alex' and let me tell you, Alex can't keep his EYES off me!

4.16 p.m.
Have decided to give him Frisky Eyes. Frisky Eyes is when you're all lusty for someone so you flutter your eyelashes at them so they know how single you are. You must flutter them properly though, 'cause if you do it too fast, it looks like a bug has flown into your eyeballs and you're trying to blink it out before it lays eggs in there.

4.17 p.m.
No reaction. Weird?

4.18 p.m.
Ah. Turns out he was staring because my lizard was hanging out.

5.32 p.m.
Nicked Tubs's best saucepan as a temporary home for my new pet. Just gotta hope she doesn't need it for tonight's dinner. It was the only thing I could find. I perch on my bed and pop the lid on, slightly askew so my lizard friend can breathe. Hope I don't kill it on its first night. Have decided I won't tell Tubs about our new 'house guest' 'cause I'm not sure she'll be too thrilled that the only friend I made today has scales . . .

5.47 p.m.
'INDI!!!!!'

Most people's mums just say 'Hello!' or 'I'm home!' when they come through the front door. Mine screams, which I think is her way of keeping me on high alert. It's proper not good for my nerves.

'Yeah?' I yell back hurriedly, closing my door from the inside so she can't see my reptile.

'How was yer first day?' she calls, hanging up her coat.

I shout through the crack in my door and push the saucepan under my bed with my foot in case she comes in. 'Hated it. Don't wanna go back.'

She tuts. 'Don't be ridiculous. I bet yer were great! Anyway, d'you want some good news? I've got yer a Saturday job!'

WHAT!?

'Er, what?' I say, opening my door and scooting after her into the living room.

Tubs sits on the sofa, unzips her boots and pulls them off. 'Well, on me way back from me interview, I popped into a few local shops and found you a *great* deal. Pay ain't bad, y'know – they offer minimum wage for someone your age, but you get regular breaks AND . . . they do yer lunch for yer! And it'll keep yer busy while I'm at work. Don't want yer getting bored, do we?'

'Where is it?'

'. . . I mean, you'll have to wear the hairnet, of course, 'cause that's just health and safety. Don't want you going up in flames, do we? Alan *did say* you're not supposed to be near the cooker at your age, although I did mention to him that getting a few lessons would be good for yer . . .'

'Who's Alan?'

I follow her into the kitchen as she rattles on, '. . . because *then* you could start makin' us tea in't evenin'! And we'll have a bit more money coming in and – oh! On top of the hairnet goes these little hats and they do actually look proper cute and—'

'TUBS, WHAT HAVE YOU SIGNED ME UP TO?'

'. . . The Jolly Fryer. Chippy, just round the corner, every Saturday,' she says, switching on the kettle and avoiding eye contact with me.

A CHIP SHOP!?!????

'JESUS CHRIST!' I roar.

'I BEG YER PARDON!?' Tubs roars back.

'Sorry! And sorry to you too, Jesus,' I say quickly. Tubs always makes me say sorry for being blasphemous. 'But no, Tubs, I'm NOT working in a chip shop. It's a violation of my human rights. Surely this goes against your Christian values!? Besides, I'm busy.'

Tubs pours hot water into two mugs. 'Busy? Doin' what? What yer doing every Saturday, Indiana?'

'Dog shelter,' I lie.

'You hate dogs.'

'I meant CAT SHELTER.'

'You're allergic to them!'

'ARGH!'

Tubs rolls her eyes and passes me my tea as a peace offering. 'Yer first shift starts next Saturday.'

Here's the thing with mums. You can't negotiate with terrorists.

11 p.m.

Can't sleep (again). Listening to The Smiths. They've got a song called 'Heaven Knows I'm Miserable Now' which is fitting, because this chip shop thing is probably gonna be the end of my life as I know it. Making a pros and cons list in my new art sketchbook.

PROS

✓ I'll be able to make some pocket money, which means I can buy my own stuff, like the boob toilet roll and Nike Air Force 1s. And a ticket to Glastonbury. The dream.

✓ Free chippy teas.

✓ I do look bloody good in an apron.

CONS

✗ The smell of fish and chip grease will seep into my hair and my skin and my bones, meaning no boy will ever fancy me and I will die alone.

Hmm, tough one. I guess it *would* help Tubs out. Over dinner, she was telling me that the job interview she had was for a cleaner at the hospital. She's always been a cleaner, Tubs. Back in London she used to clean rich people's houses, vacuuming their Persian rugs and wiping their gold statues down and polishing their corgis and stuff. Sometimes she'd be out of the house for, like, fourteen hours, and I'd always think, *Wowzers, she works loads, so we must be WELL rich!* but recently I've started to think that maybe cleaners don't get paid that much after all 'cause Tubs seems way more worried about money now than when Dad was about.

Suppose if I work at the chippy, I can give Tubs a few quid on pay day. Yeah! That would be a nice idea.

God, I am *such* a good daughter. It's a good job Tubs never had any other children because they would be second best to this angel.

CHAPTER 3

A COUPLE OF CHEEKY MEERSCHWEINCHENS

TUESDAY SEPT 8th
7.03 a.m.

'MAY THE LORD HAVE MERCY ON US ALL, GET OUT, GET OUT!'

I leap out of my warm cosy bed and fling my door open wide. There she is. My mother, the apple of my eye, screaming the entire block of flats down like a banshee. I read that word in a dictionary once. It means 'a wailing elderly female spirit'. And I hate to call Tubs a banshee, but let's be honest, she is wailing . . . and elderly.

'What's wrong?' I yell, although glancing over to the saucepan, which now has its lid ajar, I immediately know the answer . . .

'SNAKE!' she screams, using our broom to sweep my new pet lizard down the communal stairwell. 'A SNAKE, IN A BLOODY ELEVENTH-FLOOR FLAT. OH LORD, SAVE US FROM THIS EVIL SERPENT! BE GONE!'

'Noooo, Tubs, leave him alone!' I yell, quickly running over and scooping up my little baby, letting him nestle into my PJ top.

'Indiana, why is there a snake in my flat!?' she asks, horrified, wrapping her dressing gown tighter around her and visibly quivering.

'Tubs, it's not a snake,' I laugh. 'It's a lizard . . . I think . . .'

'OH MAY THE LORD HELP US!' she cries, like she's performing some sort of exorcism.

'I've sort of . . . adopted him? DON'T WORRY, I'm getting him a cage or a tank or a . . . fishpond, I dunno. I'll sort it this afternoon.'

Tubs doesn't hear that last bit because she's launched into a frantic version of The Lord's Prayer whilst crossing herself.

UGH. Got too much on my plate right now for Tubs's hysterics. Gotta sort a new home for this lizard, prepare for my impending employment, find a way to get in contact with Dad, get some better loo roll for bra-stuffing and figure out how to be an all-round better human so I can attract some friends. It's hard work being this hectic.

'. . . so bearing that in mind, I won't be going into school today, Tubs, apols.'

'Yes, you are.'

'No, I'm not.'

'YES, you are, because I got the hospital job and I start in . . . oh balls, in less than an hour . . .'

'Well, that is great news, but also YOU CAN'T MAKE ME GO TO SCHOOL!' I shout.

'Oh yes I can, 'cause I'm yer mother!' she shouts back. 'And if that snake isn't in a cage by the time I get back, I'm calling pest control!'

One–nil Tubs.

8.46 a.m.
Bus driver is a PSYCHOPATH. Proper late today, legging it down the road and it thunders past me, spraying puddle juice across my feet. BLEURGH! Right as I'm about to jump aboard, I catch him pressing the 'CLOSE DOOR' button. I manage to leap inside JUST before the doors slam shut.

'Did you try to close the doors on me just then?' I pant, accusingly.

'Yes,' he replies deadpan, without blinking.

'Even though you could SEE I was running to catch up?'

'Yes,' he says again, still without blinking.

Outrageous. Will be penning a strongly worded letter to Manchester Council at this rate.

8.49 a.m.

Today things are serious. Must. Make. A. Friend. Time to subtly give myself a toilet paper C-cup.

8.50 a.m.

'Hey, can I sit here?' says a boy's voice, just as I start pushing loo roll down my shirt. I quickly recoil and turn it into a stretch so he doesn't think I'm some kind of hideous weirdo.

NO MORE BUS-BRA-STUFFING FOR YOU, INDI RAYE.

'Er . . . you may,' I reply, fake yawning and realising I've never said the words 'you may' in my life until this moment. I reach into my bag and pull out my sketchpad and pencil and start drawing the bus driver . . . complete with devil horns poking out of the top of his head.

I feel the boy watching my pencil fly across the page and after a while he laughs out loud at my picture and says: 'Nice work! Accurate. Once he shut my whole foot in the door. Lost my shoe. He drove off before I could get it! Mum wasn't pleased. Hey, you're the girl who bought Charlie's lizard yesterday, aren't you?'

He smells good, like soap, and his dark skin is smooth apart from a few spots on his forehead.

'Er, yeah,' I reply.

'Cool.'

'Cool,' I reply, like a bloody echo. I don't know what to say next but he seems nice, so I pluck up ALL of my courage and say: 'I'm Indi, by the way.'

'Oh right, yeah, I'm Reece.' He puts his hand out for me to shake, which makes me feel about forty years old. I suspect he's in St Catherine's Debate Club and probs knows about stuff like politics.

He adjusts his thick-rimmed black glasses. 'So, second day, right? How are you finding it all?' he asks, sitting forward with a slight hunch.

'Yeah, it's great . . .' I say.

'Hmm . . . really?'

'I mean, to be honest, it's all a bit strange. We only moved recently—'

'Yeah, you don't sound like you're from round here,' he says.

'Yeah, I'm from London. It's just me and my mum at the moment, 'cause my dad . . . erm, well, he's a bit busy with work an' that . . . so we moved here, just us two . . .'

Oh god, what am I saying? It's like I've got verbal diarrhoea, why am I telling a complete stranger this stuff??

'. . . and, er, yeah, I just keep thinking, maybe, like, I don't really *need* school? Like, I'm thinking maybe I could go and save the dolphins one day, and you don't need maths and science to do that, surely?'

Reece laughs. 'Can you swim?

I nod.

'Well, that's a good start, I suppose.'

'How about you?' I ask.

'I want to be an A and E doctor.'

'What d'you say?' (This bus is really noisy: the lads at the back have started singing a Man U footie chant.)

'I said, I want to be an A and E doctor,' he repeats.

'Shut up, but what about all the blood and stuff?'

'Doesn't bother me. Quite like learning about spleens and that!'

'No offence, but that sounds like something a murderer would say!' I laugh, pushing my feet on the back of the chair in front of me.

Hmmm, in retrospect maybe I shouldn't be calling the first person to be friendly with me a killer . . .

'Ha, I'm just good at biology!' he replies.

He knows I'm joking. Phew.

'You're lucky. I don't know what I'm good at.' I shrug.

'Well, you must be good at something. You're good at drawing,' he says, nodding at my devilish bus driver sketch.

'Hmm? Yeah, s'pose. I'm currently working on a comic character called Disco Girl, hoping to turn her story into a graphic novel one day. And I'm good at catching stuff. Got proper good reflexes.

Can catch anything you throw at me: balls, eggs, babies—'

'Errrr, Disco Girl sounds cool . . . but catching babies!?'

'Yeah!' I laugh. 'I once caught my baby cousin after my Auntie Cassandra dropped her – she'd had too much wine – but I don't think there's a GCSE in catching babies, which is annoying.'

'Hmm, yeah. Dolphins it is then,' he says, smiling, and I smile back.

12.44 p.m.
Using the school computers at lunch. It's nice in this classroom; I've snuck in so I don't have to eat lunch alone or wander around the playground on my own. Munching on some crisps, which are leaving sticky prawn-cocktail dust all over my hands *and* the keyboard. I type with one finger:

DO YOU NEED SCHOOL TO WORK WITH
DOLPHINS?

Google replies:

A DEGREE IN BIOLOGICAL SCIENCE,
SPECIFICALLY MARINE BIOLOGY, IS
USUALLY REQUIRED.

Ugh. Stupid giant fish. Didn't wanna work with them anyway.

Suddenly I hear the noise of girls laughing and screaming down the corridor and the door swings open. The hockey girls from the canteen yesterday tumble in and look surprised to see me here.

'Erm, this is our space, hun. Soz, you've gotta go,' Amelia says.

'Ameliaaaa, don't be mean,' says Megan, smirking. 'You're new, right?' she says to me. 'What's your name, babe?'

'Erm, it's Indi,' I squeak. *I don't know why but I feel extremely intimidated?*

'Indi. Cute name. Nice to meet you. I'm Megan, this is Jas, Amelia and that's Maya over there. What you doing in here?'

'Erm, I was googling dolph— actually, nothing. I was just going anyway,' I say, grabbing my bag.

'Awww no, stay?' says Maya, smiling, blocking the door so I can't leave. 'We just wanna get to know you.'

'Er, no, you don't. She was rattling on about some crap band from the eighteen hundreds yesterday . . .' quips Jas, and Amelia snorts with laughter, which makes me feel a bit sick.

'I do really have to go', I say, pushing past Maya. 'See you later, girls.'

'Byeeeeeeeee, Indi!' calls Megan, in a shady way that makes me feel like she's taking the mick out of me. I bundle out and scurry down the hallway and make a note to avoid that lot like the plague.

2.34 p.m.
OMG, Reece – the boy from the bus – is in my German class! Think he felt a bit sorry for me after we chatted this morning, so he saved me a seat next to him.

Frau Schmitt is currently teaching the class how to buy a train ticket *auf Deutsch.*

'What's your favourite German word?' Reece whispers.

I whisper back: *'Hallo.'*

He leans closer and says, 'Why? Because it sounds just like "hello"?'

'Correct. Easy to remember. What's yours?'

'Meerschweinchen,' he whispers a bit louder.

Frau Schmitt shoots us both a 'Be quiet or else' look while everyone else scribbles in their workbooks.

'What's that mean?' I ask, ignoring The Frau.

'Meerschweinchen . . . is the word for guinea pig,' he replies quietly. 'But its literal translation is *little sea pig.'*

The idea of a guinea pig paddling in the ocean with a rubber ring round its middle and a pair of swimming goggles is too much to handle. I burst out laughing as Reece uses his finger to push the tip of his nose upwards, making it look like a pig snout, and motions doggy paddle with the other hand.

Actual tears are running down my face as Frau Schmitt yells at me to leave the classroom, which makes me laugh even more.

'But, miss, it wasn't even my fault,' I argue. 'Reece was being educational, and he was saying how—'

'Well then, Reece, you can leave too! *Auf Wiedersehen!*' barks The Frau.

Well, we're in hysterics now, absolutely popping off with giggles like a couple of cheeky *meerschweinchens*, and we have to spend five minutes in the corridor composing ourselves before we're let back in.

Back at our desk, I dare not look at Reece in case he sets me off again.

4.13 p.m.
I point at a wooden cabinet with a clear glass window that has all these lizard accessories inside: sandy stuff for the bottom of the tank and a big wooden branch for climbing and some shrubs. It looks like proper lizard heaven and I think to myself it'll look absolutely perfect on my shelf next to Dad's record player.

'How much is this one, please?' I ask the pet-shop assistant – a pasty man in his thirties who is wearing small round glasses and has been #blessed with the job of finding me a tank for my new adopted dino-baby.

'That one's £159.99, love. You get everything you need: your thermometer, thermostat and—'

I gulp, audibly. *It'd better come with its own jacuzzi and built-in speakers for that price . . .*

'Erm, that's a little bit out of my budget. Have you got anything . . . smaller?' I ask.

'What animal you buying it for again?'

'Lizard,' I answered.

'Oh yeah. What kind of lizard?'

'Is there *more* than one lizard . . .'

'Oh yeah, hundreds of 'em!' he says, getting his phone out and doing a quick search. He hands it to me.

'Erm, well,' I say, scrolling through. 'It's a yellow and black and speckly type. They're the ones that if you look at them from a certain angle, it looks like they're smiling. Truth be told I'm not sure I'm cut out to be a lizard mother, but someone's gotta look after him so . . .' I trail off.

'Sounds like a gecko,' he says, and takes his phone back to Google 'geckos'. He turns his phone round to face me.

'Awwwww, yeah, that's the one. Cute, isn't he?'

He leads me over to a smaller tank. 'This is good, a proper nice little starter terrarium, about sixty quid this one.'

I shake my head, embarrassed. This lizard – sorry, *gecko* – is turning out to be pricier that I imagined. Stupid Charlie didn't tell me that it would be a fiver PLUS my life savings, did he . . .

Pet-shop Assistant looks at me and sighs. 'How much you got, kid?'

I pull out my purse and count out the pounds and coppers on to the glass top of one of the tanks. A wrinkly tortoise looks up, annoyed. *Sorry, mate, but we've all got problems.*

'. . . thirty-eight, ooh, there's a penny, that's thirty-nine . . . twelve pounds and thirty-nine pence,' I declare.

'Can't help you, love,' he says. 'Maybe have a look at getting yourself a fish or something instead? Goldfish over there for a quid.'

I look down. 'Too late now. Already got this gecko, you see.'

'Hang on, what d'you mean you've already got it? I thought you were just *thinking* about buying one! Where's it living?' he says, alarmed.

'My mum's saucepan.'

'Flippin' 'eck' he cries. 'Y'can't do that! Wait over

there by the counter,' he huffs, before heading back into the stockroom. I wander around the shop, peering into the tanks of stick insects and snakes and tarantulas, and think how thankful Tubs should be that I didn't bring home a hairy eight-legged monster. Metallica plays out across the store and I note that Pet-shop Assistant seems to have decent taste in music.

He returns a couple minutes later with a manky-looking tank; the glass is algae-stained and the corners have gone rusty. He grabs a few items from the shelves and pops them inside.

He puts it down on the counter. 'Right, this is everything you need. Just give me the money you've got for the accessories, but y'can have this tank for free. Needs a good clean before you use it, alright?'

I do a little victory dance. 'Oh my god, thank you, thank you, thank you!' I say, pouring out my pathetic pennies. 'And, as a gesture of my appreciation, I'm gonna name my new pet after you!' I announce.

'Ha, you won't wanna do that . . .' He laughs, putting the goodies in a big bag.

I take it. 'It's the least I can do! Come on then, what's your name?'

He pauses for a second before saying: 'It's Gary.'

GARY!?!?! BLOODY GARY?!?

CHAPTER 4
I'M A STRESSED COURGETTE

MONDAY SEPT 14th

9 a.m.

Start of a brand-new week. I am confident. I am cool.

9.05 a.m.

I just fell down the steps heading to form.

12.45 p.m.

Wandering around the playground, trying to keep a low profile before the bell goes for maths. Footballs fly towards gangs of girls who scream at the boys because they're distracted from trying to master TikTok dances. One of them involves 'dropping it down low like it's hot'. Tubs would have a fit if she knew I was dropping anything, anywhere.

Lunchtime is the ghastliest part of the day. No one to hang out with and a whole hour to kill. Even my cheese sandwich isn't helping today, and I love cheese more than life. Seen Reece knocking about but I don't want to cling on to him like a limpet, so I wave at him instead and scurry away.

On the flipside, art is my favourite lesson already. Miss Addo teaches us and I get the feeling she's young and cool. She wears loose wide-legged trousers and soft flowing blouses, and wears her hair in thick braids. This morning she told me she really liked my painting of the sea. I used acrylics to really layer up the colour and give the water movement.

Maybe Miss Addo will be my friend?

FRIDAY SEPT 18th
3.16 p.m.
Just finished P.E.

Miss Reynolds split the class into two: *The Girls Who Play for The School Hockey Team* versus *The Rest of Us Who Can Barely Even Run.* Needless to say it was a 9–0 loss. At one point I swear Jasmine hooked her hockey stick around my ankle on purpose. I landed FACE-FIRST IN MUD and THE MUD WENT IN MY MOUTH. I can still taste earthy grit now, BLEURGH.

Whilst us losers schlep back to the changing rooms looking like a litter of pigs who'd been let out of the pigsty, Megan – who's the team captain, obviously – says loudly:

'Well, girls, THAT was embarrassing, maybe we should have given them a chance...' and Maya, Amelia and Jas all titter. Like stupid tittering... titterers.

'Eugh, Megan, would it hurt you to be nice for once?' says a voice from behind me.

'Eugh, Nisha, would it hurt YOU to stop being so basic for once?' retorts Megan.

Nisha! It's that girl from the canteen on my first day, the one who was chatting to the blonde one. I didn't recognise her underneath the huge hockey helmet. It suddenly makes sense why she didn't wear her kit at lunchtime like the other hockey girls – along with the helmet, goalkeepers wear a massive pair of shin pads and two huge paddles on their hands to protect them getting smacked with the rock-hard hockey ball. She would have barely fit through the canteen door.

I watch as Nisha pulls a grotesque face at Megan, who then runs off squealing to Miss Reynolds, and then Nisha nudges me on the arm and says, 'Probably gonna get detention now...'

She laughs and rolls her eyes. I smile back because I don't know what to say to this exceedingly cool girl who is literally talking to me. *God she'd be a mint friend.*

3.36 p.m.

'Hey Indi, few of us are going down into town, d'you want to come along?' asks Reece, jogging up behind me as I head for the school bus.

I freeze on the spot; I'm sure he can see blind fear flash across my face.

Oh my god. A social invitation. Am I ready for this? I'm not sure I am! Especially because I absolutely reek after running around like a madhead in P.E.

'Yeah, sounds good, cool, cool . . .' I reply, like I'm a cool cucumber, when in fact I'm a stressed courgette.

We stroll past the school bus as it pulls out of the carpark. I watch it drive off, wishing I was on it. Outside the front gates, feeling super awks, Reece introduces me to some of his mates.

One's called Tobias who's so tall he could be a sixth former. Or a basketball player. Or a window cleaner who doesn't need to use ladders. And then there's Marcus, who has a big head, and some others I've never even seen around before.

I see a couple of them look at me, wondering why Reece has brought me along. Marcus whispers something to Tobias, and he laughs in return, which makes me feel all self-conscious so I'm glad when a few more randoms join us, including Alice Welby, the girl who may (or may not) have ginger pubes.

3.54 p.m.

'. . . and basically *that's* why I think the Weeping Angels are essentially fallen Time Lords,' says Reece. He's telling me about *Doctor Who*, and even though I've never watched it, I try to say encouraging things like 'Oh right!' and 'Aaaah, I see!'

He lets the others walk in front and hangs back with me.

'Anyway,' he says. 'How's the new flat? Are you getting all settled in now?'

Truth be told, I've been proper homesick. Gary, on the other hand, has made himself right at home; he looks brilliant in his new tank! But I miss my old bedroom and our old house. And mainly I miss Dad and when everything was normal.

I panic. 'Yeah, it's great, thanks. Our new toaster has THREE heat settings.'

'Three, really? So, setting one is just normal toast. And setting two is . . .?'

'Erm, I dunno, toastier?'

'And setting three?'

'Ha, well, obvs toastiest!' I decide to up the ante. 'Also, we, like, have a hot tub on our balcony!' I boast. We don't have a hot tub on the balcony. We have a broken plant pot that catches rainwater. Which is almost the same. Almost . . .

'No way!' he says.

I elaborate on my massive fib. 'Yep. It's not really a flat, more like a penthouse, really. Planning a biiiiiiiiiig party for when my dad gets back; he's on a mega-fancy work trip, you see. You should come, gonna invite all my London friends up, and order tons of pizzas and my Dad will crank up our sound system extra loud, probably get complaints from the neighbours but oh well. Dad's parties just hit different.'

'Oh yeah, what what kind of music are we gonna be raving to then?'

I consider pretending I'm into rap music like everyone else at school is. But . . . I dunno . . . he seems like a bit of a geek with his love of science and *Doctor Who* and stuff, so maybe I can share the geeky stuff I like too?

'I like old music.'

'Oh right? What, like Beethoven or—'

'Nooooo, like bands and stuff,' I say. 'Have you heard of Oasis?'

'Course I have! Manchester legends. Grew up just down the road from here.'

'Yeah, well, I love them, and The Smiths and Nirvana and then there's the *newer,* older stuff like The Hives and Yeah Yeah Yeahs and then you've got emo and metal bands like—'

'—yeah you've lost me now,' he says, pushing his glasses up his nose.

'—and Arctic Monkeys as well – you know the Arctic Monkeys, don't you? I love them so much!'

'Can you play any instruments?'

'Nope. Actually, yes, the recorder!' I say.

'Not very rock and roll, the recorder . . .'

'Ha, not really,' I reply, smiling, tucking my hair behind my ear.

It goes a bit quiet after that and it was on the border of becoming a tickle awks when Marcus shouts over to us: 'Oi, you two! Chip shop?'

I feel the colour drain from my face.

Did he just say the words 'chip shop'?

It can't be.

Surely!?

4.15 p.m.
Tobias has Alice in a piggyback and a car beeps its horn angrily as we spill out on to the road to cross the street. It's still light outside but the air is starting to feel colder.

I feel like I'm gonna gip.

Surely, surely, <u>surely</u> we're not headed to The Jolly Fryer???
Imagine that!
There's just no way that the <u>one</u> chip shop that my mother has pimped me out to is the one chip shop that everyone hangs out at after school. I mean, what would be the chances???

4.16 p.m.
We turn a corner just after the off-licence and for a moment I squeeze my eyes shut and pray:

Dear God,
Please don't be The Jolly Fryer.
Please don't be The Jolly Fryer.
Please don't be The Jolly Fryer.
Amen.

I open my eyes slowly.

The shop's signage slowly comes into view, beaming its blue neon lights right into my eyes: THE JOLLY FRYER.

Outside, there's maybe ten, twenty, thirty . . . I don't know! . . . perhaps HUNDREDS of St Cath's pupils, all tucking into cones of chips. I panic. *Can't go in! Gotta go.*

'Argh, er, actually, sorry, guys, I forgot. Erm, my mum's actually doing this posh dinner tonight. *Coq au vin* apparently. Ha, gross, would much rather have chips! Gotta go—'

'Oh,' says Reece, looking a bit disappointed. 'Want me to walk you back?'

'NO, NO! No, I'm just around the corner, don't worry. Thanks, though!'

I catch a glimpse of a man in a navy-blue apron through the window handing over a takeaway bag full of fish and chips to a customer. That must be Alan then . . .

'See you guys tomorrow!' I say, practically falling over my own feet to get away.

6.01 p.m.
'Please, Tubs. Just call this Alan man and say I can't come in tomorrow after all,' I beg.

'What, and let him down last minute? Come on Indiana, yer better than that.' She looks tired after her shift at the hospital today, said it was really busy. She really doesn't need me being difficult right now but here we are . . .

I sit in the armchair and put my head in my hands. 'But you don't understand, EVERYONE from school was there. EVERYONE'S gonna be staring at me in my stupid little hat; they'll be staring at me through the glass windows, like I'm a fish in an aquarium. Except I'm not a fish in an aquarium, I'll be a fish in a fish and chip shop! A sad old trout with no friends! Is that the life you want for me, Tubs, is it!?'

She glares at me in a 'you're-being-stupid' kinda way.

'I'LL GIVE YOU ONE MILLION DOLLARS!' I scream.

'You don't even have one dollar, let alone a million of them!' replies Tubs. 'Which is why I have to go to my second job of the day. Back later. Be good!'

The door slams behind her and she heads off to one of her many new dreamy cleaning jobs where she can hang out in the toilets in peace. Some people just don't know how good they have it!

CHAPTER 5

I'M A HADDOCK IN A HAIRNET

SATURDAY SEPT 19th

8.33 a.m.

'Oh my god, Tubs, did you see that?' I gasp, staring down out of the window, grabbing her by the arm for added effect.

'What? What is it?' shes says, pulling on her work lanyard over her head.

'Bigfoot.'

'Indi . . .'

'I SWEAR, it just walked past the petrol station, Tubs! Straight past pump number five!'

'Don't be stupid, Indiana.'

'I'm not! I swear I'm not! It JUST went into the shop. I bet it popped its head in to grab a Dairy Milk and some de-icer for the car. Listen, it's up to you whether you want to believe me or not—'

'I don't—'

'. . . but, listen, I'm in a real state of shock right now,

and I don't think I should go into work today . . .'

10.58 a.m.
OK, that lie was maybe a bit far-fetched which is *possibly* why Tubs didn't fall for it. So here we are. Standing in front of a rusty mirror in the customer bogs, tucking strands of my dark hair under my brand new, crisp, white hat. *GOD, I LOOK LIKE A DIVHEAD.*

'Are yer done in there?' shouts Alan. He's a proper Northerner, is Alan.

'Yeah, coming . . .' I sigh, straightening my apron. *Well, I THOUGHT I looked good in an apron. Turns out I'd fit right in with the canteen ladies at school: I've aged about 54 years here.*

'Come on now, hurry up! What time is it? Bloody hell, almost eleven, I've got a girl on today with yer and a potwash lad who should be in shortly, but they're late, as per bloody usual . . . I tell you what, I've been running this place for thirty-odd years and young 'uns today, they don't know the meaning of hard, honest work. Anyway, that's a story for another day, let's give yer a crash course on't tills, shall we . . .'

He witters on, and I take a moment to have a good look around. Namely for an escape route for when my schoolmates inevitably come in later.

Urghhhh.

The Jolly Fryer is as retro as Alan: plastic chairs and tables with gingham checked tablecloths sit atop a black-and-white tiled floor. Each table has little, red, squeezy ketchup bottles on them. Behind the giant glass and stainless-steel counter are molten-hot deep fat fryers, and the big illuminated menu board with the names and prices of cod and plaice and steak-and-kidney pies and cans of dandelion and burdock and pickled eggs.

It smells divine, to be fair, and makes me instantly hungry.

'. . . and *then*, after yer've served the customer, you put the check up here so I know what needs to be dished up, and then yer clean those tables there. Clean 'em good, Indiana. I know it's hard work, but what is it we say?'

'Make your peace, with the grease', I repeat, monotone, for the bloody bizillionth time this morning.

'Is there a Mrs Alan?' I ask, 'cause I get nosy when I'm bored.

'Fraid not,' he says quickly – which suggests to me it's a touchy subject – before spending TEN MINUTES telling me how to fill up the vinegar bottles. TEN MINUTES, CAN YOU BELIEVE? How can someone talk for ten minutes about decanting bottles of condiments? I notice Alan's hands are scarred from the burns he must have accumulated from the deep fat fryer. I look at him and I can see my sad future.

Old, single, scaley-hands Indi Raye fondling fish forever.

11.15 a.m.
The door jangles and a girl comes bounding in.

'Sorry I'm late, Alan!' she shouts. 'There was this woman with this pram, yeah? She ran over my foot with it and—'

'Two times in three weeks, Nisha. Am I gonna have to call yer mam?'

Oh my god.

I tuck my head down as far as I can under my hideous hat so she doesn't see me, and keep low behind the counter.

'If you call my mum, she'll ground me, Alan,' says Nisha, looking sad and pouting.

'Oh give over, what are you like? Wash yer hands and apron on,' he concedes, before motioning me to stand up. 'This is Indiana. She's new today, so you'll need to show her how it all works. Lead by example, eh?'

And with that, he disappears into the back.

'Ah, it's you! Alright?' Nisha says, before getting distracted by something out of the window. 'HAHAHA, did you just see that man trip over a bin?'

I'm guessing it was one of those 'you had to be there' moments, but I laugh anyway.

This is so weird. Why would Nisha work here?

'Hahahaha, oh that's hilarious, man,' she wheezes. 'Anyway. Right. So. What do you wanna do today? Tills or tables?'

'Tables,' I reply, grabbing the refillable vinegar bottles, which are now my speciality after basically getting a GCSE in it from Alan. 'Defo tables. I'm not very good at maths. Alan asked me to add up a cone of chips with a saveloy earlier and I didn't know the answer so I pretended I needed the loo.'

'Haha, good work! Although, look,' she says, showing me the calculator next to the till. 'It's the twenty-first century, mate!'

'Ah right, yeah, cool. So, er . . . how long you worked here?'

'Ages. It's literally the best. You get to chat to everyone who comes in and I get, like, my own money and stuff. I'm saving up for new hockey kit, ennit. And also chips are my favourite food!'

'Don't they wanna make you gip? You cook them *all day*!'

'Yeah, I know, I'm THE luckiest gal in the world!'

We have a little smile together. And I start to think maybe this chippy job won't be as bad as I first thought . . .

'DON'T FORGET THE EGGS, NISHA!' shouts Alan from the kitchen.

'Ever tried one of these?' says Nisha, grabbing a fresh jar of pickled eggs from under the counter. They look rank, floating around in their juice. 'Quite nice, you know . . . Anyway, how you finding school?' She lowers her voice. 'Someone said you bought a monkey off Charlie Grenburg?'

I mean, no. I bought a lizard. But a monkey definitely sounds more exciting . . .

'Sure did,' I gamble.

'What?? Really??' she says, shocked. 'Indi, is that even legal? Not to mention moral? You know they're quite dangerous too, they've been known to attack humans, they go straight for the face—'

OH GOD!!!!!

'Woah! No!' I say, panicked. 'Sorry, no, wasn't a monkey. Just a gecko. A plain ol' innocent gecko.'

'Geckos are sick,' says a spotty boy, clanging through the door and disappearing into the back.

'Alright, Will?' says Nisha as he passes. 'That's Will, he does the pot wash. Anyway, what's a gecko?'

'A lizard or somethin'. It's actually soooooo cute, sometimes it does like a weird little dance, just rocks back and forth. Sorry, but just to confirm – I bought a <u>gecko</u>. Whoever you heard the rumour from, will you tell them it was a gecko?'

'Yeah, don't worry, babe. I'll tell 'em. Hahaha!'

I like Nisha. And maybe she likes me too now that she knows I simply bought a gecko and nothing at all suspicious.

1 p.m.
The chippy fills up by lunch. A load of Year 11s who I recogonise from the back of the school bus come in with a massive order. Alan is frying fish at the speed of lightning, Nisha is firing on all cylinders taking orders like *bang-bang-bang,* and it turns out clearing tables is actually much harder than I thought. There are trays to collect, heavy with plates and teetering teapots and cups on saucers.

Sometimes my hand accidently touches some cold mushy peas or blobs of mayo which makes me gippy, but I have to forget about it quickly, 'cause by the time I clear one table, another bunch of customers have left another bombsite for me to tidy up. Potwash Will spends the whole time with his headphones in and doesn't even look at me when I dump the dishes next to him. I keep trying to give him some Frisky Eyes whenever I enter through the swinging doors. Absolutely no Frisky Eyes back.

2.12 p.m.
The end of my shift flies (or should I say *fries*!) around pretty quickly; my mind feels full of fish rules, chip protocols and vinegar dos and don'ts. My actual physical head feels full of grease. On the upside, a man gave me a five-pound tip, which I plan to spend on Pantene.

'Right, Indiana, that's you all done. Help yourself to something to eat before you go, won't yer. Say hi to yer mam for me. And I'll see yer next Saturday,' says Alan, after he's finished taking another delivery of fish, clearly gearing up for a busy evening.

'I'm hired, then? Wowzers, I must have been *sooooooo* good today . . .' I reply cheekily.

'Go on, on with yer, before I change my mind.'

'Thanks, Al.'

But before I do, Nisha sorts me out with a large chips and cheese, smothered in ketchup. They are DELICIOUS. I'm sitting down at an empty table in the window so I can carry on talking to Nisha and just as I'm shovelling a gob-full in, Grace strides in, pulling her headphones from her ears and says: 'That's it, Nish, I'm OFFICIALLY undateable! That lad from town the other week literally hasn't texted me in days now, he clearly thinks I'm trash!'

I wonder what she's been listening to. Pop I bet. Taylor Swift.

Grace Walkden looks even more on point outside school. She's got major main character energy, is wearing a tiny crop top and she even has her bellybutton pierced. Confidence drips off her, whilst grease drips off me. She's pretty in pink, whilst I'm a haddock in a hairnet.

'Urghhh, what now? Is this another one of your cries for attention?' asks Nisha, washing her hands in the sink. '*Oh look at me, I'm so ugly*, even though EVERYBODY fancies you.'

'I think I need a face transplant!' she wails.

'Tut, shut up, man. Anyway, Gracie, this is Indi, she's just joined St Catherine's.' Nisha introduces me.

Grace waves and sits down opposite me.

'I've seen you around school, how you finding it?'

'Erm, pretty hideous, to be honest.'

'Don't worry, you'll get used to it. So, you live round here then?'

I bet Grace Walkden lives in a castle. No way I'm telling her I live on the eleventh floor at Number 64.

'Yeah, round here, sort of . . . that way . . .' I say, gesturing vaguely out of the window. 'Living in this penthouse at the top of one of the swankiest blocks of flats in Manchester. It's got a hot tub so . . . pretty cool.'

'Awesome. So, question: ever had a boyfriend?' she asks.

I gulp. *Wow, she didn't waste any time getting straight to the nitty gritty, did she?*

'Ahhh, yeah . . . once . . .' I reply.

Oh look, here's is Lies Magee with her pack of lies. For the record, no. No, I've never had a boyfriend. But despo times call for despo measures. I can't have them think I'm a Basic Betty, can I . . .?

'Oh my G, really!?! TELL US EVERYTHING,' says Grace, looking at me dead in the eyes, thrilled.

Oh god.

I think fast. 'Well, there was this boy . . . in . . . Barcelona . . .'

'Wow, Spanish!' says Nisha, grabbing the seat next to Grace, even though she should still be working.

I look them both dead in the eyes. 'Yeah, Spanish.

70

And his name was . . . Enrique.' I roll the 'r' in Enrique with my tongue to make him sound even more Spanish, like 'rrrrrrrr'.

'SHUT UP!!?' squeals Nisha.

'So, what happened?' asks Grace. 'How come you aren't together now?'

I DON'T KNOW, HE'S MADE UP, ISN'T HE?

Think Indi, think . . .

'Er . . . so . . . he . . . fell off a horse? Lost all of his memories. Doesn't even know who I am any more.'

I stare out of the window into the middle distance, proper whimsically, like I'm in some kind of Hollywood movie.

'My amigo,' I say sadly. 'My amigo . . .'

'Wow,' says Nisha, solemnly.

'Tragic,' says Grace, shaking her head.

AMIGO!? BLOODY HELL, INDI RAYE!

4.34 p.m.
OH MY GOD, I ACTUALLY SMELL LIKE A FISH!

No amount of Pantene will save me; I've scrubbed my scalp so much it feels like it's on fire. Told Tubs to tell me if it looks all red and she just said it isn't, even though it's literally the colour of a lobster on fire.

WEDNESDAY SEPT 30th
4.02 p.m.

Just got home from school. Can hear Tubs in the bath, which is so weird 'cause she never has a bath. And it's four o'clock in the afternoon. She's listening to this dead sad Adele song. In the music video – which is black and white, by the way, for added sorrow – Adele looks proper miserable and the lyrics are all like, 'Ooh, you're gone and I'm all bummed out,' so just one play of this tune is enough to make you feel proper depressed, and Tubs has got it on repeat.

4.27 p.m.

It's still going on. Doing my head in now.

4.31 p.m.

She just got out of the bath, but she was in there so long, I reckon she'll be all dehydrated and wrinkly like an old sultana. I'm gonna go check on her.

4.41 p.m.

Creep down the hallway and peep my head around Tubs's bedroom door. She is trying on dresses, even though it's a Wednesday evening and she's got a shift cleaning at the hospital later. I tell you what, if she starts her cleaning shift in high heels like that, she might end up having a mishap with the vacuum, it's a real health and safety hazard.

'Going out, Tubs?' I ask.

'Eh? Oh, er, no,' she replied, tugging at the hem of a particularly hideous floral number. 'Just trying on some of me old favourites before I put them on the eBay . . . look at THIS ONE!'

She whips out a silky silver slip dress and gazes at it lovingly. 'Yer father loved me in this. Try it on.'

'Guess what, school today, my headteacher, Mrs Jenkinson, said I have a larger than average IQ!' I interrupt with a big fat lie.

'Come on, try it,' pushes Tubs, ignoring me.

'Noooo, it won't suit me.'

'Come on, let's get this school uniform off and—' (she starts trying to undress me at this point . . .)

'TUBS, STOP TRYING TO GET ME NAKED, IT'S WEIRD.'

She turns to her side, pushing her hands down her hips, as if trying to flatten them out. She sighs.

'Am I fat, Indi?' she asks, bluntly.

Now, you may think the lies I tell are morally

incomprehensible. But *sometimes*, lies are useful. Sometimes I need to lie for the greater good. To protect Tubs's feelings.

'Errrrr . . . are . . . yoooou . . . fat . . . hmmm? I mean, it's a big question, one that philosophers have debated for many centuries . . .' I waffle. '. . . on the balance of probability, I'm gonna saaaaaaay . . . no?'

'Oh, so I AM, then. Well, thanks very much!'

'I DIDN'T SAY THAT, DID I?'

I can feel my impatience growing.

'Why are you asking me anyway?? You *do* know that it's been scientifically proven that parents can pass their insecurities down to their children. You're essentially ensuring I'll need years of therapy in years to come, Tubs, so actually, thank YOU very much.'

We sit in silence for a second until she turns back to the mirror and pulls at the side zip. It's super awks so I say: 'If you go to work wearing those heels, you might have a mishap with the vacuum. Oh, and by the way, I need you to wash my bed covers 'cause Gary pooed on my pillow, BYE!'

Then I run out of the door before she can ask me any more questions.

4.49 p.m.

I storm into the kitchen. I need a glass of water. None are washed so I run the tap and slurp from underneath it.

Then I have to bite my lip hard so I don't cry. I hate when she's like this. All melancholy. Sometimes when she's not working she curls up under a blanket on the sofa and she leaves ITV2 on all day long and she just stays there all day and doesn't speak very much. I get it, she's sad about Dad not being here. But she's not the only one.

I glance over to the hob. There's a saucepan of cold soup that Tubs made earlier today. I grab it, crack the window open, and throw the whole thing out. I slam the window shut then march back past Tubs's bedroom and say: 'A squirrel just broke in and threw the soup out of the window. I'm going to bed. GOODNIGHT.'

THURSDAY OCT 1ˢᵗ
7.11 a.m.

I slide a five-pound note across the kitchen table to Tubs. Got my first set of wages at the weekend. Really wanted to keep it all for myself – trying to save up for Glastonbury – and also I saw a flyer at the bus stop for this big record fayre in town – bet there's loads of rare vinyl to pick up there – but I said I'd give

Tubs some to contribute to the food shop and the electricity and that, didn't I? And now seems like a good time to do it . . .

'Sorry about last night . . .' I mumble.

She says nothing but takes the fiver, rolls it up and puts it in her jeans pocket. In return, she points to a mop and bucket and I head downstairs to clean up the bright orange soup that splashed across the courtyard like giant bird poo.

Well done, Ind. Not one of your better lies, was it?

SATURDAY OCT 10TH
2.46 p.m.

Starting to get the hang of things at the chippy now. Bit quieter today so I've had the chance to learn how to restock the fridge, making sure all the shiny cans of Coke and dandelion and burdock are in the right order. Managed to carry TWO trays back to the kitchen today, one on each arm. Didn't drop a single fork. Also less gippy at the sight of blobs of old mayo.

And even better, Grace is in again and has just asked me to play dares with them. I know, I know, I'm brand new, I should be keeping my head down, doing my jobs, trying to impress Alan and getting paid. But I also really want friends, so . . .

'OK, Grace, I dare you,' ponders Nisha, 'to tell Alan he has the most beautiful eyes you've ever seen.'

We crack up laughing as Alan emerges from the back room with a big tub of battered fish ready for the fryer.

'Erm, Alan . . .' calls Grace, hardly suppressing her giggles. 'You have wonderful eyes.'

We shriek with laughter. Alan takes it in good spirits and laughs with us.

'D'you know, I've always thought that, thank you, Grace!'

'OK, Indi, your turn!' says Grace. 'I dare you to go and talk to Will about haddock . . . for a whole THIRTY SECONDS. No pauses.'

'Oh my god, OK!' I say, squirming.

We tumble into the kitchen and find Will racking up the dishwasher, earpods in. I gesture at him to pull them out so he can hear me.

'Er, Will. I just was popping in to say—'

Grace holds up her phone which has a 30 second time on it and says, 'Three, two, one, GO!'

'The history of the haddock is an intriguing and important one. Typically found in the sea, haddocks are often confused with cod due to their similar white flesh but, no, Will, for these are two very different species—'

Will puts his earpods back in his ears and starts scrubbing a big metal pan.

'Damn! Eleven seconds. Nice try, though!' says Grace.

'That's eleven more seconds of haddock knowledge than I've got!' laughs Nisha.

Grace glances back at her phone. 'Nish, we need to get going!'

'OK, cool, let me tell Alan I'm off,' she says, removing her apron.

'Where are you guys going?' I ask. Secretly hoping they might invite me along.

'Got a big game today against Manor High. Grace is coming to be my cheerleader, aren't you, Gracie? Then cinema later. New Marvel film, ennit,' says Nisha excitedly.

'You got any plans this afternoon, Indi?' asks Grace. Which is kind of her, to be fair.

'Erm, nah, just gonna do my art homework. Doing still-life drawings this week, so gonna draw Gary the gecko, I reckon. Listen to some music and stuff, nothing much.'

Wish I had something more impressive to say. Should have lied. Should have said I was off to Alton Towers or had a hot air balloon ride booked or something.

'OK, cool! Well, have fun! See you next week,' calls Nisha, as they head off, leaving me listening to the hum of the dishwasher next to Potwash Will – who now thinks I'm obsessed with haddock. Looks like my dream of getting Frisky Eyes from him is over before it even started.

SUNDAY OCT 18th
12.35 p.m.

The needle of Dad's record player makes a satisfying scratchy sound as it rests on the vinyl record. Patti Smith today. Queen of punk rock. It's proper hideous outside, pelting with rain and Tubs is refusing to let us have the heating on in Number 64. She says unless it's snowing, we can just put extra layers on. It's, like, two degrees. Even Gary looks cold. I swear I saw him hold his scaly feet out towards his heat lamp for extra warmth, a bit like a human would do to a campfire on an Arctic expedition.

12.38 p.m.

I've snuggled under my duvet for warmth, doing my art homework. I should probably crack on with my R.E. homework first, get it out of the way, but replicating the work of Claude Monet is much more fun to me than The Pope. (No offence, Pope.)

School's been alright, I guess. Me and Reece don't have many lessons together, really, which is a shame. German is the best one 'cause we can sit next to each other and it's always proper fun. The other day Reece was supposed to be a shopkeeper selling apples and I was supposed to be the customer buying one. We were supposed to have the whole conversation in German but instead of using the word *apfel,* I just said the word 'bum' instead. I said, '*Kann ich bitte einen* bum *haben?*' and Reece replied, '*Jah, hier ist ein* bum.' It made no sense, but kept us entertained because 'bum' is a very funny word when you think about it.

Spend a lot of my breaks and lunches on the prowl around school trying to bump into Nisha or Grace. When we do see each other in school, they give me a little half-smile, but that's it. They're obviously best friends and they say three's a crowd, don't they, so I don't want to stick *mein* bum in.

OMG, forgot to mention, on Wednesday, some Year 10 lad used the library computer to print off a picture of a proper naked woman – not a cloth on her! She had her leg twisted up into a super-strange position which revealed *a lot* and the print-out spent its day getting passed around underneath desks during science lessons.

12.42 p.m.

Decide to see if I'm as flexible as that woman. I lie on the floor and lift my leg up. Lift it forwards, to the side, upwards but I'm sorry but there's no way in HELL I'm getting it over my head – IT IS IMPOSSIBLE. If that's what *'doing it'* is like, I am doomed.

Tubs knocks on my door. 'Ind, I need to go and pick up some bits, yer wanna come?'

'DON'T COME IN!!!!' I scream but she's already inside. Tubs has little-to-no respect for personal space.

'What *are* yer doing, Indiana?'

I look up at her from my upside-down position. 'Oh, this . . .' I lie, breathlessly, '. . . is a rare form of Mongolian yoga. Saw it on YouTube.'

'Ooh, come on then, show us how it's done,' said Tubs, getting down on the floor.

WRONG.

WRONG, WRONG, WRONG, ON <u>SO</u> MANY LEVELS.

'So, you wanna come to ASDA with me, get summit for tea?' she says, raising her leg over her head no problem.

'YES. PLEASE. LET'S GO NOW, I LOVE ASDA,' I shout, putting a swift end to the moment my mother accidently impersonated a naked internet lady.

CHAPTER 6

HE'S NOT A KILLER, HE'S CALLED JONATHAN

SATURDAY OCT 31st
2.05 p.m.

Boring shift at the chippy today. Nisha is at a family wedding – Alan says it's a big three-day celebration for one of her cousins. So obvs there's no sign of Grace either. Would have been nice if she'd popped in; we could have had a chat or something.

'See you, Al,' I call.

'Ta-ra, love.' He waves.

I push the door open and the cold air hits me right in the face, instantly cooling me down; it's refreshing after standing next to deep fat fryers all day, so I suck it in.

'Nice hat, mate,' Reece says, cycling up beside me, his brakes screeching.

Oh god, what is he doing here!? It's so weird seeing him in non-school uniform. He's wearing black jeans and a

83

white T-shirt with a checked shirt thrown over the top. Cycling helmet on, neon yellow. Same thick-rimmed glasses though.

OBVS when we ended up here that day after school I didn't reveal to him that Tubs had full-on thrown me under the bus and signed me up to be Captain Birdseye, Queen of Fish every Saturday. And I've been meaning to mention it to him, but I've been worried he might . . . like, judge me, or whatever.

'Oh god, don't, Reece . . .' I moan, looking at the pavement.

'No, I'm being serious. It actually suits you! So, you're working here, I'm guessing?'

The lie just falls out of me: 'No, no, I'm not working here, no.'

'You *don't* work here?' he asks sceptically, glancing back at the hat and then to the apron which both bear the Jolly Fryer logo on it.

'OK, no . . . er, you see . . . I don't, I mean, I didn't . . . well, my mum, Tubs, she sort of made me do it so I guess . . . now I *do* work here but only on Saturdays so . . .' I fumble.

Reece grins. 'That's awesome! I want a job. It's proper adulting, isn't it,' he says.

Oh. Not the reaction I was expecting.

'Well, you could come and work at the chippy but apparently there's a requirement that you HAVE to look cute in the hat so . . .' I say, with a bit too much sass for someone's whose hair absolutely hums of cod.

'Ah, probably not for me then,' he jokes, jumping off his saddle and pushing his bike alongside me as we walk. 'So, got any Halloween plans for later?'

Obviously not. You need friends for Halloween plans.

'Oh yeah, totally, just heading out trick-or-treating with Tubs . . . erm . . . my mum.'

God, that sounds SO tragic.

'Aw. Nice. Listen, been meaning to say . . . you don't have to, but my mum told me to ask you . . . do you wanna come over for tea?'

I'm so taken aback, my mouth drops open. 'Your mum asked? How does your mum know who I am?'

'Well, I told her about you, stupid! I said, "*There's this new girl in school and she's a total freak, really quite annoying . . .*"'

'Shut up, am I? Oh my god, am I really annoying??' I whinge.

'SO annoying. You're being annoying now!'

I grin at him.

'So, let's say next Saturday night then? Six-ish? It'll probably be chicken or something.'

This is what I've been wanting. A real friend. But I'm still high-key panicking. This is weird. Isn't it? We've only known each other a couple months. And Reece is a boy; I can't just go to a boy's house. Can I?

I think about lying, making up some kind of random excuse like 'Sorry, no can do, I've got the bubonic plague' or something. But instead, I take a deep breath and say, 'Yeah, OK. I like chicken. Bwark, bwark.' *Oh good, I just bwarked in a chicken voice.* 'I mean, that would be proper nice. Say thanks to your mum, yeah?'

'You can tell her yourself! Anyway, gotta go, going round Tobe's to play the new *Star Wars* PS game!'

'Have fun, nerds,' I say, as he mounts back onto his bike and cycles off, leaving me feeling somewhere between excited and terrified.

7.07 p.m.
A short list of some of the best lies I've told recently:

1. I told Amelia Jacobs that I'd been featured in the Japanese version of Vogue magazine.
2. I pretended that I'd swallowed a whole boiled egg during lunch and needed medical assistance. The school nurse said that eggs were soft and I'd be fine.

3. I told Charlie Grenburg that Gary had grown to the size of a cat even though my lickle gecko is still just 10cm long.

4. I told my art class that the man who owns Starbucks is my uncle. I told everyone he'd sort them out with free Gingerbread Lattes for life if they mentioned 'Uncle Bucky' at the till.

5. I told Maya Richards that I went on a date with both Harry Styles AND Niall Horan. I WISH.

It's been getting a little bit out of control to be honest, but my schoolmates seem to be lapping it up . . .

7.16 p.m.
Just watched a boy wearing a white bedsheet with eyeholes kick a pumpkin over and run away.

Honestly, this country.

I used to love Halloween. Dad used to take me out trick-or-treating all the time. Once I dressed up as Ant AND Dec (yes, both of them) and I looked so good. I got LOADS of sweets and ate them until I vommed. Turns out Halloween isn't half as fun when you're a friendless thirteen-year-old. Looks like it's me, Tubs and *Strictly* again tonight.

7.18 p.m.

Wonder if Nisha and Grace went trick-or-treating tonight. Probably had a sleepover at Grace's actually and watched loads of horror films. Or had a fancy-dress party.

7.25 p.m.

Speaking of spooky things, there's this man who lives opposite us at Number 68. A few times now, I've caught him peeking out from behind his curtains when me and Tubs leave Number 64.

'He might be a killer, Tubs,' I hiss. 'And tonight's Halloween, it's the perfect night for him. Lock the doors!'

Tubs laughs and waves at Number 68. 'He's not a killer, he's called Jonathan.'

'WHAT DOES THAT EVEN MEAN!?'

'Well ... I just don't think murderers would be called something like Jonathan. It's a nice name.'

'Oh well! That's that then! Imagine that in a court of law. "*I hereby declare,*"' I say, imitating a courtroom judge, '"*that the jury find the defendant NOT GUILTY because he goes by the name of Jonathan!*"'

'Correct,' says Tubs.

'OK, so what would you say IS a *murdery name*?'

She looks thoughtful for a moment and then says: 'Satan.'

My mother, ladies and gentlemen, thinking that people in this day and age call their babies after The Devil. Unbelievable.

'Look,' I say. 'I just don't think THE FATHER OF YOUR CHILD would be best pleased with a murderer sniffing around, that's all.'

'Well, *the father of my child's* not here, is he?' she retorts.

'Hmm. Hey, guess what? I've been put forward for this art prize at school,' I lie. 'Miss Addo said if I keep doing well, I could get a scholarship for art school one day!'

'Oh, Indiana! That's fantastic news! Wooooo, imagine that! *My girl* off to art school! I can see it now!' she laughs, taking my hands and making me dance with her to the *Strictly* theme tune playing on the TV in the corner.

And I dance with her too because she doesn't have to know it's one of my hideous lies, not right now. She's distracted from Dad-chat and that's all that matters.

9.11 p.m.
Seriously though, I'm not being funny, but who is that man, hm?

Dad would be livid if he knew there was a man so local to us. A local man. Doing local things like peering out of his window. I don't like the sound of it, not one bit, and neither would Dad.

It's been weeks now and not even a phone call from him. I've started worrying about him.

Like, what if he's not OK?

What if he's had an accident, like a plane crash, or fallen off a mountain and we don't even know? When I start to think that might be the worst thing ever ... I think of something arguably worse: that maybe he's alive and well and just doesn't want to see me.

TUESDAY NOV 3rd
3.34 p.m.

Walking to the bus after school. Grace runs up behind me. It's the first time she's actually spoken to me properly outside the chippy and little do I know, it's about to be the most amazing moment of my life so far.

'Indi! So, listen ... my brother, he's in a *really* cringe band but they're doing a gig at this place in town next Friday. It's actually quite cool – it's a pub called The Crown and Castle – anyway, he wants me to bring some friends so it looks like there's a big crowd, you know, so they look like they *actually* have fans.' She laughs. 'Which they don't but . . .'

She's probs gonna ask me to do her homework for her, or something, so she has time to go to the gig . . .

'ANYWAY – you like that kind of stuff. Music and that. I mean, I'm more of an Ed Sheeran type of gal but . . . you wanna come with me and Nish?'

SCREAMS INTERNALLY

I try not to pop off with excitement. This might be the best thing I've EVER heard.

'Er, yeah, whatever, I mean I've pretty much seen *all* the bands but—'

'Oh. Well, you don't have to, babe,' retorts Grace, tucking her blonde hair behind her ear, looking slightly affronted.

'ER, NO, I MEAN, I'D LOVE TO. That'd be cool, I mean, that'd be mint.'

'OK, cool, so . . .' says Grace, thrusting her hand into her blazer pocket and shoving her shiny iPhone into my hand. '. . . put your number in my phone and I'll text you the deets.'

Uh oh.

I grip her phone tight, worried that my nervous, trembly hand might drop it. It's perfect. A flawless screen, no cracks, with a purple glittery case that's squidgy; when you squeeze it, the sparkles move about like lava. Proper pretty. Proper Grace. I look at her background image.

'That's Roger and Dodger, my Persian cats. Literally *the* cutest . . .' she says, smiling.

'Cute,' I reply.

EVERYONE in my year group has a phone. They're banned but everyone sneaks them in anyway, sending messages at breaktime and sneaking in selfies in the corridors. I reckon it would be weirder for someone to have no head rather than no phone. Someone could come into school with no head and people would be like, 'Oh yeah, that's the girl with no head' but if someone came into school with no phone, people would be like, 'OH MY GOD, CALL THE POLICE, SHE HASN'T GOT A PHONE!!!!'

I, obvs, am one of those phoneless losers and I just KNOW Grace is gonna think I'm *such* a baby for not having one. So I say:

'Oh! Bloody hell . . .' I roll my eyes in faux-despair, buying myself some time. '. . . stupid me . . .'

'What?' Grace asks.

'I've gone and left my phone at home, haven't I . . .' I lie, like the Big Liar I am.

'So? Just pop your number in, I'll text you later?' says Grace.

'Ah, no . . . but . . . the thing is . . . I can't *remember* my number, can I? I always forget what it is, stupid divhead!' I laugh. '07512 . . . or is it 215? I always get confused! How about,' I suggest, 'we just decide when and where to meet? Say, six-thirty p.m. outside Maccies?'

'I mean, I can always get my mum to come and pick you up from yours?'

ERM, NOPE. NO WAY YOU'RE COMING TO SEE NUMBER 64.

'No, it's all good. More fun like this, anyway! I WON'T BE LATE. I'LL GET THERE PROPER EARLY, LIKE AN HOUR EARLY.'

High-key aware that I'm coming off despo at this point, but I don't care. I'm going to this gig even if I have to die trying.

3.44 p.m.

I park myself on the school bus home. I start thinking that maybe this is the happiest I'll ever be, until I realise . . . I *despo* need a mobile phone.

It's stupid really, how come I haven't got one already? I must be the only teenager in the whole country without one. Even bloody babies have mobile phones these days! I mean, how does Tubs expect me to keep in contact with my new friends? A telegram? Homing pigeons? Two tin cans on a piece of string!?

4.05 p.m.

As soon as we pull up at my stop, I tumble off and sprint home. I run up the stairwell to Number 64, taking two steps at a time. Tubs will be home from work in exactly 1 hour and 25 minutes.

The key to asking for something you know your parents will never buy you is to catch them in a good mood.

I raid my money-saving tin, pulling out a tenner. Once again Glasto will have to wait: we have a new and more important priority. I leg it down to the big ASDA and purchase the following:

- 1 x packet pasta (little bow-tie ones, they're the best, am I right?)
- 1 x Smart Price tinned tomatoes
- 1 x packet of wafer-thin ham
- 1 x net-full of Babybel

Oh yeaaaaaah, we're having pasta bake tonight and what I lack in culinary skills, I will make up for in cheese.

5.30 p.m.
I stick water on the hob to boil, switch BBC Radio 2 on (old people LOVE Radio 2) and put a load of dirty clothes in the washing machine. Can't find the washing powder, so squirt a load of washing-up liquid in there instead, which will probs be fine.

I hear Tubs fumble with keys and open the front door, sighing heavily as she does so.

'HEY, MUMMY!' I yell.

'Indiana, do not start,' she barks back immediately.

Hm. This might be a tough gig . . .

'I've got tea on, washing in the machine and *et voila madame*, may I pour you a glass of wine?'

'Wine? Where did YOU get wine from?' She comes into the kitchen and sits down at the table, pulling off her boots and rubbing her sore feet.

'Found it under the sink! Must have been here before we arrived.'

'What is it?'

'Says here . . .' I read the label. '. . . says it's called *Vine Gar* – sounds French to me?'

'Lemme see?' says Tubs, reaching for the bottle.

She peers at the label. 'INDIANA, THAT'S VINEGAR! The stuff what you put on yer chips!'

'Haha, whoops, well never mind that – dinner is almost served!' I say, flourishing a tea towel.

'What are you up to?' she says accusingly.

'OH! OH, HO, HO! I see how it is! A LOVING daughter tries to do something NICE for her hardworking mother . . .' I stand behind her and start massaging her shoulders. '. . . and all I get is suspicion. I see how it is. Ooh, you feel tense . . .'

'Indi Raye . . .'

'Ohhh-kay . . . alright . . . it's just a small thing . . .'

She looks at me dead in the eye, frowning. She isn't here for my games so I get straight to the point.

'I need a mobile phone. Newest iPhone if possible. Now, I *know* it's expensive which is why I've taken the liberty of looking into all the best packages so that we can get the cheapest deal and really, we shouldn't need to pay more than £43.99 a month for it, so . . .'

Tubs ROARS with laughter as she heads to her bedroom to change.

'Erm, I'm struggling to see what's so bloody funny here, Tubs.'

'Forty quid a month?'

'Actually it's more like forty-four . . .'

'Oh, Indi, you are SO FUNNY, d'you know that? How long 'til dinner?'

'Ten minutes,' I reply, flatly. And she closes her door.

I suspect getting my hands on a phone is gonna be harder than I thought.

6.51 p.m.
Oh, turns out if you put washing-up liquid in a washing machine, it makes a flood of bubbles, which will overflow out of the washing machine and all over the kitchen floor. Which happened halfway through dinner. Which I'd burnt btw.

SATURDAY NOV 7th
10.30 a.m.
'So I was thinking . . . maybe we could get ready round your house next week, Indi, before the gig. Come and say hello to Mr and Mrs Raye. I bet your dad is boyfriend goals . . .' jokes Grace. She's swung by the chippy to talk logistics ahead of her brother's big gig on Friday.

'Ewwww, stop, that is massively giving me the ick, why would you say that?' I shriek, pushing white napkins into their silver holders.

''Cause you're pretty. So your dad must be handsome. It's literally genetics.'

Grace just said I was pretty. That's nice.

I really feel like our friendship – *can I call it that?* – has turned a corner. We even say hi in the corridors at school now. I'm not saying we're besties yet, but . . . there's hope. But they can't come round. Not yet.

'Ahhhh, the thing is, we're basically redecorating at ours. The whole place is a tip. I'm getting a walk-in wardrobe so . . .'

I clock Nisha and Grace give each other a side eye.

'Also it's just me and my mum at the minute. Dad's away,' I say.

Look at me, being all honest with my new friends.

'Oh right,' says Nisha, joining us. 'So, where is he then?'

'Australia,' I lie. 'We spoke the other night and he was like, "G'day, mate!" and I was like, "G'day, Dad!"'

'Woah, wait, so . . . how come he's there?' asks Grace.

'OK, so . . .' I say, sitting down opposite Grace. 'My Dad came to the UK when he was, like, twenty and he met Tubs and they *seriously* fell in love and had me . . .' (this part is actually true). 'Ever since then, we've just travelled the world like one big, happy, wandering family!'

'Wow, really?' says Nisha. 'I thought you were from London?'

'Naaaah, that was, like, just a temporary thing. So 'cause of my dad's job, one year we'd be in Shanghai, the next it would be Madrid. We'd stay there for eighteen months and next thing, we'd pack up to Johannesburg. One time, right, Tubs found an *actual snake* in the garden; I don't think it was dangerous or anything but she screamed at Dad until he requested a transfer to somewhere less "reptilian".'

The words just tumble out of my mouth, getting more and more elaborate with each sentence.

'We've been to Latvia . . . Tokyo . . . I've lived in the jungle and New York in one of those massive skyscrapers. Yeah. It's been busy. Anyway, we've come back to Manchester for a bit and Dad's still out there, working away, BUT I get so many amazing presents when he comes back. Something is currently being shipped to me from Down Under right now, but I have NO idea what it is.'

I look at their faces, concerned they don't believe me. But they Eat. It. Up.

'Oh my G, that is literally the COOLEST thing I have EVER heard, Indi!' squeals Grace. 'Maybe he'll send you a baby kangaroo?!'

'Think it's pretty illegal to post a kangaroo, Grace, but sure,' scoffs Nisha. 'Nah, that is pretty amazing, though, Ind. Your dad sounds soooooo cool.'

'Yeah, he is. He's the actual best,' I boast.

This is by far the biggest lie I've told Nisha and Grace and I should feel bad, but they've fallen for it hook, line and sinker. And what's more, they think I'm interesting! And cool!

'Oh my god, I'm gonna tell you something really embarrassing now, though, OK . . .' I continue. 'So I'm called Indiana, because it's the name of a place in America where . . . my parents, you know . . .'

I pull a grimacing face.

'Oh my G, WHAT?' screams Nisha.

'Yeah, my parents told me a few Christmases ago, across the dinner table, would you believe . . .'

Grace laughs. 'Ewwwww! Surely that means that every time someone says your name, a tiny part of you will always be reminded that your mum and dad—'

'No, don't say it!'

'. . . your mum and dad . . .'

'. . . *la la la*, don't wanna think about it!'

'. . . DID IT!'

'Nooooo, please, never say that again, I beg!' I squeal, putting my fingers in my ears.

Nisha cackles. 'Eh, it's not all bad, babe. At least you weren't conceived in Chichester, ennit!'

11.30 a.m.

Grace has gone shopping and Nisha and I are left clearing out the big fridge, which is good 'cause half of St Cath's seems to have turned up for lunch and I'm not in the mood for pleasantries when I've got other things on my mind. It's probably a good time to tell her I'm off to Reece's tonight. Also it bloody stinks in here so will be a good topic of conversation to take our minds off it.

'Maybe he *fancies* you!?' says Nisha.

'Reece Williams does NOT fancy me; he's just being nice, I think. I, er, haven't really made many friends in Manchester as yet so I think he's just taking *pity* on me, ha.'

I wipe down the sides of the fridge, and say that last bit with a deliberate bit of sadness in my voice, to let Nisha know that I'm still despo for us to be besties.

I hope she might say 'Well, we're friends!' back . . . but she doesn't.

She raises her eyebrows. 'OK, but you've got to admit, it WELL sounds like a first date, ennit,'

'No way! His parents will be there! It's not a date.'

'OK! . . . It might be true looooove, though!'

'Oh my god, STOP IT!' I yell, sloshing water from the bucket at her.

'You stop it!' she screams back, squeezing her sponge out on my hair, a back and forth that continues until Alan comes in and gives us a right royal telling-off. Poor Alan. I think he regrets the day he hired me.

2.19 p.m.

'Oh my GGGGGGG, that is soooooooooo nice, that's *just* your colour!' says Nisha, holding up a pink Rimmel lipstick. Grace went on a rampage in Boots and she's bought LOADS of make-up. I'm so jealous that she can afford mascara without deep frying on the weekends like us.

'Daddy literally gave me twenty quid as I was leaving the house this morning,' she says, emptying the rest of the bag out on to the table. Nisha shrieks with joy. Bottles of this, tubes of that. Glittery eyeshadow and glossy lipbalms.

'Cute, right?' gushes Grace. She turns to Nisha. 'And I was thinking, *how* nice will this go with my new top, the one with the off-the-shoulders, y'know, the lilac one? Thinking I might wear it to the gig next weekend.'

'Oh my G, yessssss it SO will,' says Nisha.

Oh god, what am I gonna wear? Standard hoodie and leggings I guess . . . if my leggings are clean . . .

'Have yer got my colour there, Grace?' jokes Alan.

'Ermmmm, let me see, I think this one for you, Al, it's called *Saucy Lady*, this lippy. You want some on?' she laughs.

'Maybe later,' he chuckles.

I pick up a cream blusher and inspect it.

'Indi?' asks Grace. 'Like, no offence, yeah, but how come you don't wear make-up?'

It's a fair question. Girls at St Cath's are OBSESSED with the way they look. They roll their skirts up on the way to school to make them shorter (and then roll them back down when they *enter* school before they get busted by Mrs Angus, history teacher, who goes around with a ruler checking the length). Make-up is banned but *everyone's* wearing foundation and concealer, lipgloss and mascara, minimum.

Last week, Maya Richards came in with so much blusher, her cheeks looked like two rashers of bacon, and her form tutor made her scrub it all off in the girls' toilets but she got soap in her eyes and then she spent the day looking like she had two stink-eyes, so really, she ended up looking worse.

Truth is, make-up and hairspray and Nike trainers and phones and everything else I want is just . . . expensive. There's no way Tubs would ever be able to buy this stuff for me. Not gonna tell Grace and Nisha that, obvs, so I just shrug.

'LET'S GIVE YOU A MAKEOVER!' yells Grace.

'YAAAAAAAAAAAAAAAASS!' shouts Nisha. 'For your DATE tonight!'

Grace's mouth drops. Nisha mouths 'sorry' to me.

'OH EM GGGG, who are you going on a date with?'

I roll my eyes. 'NO, seriously, it isn't a date. I'm going over to Reece's for tea, that's all.'

'OK . . .' smiles Grace, somewhat sceptically. 'Well, you still want to look nice, don't you? He's cute.'

Is he? Is Reece cute?

Nish and Grace set to work, adding lotions and powders and slicks of this-and-that to my face, buffing with brushes and smudging with thumbs, making my face feel dry and a bit tight. They'd better not give me Maya Richards' bacon cheeks. I just *know* I'm gonna look ridiculous. Make-up is for girls like Grace, not girls like me. But it's kinda nice, being experimented on like this.

'Oh my gee, you look SNATCHED. Ready to have a look?' asks Nisha finally. She flicks open a mirror compact and reveals my reflection.

I've got gold eyeshadow up to my eyebrows.

Big spidery false eyelashes.

There's layer upon layer of neon pink lipstick.

I LOOK LIKE A BLOODY CLOWN.

I LOVE IT.

4.16 p.m.
Dancing round my bedroom to the Foo Fighters. I say dancing, *thrashing* would be a better word. Gary is currently staring at me from on top of my chest of drawers. His big old bulbous eyes locking mine from his terrarium.

'What is it, Gary?' I say, out loud.

'No, nothing, my love . . .' he seems to reply, camply.

I jump off my bed and get closer to him. 'No, go on, spit it out.'

He puts his foot up on the glass. *'You look like a low-quality Instagram model.'*

'Errrrr, rude!' I gasp.

'Listen, I'm just trying to be a good little dragon baby, I'm here to tell you how it is, my dahling!'

I tip some crickets into his tank to shut him up.

CHAPTER 7
JOHNNY HOTPANTS

SATURDAY NOV 7th
6.01 p.m.

Strolling up the pebbled driveway, past a shiny, silver car which has an Audi badge on the front. *These are swanky cars, Dad always wanted one.* The house, a fancy detached with a big red door, is tucked in the corner of Greenbank Drive, a cul de sac with a collection of ten, maybe twelve super-nice houses.

There's a doormat at my feet that says *Welcome.* I clock my dirty trainers and give them a vigorous rub. It doesn't help matters, so I kick them off and hide them behind a long umbrella that's leaning against the wall and ring the doorbell, which chimes the tune of Big Ben.

Fancy.

'Oh, hello,' Reece says, a bit self-consciously as he opens the door, almost as if he wasn't expecting me. He's wearing a light blue cotton shirt, which seems a bit formal for home-wear.

'Er, hi. Wasn't sure if this was the right address . . .'

'Should have just used Google Maps!'

WELL, THAT WOULD BE NICE, BUT I DON'T HAVE A PHONE, DO I?

'What have you put on your face?' he asks.

'Make-up, obvs. Grace did it. Does it look alright?'

He gulps and then says, 'Yes. Fine.'

Reece's mum swings round the door at the far end of the entrance hall. She has a wooden spoon in one hand and is wearing a blue striped apron. She's got super-short blonde afro hair and a big smile. She looks like the type of woman who bakes on a weekend, like a proper mum. Tubs only bakes when *The Great British Bake Off* is on, and I'm pretty sure it's because she's lustful for Paul Hollywood.

'Ah, you must be Indiana! I'm Gloria! Come, come in! Reece, open the door properly!' she fusses.

I spot a chandelier in the hallway.

Oh god, oh god, oh god, I'm not posh enough to be here. Think quick, Indi.

'Ah, good EVENING, Mrs Williams!' I exclaim, following Reece down the hallway. And in my POSHEST voice I say, 'Please will *one* forgive me, *one's* removed *one's* shoes already. Little bit muddy after a spot of horse riding this arvo!'

Reece's jaw more or less hits the floor.

'Horse ridin', eh?' says Gloria. 'Well, good for you. Can't say I've ever ridden a horse before. Listen, you two, set the table for me, please. Dinner's in five.'

Reece grabs me by the wrist and pulls me into the dining room. *They have a DINING ROOM.*

'What are you doing!?' he hisses.

'What? I mean . . . *pardon*?' I reply, tittering.

He leans forward on the table in front of us. 'Why has the Duchess of England appeared at my house?'

'What does thou mean? I always speaketh like this . . .' I reply, flourishing a hand.

Reece rolls his eyes. 'No, you don't, just be normal, you weirdo!'

'One cannot.'

Reece looks like he's about to laugh. 'Why?'

'Because, Reece,' I hiss back, breaking character, '. . . because I need to make a good impression! You've got a chandelier in your hallway and we're standing in your DINING ROOM. Your family are posh!'

'No, we're not. We're just dead normal. Also, didn't YOU say that you've got a hot tub on your balcony?'

Good point. It was a lie, though . . .

'I . . . er . . . erm . . .' I stutter.

Reece shoves some forks into my hand. 'We're not posh. My mum works for the NHS and my dad works in cars.'

I help lay them out. 'Oh what, like a mechanic?' I ask accusingly. 'Sorts out greasy engines, does he? Head under the bonnet, wearing overalls?'

'No . . .'

'So, he works in an office? Like the people who SELL the cars?'

'Yeah . . .' Reece replies, shuffling uncomfortably.

'Does he MANAGE A TEAM?' I ask, pointing a fork at Reece perhaps a bit too aggressively.

'Yeah, like a group of, like, thirty people or something, but they're proper lads, they are—'

'DOES HE HAVE A BRIEFCASE?'

'Well, no, it's more like a *manbag* if anything—'

'HE'S POSH. AKA so are you and so's your mum by association and *one is not about to make a fool of oneself in front of Britain's elite so—*'

'Alriiiiiiight, take a seat, grub's up!' says Reece's dad, clapping his hands together as he enters. 'Ah, ya must be Indi! Pleased to meet ya, I'm Anthony, but everyone calls me Tony.'

He reaches out a hand and I shake it. He's got big hands, but then again, he's a big dad; his head almost hit the doorframe as he came in.

'Tony! The pleasure's all mine,' I reply in my posh accent. 'May I comment on what a beautiful home you have!'

Tony peers at me over his glasses, trying to work me out. 'Oh, thank you. Been here eleven years now . . .'

'Sit, sit everyone,' says Gloria.

'Did you do the gravy, Glor?' asks Tony.

Gloria sits down.

'Yes, yes, over there at the end of the table, look. SO, Indiana . . . spuds for ya?' She dumps a spoonful on my plate without waiting for an answer. 'How's St Catherine's treatin' ya?'

I grind some pepper on my chicken, all sophisticated. 'Oh, just marvellous!' I lie. 'I must say I was a little dubious having spent many years at Eton, but I've been rather pleasantly surprised!'

Everyone stops what they're doing and looks right at me. Reece rolls his eyes hard.

'Eton?' asks Gloria. 'I thought Eton was an all-boys school? Didn't the prime minister go there, Tony?'

'Yeah, I think that's right. Eton, you say?'

Uh oh, caught out already . . .

'Well, they made an *exception* for me you see, said I had an exceedingly bigger brain . . .'

Tony looks at Gloria with a little smile, raising his eyebrow. 'Ah, is that right?'

I raise my glass. 'Anyway, all, chin-chin, many thanks for your hospitality!' I say. Everyone cheers and clinks my glass.

'So, Eton, eh . . . what is it ya parents do, Indiana?' Gloria asks, taking a sip of wine.

'Well,' I say, lowering my voice. 'I shouldn't really tell you this, but between us; they both work for Her Majesty's Super Secret Service. MI6. All super hush-hush, you know how it is.'

'I see! You really are very well-bred, aren't you, Indiana . . .' says Gloria and it looks like Tony kicks her under the table playfully.

'Oh yes,' I reply, picking up a chicken drumstick and chomping into it, like a caveman.

'Well listen, round here, we just like everyone to feel comfortable, don't we, Tone?'

Tony burps loudly. 'That's right. No airs and graces from me,' he says.

'Dad!' cries Reece, laughing. 'So embarrassing.'

As dinner continues, I learn loads of stuff about Reece and his family.

Tony's a massive Burnley fan; he's gone to every home game for the last fifteen years. Gloria works in a fancy office in town but also has an Etsy shop selling tables and chairs and dressers which she refurbishes herself in the garage.

We talk about the fact I haven't worked out what I want to do when I finish school and Reece talks about his big plan to study medicine and become a doctor. Tony and Gloria look proper proud of him and stop eating while he speaks, savouring every word.

It makes me wonder what my dad is doing right now.

I suppose he might be proud of me, if he knew what I was up to. I wish I could tell him about my job at The Jolly Fryer and having dinner with the Williamses and eating with their fancy cutlery, and about my new mate Reece. And Gary too, who definitely doesn't eat with a fork but . . . OOO, IMAGINE A LITTLE GECKO CUTLERY SET!

Someone should invent that.

8.42 p.m.
Sitting on the doorstep pulling my grubby trainers back on. Really need those Nikes y'know.

'What was all that posh act about, then?' asks Reece. 'Pretty obvious you didn't go to Eton, mate.'

I decide to ignore his specific question, and distract him by asking, 'Did they like me!?'

Reece looks at me quizzically. 'Course they did, stupid. When you were being yourself, like. You really are a weirdo, Indi Raye. Anyway, you'll have to invite me round yours next, to meet your mum and dad.'

His mention of Dad makes my heart race for a second.

'Erm, yeah, we must do that . . . sometime,' I reply, non-committedly. 'Although it's just my mum. Just me and Tubs.'

'Oh yeah, sorry. You said before. Dad's on a work trip, right?'

'Yeah. I mean, he travels the world and that so . . . But I thought he might have . . . y'know . . . come to Manchester by now. 'Cause like, it's my birthday soon and that and I know he wouldn't want to miss it. But, erm, yeah, he hasn't . . .'

God I'm blabbing on like such a loser.

'Sorry, I don't know why I'm telling you this. Bit weird, soz . . .' I say, flustered.

Oh god, I've made it awks.

'No, it's fine,' Reece replies calmly. 'I don't mind.'

10.11 p.m.

Tucked up in bed, under my blue spotty duvet cover. Doodling a bit more Disco Girl. Must admit the poor lass has been on the backburner recently. Too much going on. Tubs is on lates tonight. Thought I might stay up and wait for her. Also have these weird butterflies in my stomach. Suppose that's what you get when you've had a good day.

Reece is really nice.

I just feel a bit stupid about pretending to be posh. *Why do I do stuff like that?* Even around people I like, I just can't seem to stop myself lying. Oh, I just wish I could walk in there and be myself! And just tell him about Dad and that there's no big work trip, and that truthfully, I don't know where the bloody hell he is.

But the words just don't seem to come out.

TUESDAY NOV 10th
1.07 p.m.

Off to check in with Mrs Jenkinson – or Jenko as I've started calling her – about how I've settled in, but I have LITERALLY BEEN STOPPED IN MY TRACKS BY LOVE.

There's a boy. Sitting on the chairs outside Jenko's office.

I've never seen him before. Never seen him around school. Never been in the chippy. Must be in one of the years above.

He has sandy brown hair and blue eyes, milky, freckly skin with THE nicest, whitest teeth. He's chewing gum and picking at a scab on his arm.

Probs got his injury from doing skateboarding or another sexy sport like . . . like . . . badminton. Mmmm, badminton.

He looks up, smiles and says, 'Here comes trouble.' I've always wondered if love at first sight exists, but I think it might 'cause it feels like someone's dialled down all the sounds in the corridor. Everything around me is fuzzy and my mouth is all dry and I have to gulp to find moisture.

'What?' I ask.

'Seen you about. You bought that lizard, yeah?'

I can't even respond because of how beautiful he is, so I just stutter, 'I, er, erm . . .?' and then Jenko calls me into her office and off I go, KICKING MYSELF FOR BEING SO BLOODY DULL IN FRONT THE MOST UNREAL BOY I'VE EVER LAID MY EYES ON.

2.11 p.m.

In science.

Can't concentrate.

Mrs Arkwright is trying to teach us about the physics of the universe today but she may as well give up on me now because my brain is another planet, the Planet of Love. Forget black holes and Milky Ways, all I can think about is necking on.

He was absolute boyfriend goals.

Should have given him Frisky Eyes.

2.16 p.m.

I'm gonna call him Johnny Hotpants until I find out his name.

CHAPTER 8

THE HOT RECRUITS

FRIDAY NOV 13th

5.02 p.m.

'Home by eight o'clock sharp, OK?' says Tubs. 'I'm on lates and I want yer back before me.'

'Tubs, the gig doesn't start until seven . . .' I shout over the hairdryer. The hair is freshly washed, no hint of haddock tonight.

'OK, nine p.m.'

'Eleven p.m.!' I bargain.

'Ten p.m., that's my last offer. Calling the police if you're not back by then.'

'Deal,' I say before literally skipping out of the flat.

5.29 p.m.

I love going on the tram in Manchester.

What is a tram anyway? Is it a bus? Is it a train?

NEITHER. IT'S A TRAM.

It picks up grandmas with tartan shopping trolleys and mums with five kids in tow and sweary teenage boys. I love watching the city that's become my new home go whizzing past.

There's cool old buildings with graffiti on them and there's the emblem of bees on everything; bees on public bins and bee statues and bees on bollards. Apparently, it's because people in Manchester have always been hard workers so the worker bee has become their little mascot.

I wish I was a hard worker. My mascot would probably be a sloth or a slow worm.

There's people with bags and bags of Primark goodies and people hanging around the town hall drinking cans of lager and football fans off to the City game.

5.41 p.m.

I'm nervous.

Today we move into Real Friends Territory.

Which is much different from School Territory or Chippy Territory.

Here's a collection of random thoughts you have when you're nervous:

Please don't make a div of yourself today.
Hope I'm wearing the right fit.
What if the other girls turn up in mini-dresses?

Grace loves a mini-dress.

There's a charity shop across the road and there's a red mini-dress in the window.

I could go and buy it and do a quick change in Maccies toilets?

Actually, probs not.

An eighty-year-old grandma probs died in that red mini-dress.

R.I.P. granny.

Getting hangry now. I'm off to go and buy some McNuggets.

5.50 p.m.
Six chicken nuggets just cost me £3.19 but they are bloody delicious.

5.57 p.m.
Just bought six MORE nuggets.

I'm gonna end up looking like a walking McNugget at this rate.

Would you rather look like a chicken nugget or an actual chicken?

6.27 p.m.

Eeek, they're here. I can see them walking down the high street.

THIS IS IT.

OK, be chill, Indi Raye.

I decide to lean against the frontage of Maccies, one leg tucked up behind me, looking in the opposite direction to make me appear all cool and blasé even though I am sweating, *oh my god, I'm sweating HARD* and we haven't even danced yet.

'Hey sis!' Nisha shouts over to me.

'Oh! Oh, hey you guys!' I call back, acting like I hadn't intently watched them approach. We have a quick hug, which feels a bit awks 'cause we haven't done that before, but I guess that's what proper girlfriends do.

Grace sniffs my coat and crinkles her nose.

'Wow, you literally smell of chicken nuggets, Indi . . . here, have a chewing gum . . .' says Grace, reaching into her bag and squeezing me a spearmint one out of the packet.

I take the gum and pop it in my mouth. 'Thanks. Yeah, I had twelve of them while I was waiting.'

'TWELVE!? You gotta be careful, you're gonna get chunky, babe!' laughs Grace.

Nisha rolls her eyes and I copy, rolling mine too.

Grace seems to care a lot about her weight. She'd look stunnin' no matter what weight she was. Tonight she's wearing a pink mini-dress and Converse trainers and a pink, fluffy bomber jacket with her blonde hair in a high-pony with a gold scrunchie, and black eyeliner smudged along her lashline. She looks iconic.

I thank god for Nisha who's a bit more dressed down: a black puffer jacket, purple-and-blue tie-dye tee and platform trainers, but I still feel underdressed in my old jeans and bottle-green hoodie.

'Would you rather look like a chicken nugget or an actual chicken?' I ask.

'Hmm, well, if you were a nugget, people would try and bite you all the time, ennit, but if you were a chicken you'd have one of those wattles,' says Nisha, taking my silly question much more seriously than I imagined she would.

'What the hell is a wattle?' laughs Grace.

'A wattle,' states Nisha, '. . . is the funny red thing under their chins. It flaps about going goggle-loggle-loggle.'

She's making an imaginary wattle with her hand, flapping it about under her chin, and then at Grace's face, who shrieks.

'Right, wattles aside, girls, here's the plan. We rave. We rave hard,' says Nisha.

'OK,' I say breathlessly. *I'm so excited I need to pee. Tell you what, if I DID have a wattle, it would be goggling like a crazy right now!*

'LET'S GO!' shouts Grace.

6.34 p.m.

We ramble through the streets of Manchester and from a hundred metres away, we spot the shiny green tiles that embellish the outside walls of The Crown & Castle. Floral hanging baskets are suspended above the pathway. On first glance, it looks pretty for a pub, but on closer inspection, the tiles are cracked, the flowers are plastic and the word 'Crown' is missing it's 'w' so it actually reads 'Cron'.

There are two bouncers on the door, who nod us in even though they know we're underage – our names are down on the GUEST LIST! *We're with the band, baby!*

Once we're inside, I have to try proper hard not to squeal with excitement. WE'RE IN A PROPER, GROWN-UPS' PUB! It smells musty, like the beer Dad used to drink, blended with old smoke.

The walls are adorned with photos of Manchester icons: *Coronation Street* actors, bands (Oasis, of course!), comedians and Man United footballers, every photograph with their autograph squiggled across hurriedly in black permanent marker.

Out of nowhere, this *ridiculously* stunning boy saunters towards us through the crowd surrounding the bar. He's tall, has floppy *pink* hair that he pushes back with his hand, wears an oversized denim bomber jacket and has a pint in his hand.

'Oi, oi,' he says to us and I look around at the girls, perplexed.

Is HE talking to US?

'Alright,' says Grace.

'Hey, Oliver,' waves Nisha.

'Indi, this is Oliver, my big bro.'

Ohhhhhh, Grace's brother. Of course her brother is boyfriend goals. Good genetics run in the Walkden family too.

'Welcome to where the magic happens, girls,' he says.

'Right, come on, you're eighteen now, Ol. Buy us some beers, then?' asks Grace.

'No way, you're underage.'

'So?'

'Listen, this is a big one for us. *The Hot Recruits*—' he begins.

Nisha and I both snigger.

'What?' he asks, deadpan.

'Nowt!' laughs Nisha.

'Come on, get it out your system . . .'

'*The Hot Recruits!?* That's your band name!?' I giggle.

'Whatever. Listen, you girls are here to do one job, OK? Just make sure, when we're on, you dance for us right down the front and scream loudly and stuff, OK? Matty's filming this for our YouTube. Oh, and don't dance for the other bands, 'cause we want them to look like they've got no fans.'

7.13 p.m.

The first band – who has decided to wear matching oversized tweed blazers – strikes up and . . . oh wow, they're hideous!

SO, SO BAD.

The lead singer is screaming more than singing and the barman winces slightly at the noise. But I don't care. This is my first gig and it's amazing! The pub fills up with uni students, mums and dads of teenage band members, clapping and whooping with pride, old rockers in band tees and us.

The three of us.

Dancing like crazy, doing air guitars and throwing our heads back and forward in time to the music totally ignoring Oliver's request not to dance for his rival musicians. We chug glasses of Coca Cola fast. Nisha burps loudly every five seconds, making us hoot with laughter.

'Nisha, stop! That woman over there literally just GLARED at you!' laughs Grace, gesturing behind us.

'Oh my G, don't look, don't look, she's furious!' I laugh over the drumbeat.

Grace tries to upgrade us with some fruity ciders at the bar, doing Frisky Eyes and giggling with the barman, but he knows she's Oliver's little sister and she comes back with three more Cokes instead. We sway to the music, arms round each other's waists.

The Hot Recruits come on and Grace gives Oliver a little thumbs up which is cute. He actually looks *AMAZING* on bass guitar. I don't tell Grace that, obvs, 'cause she'll be grossed out . . . but the way his mouth hangs ajar slightly as he plays . . . *wowzers.*

'Girls, I need to tell you something!' I shout. 'I saw a boy, at school, and oh my G, he was . . . like . . . beautiful!'

'Who!?' yells Nisha.

'I dunno! That's the problem! I'm new, remember??'

'What's he look like?' shouts Grace. 'I'm a great detective, I'll work it out!'

'He had really white teeth!' I shout back.

'What?' yells Nisha, over the noise of a ferocious

guitar solo.

'I said, he had really white – ah, never mind!' I yell back.

'Errrrrr, what about Reeeeeeeece anyway?' shouts Nisha. 'How did your big date go?'

'Yeaaaaah! Did you neck on?' shouts Grace.

'How many times, it wasn't a date!' I protest.

It really wasn't. Why do they they keep saying that? Me and Reece are just friends? Friends can have dinner at each other's houses, can't they? Or maybe they can't? Maybe people don't do that at St Cath's? Oh god, I hope people aren't gossiping about us. There's really nothing going on. Nothing.

If I was sweaty with nerves when I started the evening, the raving leaves me proper drenched as we leave. The cold, wintery air is a welcome relief for my sweaty fringe, stuck to my forehead, and for Nisha and Grace who both look like a pair of tomatoes. We spill out of the pub, gabbling away like a flock of hens.

'Oh my G, I'm a hot mess!' sighs Grace. 'Let's take an end-of-night selfie! Nisha, you do it, you've got the longest arm.'

'Kay,' says Nisha, pulling out her Samsung. As she lifts the phone up high to make sure we can all get in, a message flashes across the screen. Whoever it's from is saved in her phone with three red heart emojis and the message reads:

> kk night night spk tomorrow bby

Grace screams into the night.

'NIIIIIISSSSSSSSSSSSSSHHHHHHHHHH HHAAAAAAAAAAAA!'

She jumps up and snatches Nisha's phone from her hand.

'WHOOOOOOOOOO is THHIIIIIIIIIIIIS!?!?!?!?!?!'

The colour drains from Nisha's face and she says seriously: 'Give it back. It's no one, honest.'

'Nope!' Grace says gleefully. 'Not until you tell me who your boyfriiiiiiend is? Indi, catch!'

Grace throws the phone to me, and I grapple for it, trying not to let it fall to the ground and smash.

Nisha says, 'Indi, give it?' but if I do that, Grace will think I'm proper lame, ruining the fun, and we've had such a good night.

But Nish is starting to look a bit distraught.

I tease her with it for a moment, just to prove I'm not a Boring Betty, and then hand it back to her. Grace tuts, but Nisha looks so relieved, I think I made the right decision.

'You two are idiots, you know . . .' grumbles Nisha, but she's smiling so there's no hard feelings.

Grace smiles back but I can tell she's disappointed that Nisha's clearly got a secret. I always thought Grace and Nisha knew everything about each other . . . but apparently not.

'Got my eye on you, Nisha Chowdhury, you sly dog,' she teases.

'Yeah, OK, OK, can we go now? Big Diwali celebrations tomorrow, ennit. Got half of Manchester coming round my house,' she says, linking both of us by the arms and we skip down the lamp-lit streets towards home.

10.58 p.m.
Best night ever.

Told Gary all about it and he said, *'Pics, or it didn't happen.'*

Not sure how I got lumbered with such a sassy gecko.

CHAPTER 9

DO YOU WANNA COME OVER TONIGHT AND CHECK OUT MY GECKO?

MONDAY NOV 23rd
5.58 a.m.

I'm up early today by my standards and there's one reason for that, and one reason only: TODAY IS MY BIRTHDAY!

Happy birthday to me! Fourteen years old!

I brandish a tape measure.

Tubs has got this sewing tin which she keeps in the cupboard for stitching up socks with holes in them and also for the time she squatted down in Tesco to reach for a packet of rice and ripped the crotch of her work trousers. It was proper cringey. I had to use her coat to shield her bum as we went through the checkout. Anyway, inside the sewing tin is this tape measure which I've nicked so that I can check my boobs for growth as a little birthday treat.

There's a knack to it. You see, if you breathe out, it makes your measurement slightly bigger, by a few millimetres. You look like a puffer fish, all huffing and puffing as you do it, but every millimetre counts! Tell you what, my boobs do *feel* bigger. Maybe I am turning into a woman after all!

All this adulting *does* mean I proper need to get a move on with finding a boyfriend though.

'That would be a nice birthday treat, wouldn't it?' I say to Gary, who's currently basking in his tank, on the rock right under the heat lamp.

'One can only hope, dear,' he drones.

6.33 a.m.
Dippy eggs and toast are waiting for me on the kitchen table with a glass of orange juice. Mine and Tubs's birthday tradition. There's one solo birthday card too. Was hoping it's from Dad but I can tell from the handwriting that it's from my Auntie Cassandra.

Tubs gestures for me to take a seat. She's acting a bit weird, her lips pursed together; like, you'd think she'd have wished me a happy birthday by now?

I watch her, puzzled, cracking the top of my egg with my spoon.

She reaches into her handbag hanging on the doorhandle and pulls out a small rectangular box, wrapped in green paper with metallic silver stars, and places it next to my egg. It's small . . . but when I pick it up, I realise it's also quite weighty for its size . . .

My hands are proper trembling as I tear the paper off it. *Oh my G. Is this what I think it is . . .*

'For goodness' sake, Indi, please look after it . . .'

Oh my GGGGG, IT'S A MOBILE PHONE! AN IPHONE! I AM OFFICIALLY DEEEEAAAAD!

'Jesus Christ!' I shout.

'LANGUAGE!' shouts Tubs back.

'How did you even afford this though!?' I shriek.

'Ask no questions and I will tell you no lies. Happy birthday.'

I can't believe it. *I CAN'T BELIEVE IT.* I would have bet you one million U.S. dollars that Tubs would have bought me an old second-hand Motorola from the Mobiles 4 Us shop down Withington Road.

I smile at her ecstatically, but quickly realise we need to give it back to the shop.

'Thanks, Tubs. But we can't afford this,' I say, carefully placing the box down again.

'Well, look, I managed to sort out the credit card and I spoke to work about getting an advance on this month's pay and . . . look, doesn't matter. Consider it your birthday *and your* Christmas present. For the next three years.'

'THANK YOU, THANK YOU, THANK YOUUUU!'

I hug her so tightly. This might be the BEST thing she's ever done for me! She tells me I'm not allowed to take it to school in case I lose it, and she's right; it would probs end up down the loos at St Cath's before 10 a.m. so I leave it under Gary's watchful eye, but WOOHOOOOOOOO!

I, INDI RAYE, AM THE OWNER OF A REAL-LIFE MOBILE PHONE!

10.30 a.m.

Today just gets better and better. First lesson is art and Miss Addo just gave me top marks for the papier-mâché version of our own heads we've been making. Everyone else's looked like they'd been run over by an articulated lorry. Mine, with its dodgy nose and green woollen hair, looked like it had been hit by a small family car, like a Skoda or something, making it the best in the class.

1.27 p.m.

Reece pulls out a present from his rucksack at lunchtime. It's wrapped in beautiful gold paper and tied with a red velvet bow.

I suddenly feel butterflies in my stomach as I open it. Been feeling a bit weird about Grace and Nisha saying Reece fancies me and now we're in the busiest corridor where *everyone* can see us. Alice Welby just slows down her walk on her way to the loos to get a glance.

'You didn't wrap this . . .' I tease.

'No, you're right, Mum did . . .'

I pull out a black beret. 'It's . . . a . . . hat?' I say.

'Ta-daaaa!' he declares. Reece shoves me playfully. 'I know how much you *love* your fish-and-chip-shop hat, I thought you might like a different one to wear outside working hours. My mum helped me pick it.'

It's actually proper cool. It reminds me of a hat worn by Debbie Harry from Blondie, who is *actual* fashion goals.

'It's proper nice, thanks, Reece. But you know you didn't have to . . .'

'Of course I did, mate, it's your birthday,' he says smiling and re-adjusting his glasses. 'Try it on then.'

'Nah, not yet,' I say, embarrassed. 'Thanks, though.'

'Try the hat! Try the hat!' he starts shouting giddily, and EVERYONE in the corridor turns around. 'TRY THE HAT!'

'Reece, pack it in!' I hiss angrily. 'I'll try it later, OK?'

His face looks like I've just slapped him. The bell rings for class and he slopes off, leaving me standing here with my new beret and a deep sense of regret.

2.07 p.m.

Sitting in maths feeling the most hideous I've felt in a long time. The beret is on the table in front of me and I feel like it's staring at me.

Reece did a proper nice thing, buying me a present. He probs used his own pocket money and everything.

But . . . but isn't it a bit soon to buy me a present?

I stuff it to the bottom of my schoolbag. If I can't see it, I don't have to think about what it all means.

3.48 p.m.

The whole school bus is playing volleyball with a deflated football. We're all ignoring Bus Driver who's telling us to stop and everyone cheers when I give it an almighty punch and it goes flying towards some Year 11s. Liam Horrace shouts: 'It's Indi's birthday, everyone!' and he kicks off a rendition of 'Happy Birthday' for me and the whole bus sings and I'm just so happy and excited to be going home to play on my new phone, that I momentarily forget about the Reece drama.

I even saw Johnny Hotpants today near the P.E. block. He was in his green-and-white football kit. There should have been a warning about that, 'cause, wowzers, he looked unreal. Happy birthday indeed.

4.16 p.m.
I swig from the orange juice carton whilst shoving my new beret to the bottom of my wardrobe.

In you go, mate. I'll deal with you later.

And then, I turn my attention to a much better present, one that fills me with giddy excitement.

An actual phone.

All for me.

A world of possibility is at my fingertips.

I hold down the 'ON' button and the blackness of the screen illuminates with a searing white light. The display reads 'Hello' and I whisper 'hello' back.

I'm captivated.

I swipe through to the home screen and tap through the various apps; I download Spotify straight away – a world of new and old songs at my fingertips.

Imagine the millions of amazing B-sides and live recordings I'll be able to listen to! I take a photo of Gary who looks sooooo cute on camera (and make him my lock-screen AND home-screen), then I put Tubs's number in the contacts. It's the only number I know by heart.

Although *in theory*, I *could* contact anyone in the world right now . . .

4.20 p.m.
I've had an idea.

Tubs won't be back until at least nine o'clock tonight. She's left me some McDonald's vouchers for a birthday tea, win.

I sneak into her bedroom and search her bedside table. A little jar of stuff that smells like lavender . . . a packet of paracetamol . . . a book called *The Erotic Mind* (!?!?!) and then . . . BINGO. An old address book.

Who even owns these any more?

I flip through it – it's alphabetised – and get to 'P'. P for Paul.

Except Tubs has scrubbed out his name and relabelled it with the word 'Pig'.

She must be really angry . . .

138

And there it is. His mobile number, staring back at me.

My hands suddenly go all shaky.

I mean, what do I say?

> heeeeeyy dad! tubs got me a phone
> for my bday! thought i'd text to say hello!

No. That's not right. He's the dad. He should have contacted me, right?

> heeeeeeeey bestie think you forgot my
> bday today but never mind! tubs got me a
> new phone and this is my number so . . .

Nope. Too nice.

> hey dad. its my birthday today.
> did you forget?

But that looks like I'm moody with him and I don't want him to think I'm in a grump.

Even though I am.

I'm bloody furious with him.

It's gone six o'clock at night and he's not even sent a card, let alone a present. Not even a phonecall? Who forgets their daughter's birthday???

I keep writing and deleting, writing and deleting, not quite knowing how to say it. In the end, I settle with:

> this is my new number. id love to see you soon. love indi x

11.59 p.m.
Can't sleep. Keep checking for a text back.

Tubs is right. Paul is a pig.

I stick my foot out of my bed and kick over a box of Dad's treasured LPs. Some of them will probably be scratched now, but who cares anyway.

I've been ghosted by my own dad.

THURSDAY NOV 26th
9.05 p.m.
This morning's assembly is run by Mrs Jenkinson who is currently giving us a lecture on 'self-care', which is a bit of a joke seeing as there's always a shortage of loo roll in the St Cath's girls toilets. Tell

that to my nether regions who are frequently forced to drip-dry, Jenko.

Luckily I've got a new phone and some earphones to drown her out with the sound of some Iron Maiden.

Stupid Jenko.

Yes, I'm in a bad mood today.

Also, Reece is defo ignoring me after beret-gate. On Tuesday afternoon, I got on the bus and saved him a place. Tapped the orange seat next to me as he approached, but he pretended he hadn't seen me and went to the upstairs deck, WHICH CAN I JUST SAY, he NEVER does.

And yesterday in German, I whispered 'meerschweiiiiiiinchen' at him in a ghostly voice and he didn't respond so I did it again and he whispered back, 'Shush. I'm trying to listen.'

He's DEFO well angry with me. Sort of miss him a bit.

FRIDAY NOV 27th
1.52 p.m.

Grace runs really weirdly. She's all arms and legs. It's quite a sight to behold. Like a big octopus. Within five minutes of athletics, she manages to ditch it altogether and head back inside, claiming her period cramps are too intense, although I think she's lying 'cause she winked at me as she departed the school field. I wish I had a period to use as an excuse to avoid P.E. I'm literally the latest developer in the entire world. What if I just stay like a big overgrown baby forever?

'I just find tampons, y'know, more adulty,' Grace says in the changing rooms.

'If I wore tampons, they wouldn't stand a chance against my flow,' says Nisha, which makes me snort with laughter. 'I'm serious! I have to wear those heavy-duty night-time pads 'cause my periods are so bad. Feel like I'm wearing a nappy, ennit.'

I'm really trying not to lie to the girls so much, so I join in with the periods chat, but I don't let on that *I haven't actually started* my period as yet. I mean, they don't exactly sound fun. But you bet I check my knickers every time I go to the loo, hoping for a little bloodstain, welcoming me to womanhood.

'The idea of tampons freaks me out a bit,' I laugh. 'I don't even really know . . . you know . . . how you'd . . . y'know, get one up there!'

'It's super-easy. I'll explain it to you,' says Grace. 'Whenever you invite me round to your house.'

SATURDAY NOV 28ᵗʰ

11.05 a.m.

Grace is sitting at our table at the chippy, wanging on about *her* birthday next week. She usually comes towards the end of our shift, but she's turned up *right* as I'm putting the plaice out, and it's a bit distracting. Alan scowls at her, and me, but I know he'd never kick Grace out. We're like his adopted daughters.

'And basically, Mum said I can have a big sleepover, and I can literally order any cake from Green's and, like, anyone can stay over. Even the lads.'

Green's Bakery make the most amazing cakes, in any kind of design you want: they can make your birthday cake look like a big teddy bear or a car or a handbag . . .

'I wonder if Megan and Jas and those lot will come? I'll send invites. Do you think I should just WhatsApp them or get those sparkly card ones from WHSmiths?'

Nisha throws down the blue cloth she's wiping tables with. 'URGH, for god's sake, don't invite them, Grace. Why do you have to ruin it by inviting them?' she huffs.

Grace looks put out. 'Because! I just think, water under the bridge, and maybe . . . I dunno, maybe I should just be friends with them again.'

Nisha looks hurt for a second, and then says: 'Right, Indi, it looks like it's just me and you then. We don't need Grace, do we? I mean, *who knows* if we're even invited to Grace's big sleepover anyway.'

My face breaks into a smile. It's nice to know I'm second best to Grace. *I'll take it!* 'Of course you're invited, you stupid idiots,' says Grace, rolling her eyes. 'ANYWAY, that aside, I've asked Daddy for a car.'

'A CAR?' Nisha and I both cry in unison.

'Mm-hm.'

'Grace, you can't drive until you're seventeen!' I laugh.

'Nope, not true, babe. You can apply for a provisional driving licence when you're fifteen years and nine months old. So I thought it would be really good, before I start driving, to get a car and spend some time just sitting in it, in the garage, like turning the headlights on, practising my seatbelt technique and stuff . . . you know, get a feel for it before I hit the road.'

She says this deadly serious, like it's the most sensible plan in the world.

Nisha laughs and shakes her head. 'So you want your dad to buy you a car, which you won't even drive for three years. Yeah, good plan, ennit . . .'

'Well, it's that or a puppy so . . . Anyway. What did your dad get you this year, Indi? Give me some inspo,' says Grace.

I start to feel hot around my neck as soon as she says it. But we're real friends now. And real friends should be able to tell each other everything, right?

Tell the truth, Indi.

'Well, erm, things are a bit complicated at home so . . .'

Grace and Nisha both suddenly look *really* uncomfortable and say, 'Oh god. Oh, sorry! You don't have to tell us—'

I feel sick. I can't bear it. I want to crawl out of my own skin. They're *pitying* me and I hate it.

Their home lives always sound so amazing.

Grace's dad is actually her stepdad. He and her mum got married when Grace was seven and she loves him so much, she *actually* calls him Daddy.

And Nisha's family seem like the happiest family in the world: two parents, three kids, all happily tucked in under one roof. Like a BBC One sitcom.

Me, however . . . I just feel embarrassed.

So I totally bottle it.

And I say: 'He's bringing me a super-rare Egyptian necklace when he's back next and, last week, I got a surfboard from his trip to Hawaii so . . . two presents.'

WEDNESDAY DECEMBER 2nd

1.13 p.m.

Spot Reece talking to Tobias on the playground. They're wearing their big puffer jackets because it's super-cold today. I can see my breath. Me and Reece haven't spoken much since hat-gate and it feels weird. I need to break the ice between us so I stomp over and interrupt the boys by saying: 'Do you wanna come over tonight and check out my gecko?'

'Pardon!?' Reece splutters, spitting his apple juice out, as Tobias's face breaks out into a cheeky grin.

Hmm, that didn't sound like how I meant it to sound.

5.28 p.m.

Reece, Tubs and I are currently cramped around the kitchen table eating fish fingers, chips and beans.

A bold move for Indi Raye. Never has someone from school come round before. There's also the *teeny tiny fabrication* I told Reece about living in a penthouse with a hot tub. Which he clearly now knows is not true. He looked slightly surprised when he arrived but had the decency to say nothing. I suppose he doesn't want to embarrass me.

Tubs is doing enough of that for the both of

us tonight. She's lit a candle and put a fancy white tablecloth on . . .

'It's just SO nice that Indiana has brought a boyfriend home. I never thought I'd see the day!'

'Tubs!' I scream. 'For the thousandth time, Reece is NOT my boyfriend. Just a friend!'

'He's a boy, isn't he? You're a boy, aren't yer, Reece?'

Reece's glasses have steamed up. 'Er, yes, I think so . . .' he stutters.

'And you're both friends?'

'Yes.'

'Well then! He is a boy who is a friend! A BOYFRIEND. How's the fish fingers, Reece?'

'Very nice, thanks, Mrs . . . Tubs?' he ventures.

'You can call me Joy, my darlin',' she gushes, before asking how he plans to take my hand in marriage.

6.13 p.m.
'Hold your hands out flat,' I say.

'What if it bites me?' shrieks Reece, his voice much higher-pitched than normal, which makes me giggle.

'He won't! He's tame. Just keep still else you'll spook him,' I reply, gently lowering Gary into Reece's flat palms.

Gary looks at me as if to say, *'What the hell do you think you're doing with me?'*

'So you gonna tell everyone at school I don't have a hot tub then?' I mutter.

'No? Why would I do that?'

''Cause I was rude to you about the beret. You might wanna get back at me or something. Take revenge.'

'Hmmm, I thought about it! But naaaah. It's fine. You know you don't have to make stuff up to impress people, though, don't you?' he asks, earnestly.

I think for a moment and say: 'Yeah, I know. I just want people to like me, y'know?'

'Yeah, I know. Everyone wants to be liked. Sometimes I think it'd be cool to be on the footie team with the lads and that.'

'Mm. Hey, you reckon you could . . . maybe . . . just keep it quiet. About where I live and the hot tub thing and stuff?'

'If you want me to, I will.'

'Thanks. *Fruende*?' I say, stretching out my hand.

He transfers Gary on to one palm and uses the free hand to grab mine. We shake on it.

'*Freundin*. Your mum's nice, by the way,' he says.

'She's insane, is what she is.'

'So . . . erm . . . did you . . . er . . . did you tell her I was your boyfriend?' he asks awkwardly.

'NO! GOD NO!'

'OK, good. 'Cause we haven't even had a first date yet,' he jokes. *At least I think he's joking* . . .

'Don't worry, I'm not planning on turning up at school tomorrow in a white dress . . .'

'Ha, god, yeah, me and you, yuck!' he laughs, keeping his eyes fixed on Gary.

CHAPTER 10

SUPER BOYF GOALS

SATURDAY DEC 5th

5.55 p.m.

It's Grace's birthday sleepover tonight.

I have NOT told Tubs that boys might be there.

I think she'd start dousing me in holy water.

Googling Grace's address on my phone.

She lives on a street called The Avenues, which can't be right because there's rumours that's where Marcus Rashford's house is . . .

6.10 p.m.

Urgh, I've just realised the only PJs I've got are the ones with cartoon pugs all over them, which is sooooo babyish. I'm fourteen years old but I'm gonna look like I've just come out of the womb in these.

7.16 p.m.

JESUS CHRIST (sorry, Tubs and Jesus) – but Grace lives in a mansion! An actual mansion!

I press a buzzer which opens the gate to the Walkden residence. A long pebbled driveway leads up to what looks like a stately home: whitewashed exterior walls with ten windows staring back at me. Ivy creeps up the right-hand side, twisting around the chimney. There's not one, but TWO garages and the whole place is illuminated with lights from the ground. AS IF I thought Reece's house was posh! Reece's house is practically a prison compared to this!

No wonder she doesn't need to work at the chippy with me and Nisha, she's probs a millionaire!

OH MY G THERE'S A CHERUB STATUE WEEING ON THE FRONT LAWN!

Wait until I tell Tubs about this!

Grace said we're having pizza for dinner, but I BET it's bloody caviar-infused quail or something.

I just can't believe how different our lives are.

Grace lives next door to a professional footballer, I live in a damp flat.

Grace's family play cricket.

I play *The Chase* (ITV, weekdays at 5 p.m. Once I got four questions in a row correct!).

Grace brings breaktime snacks from *Waitrose*.

I eat slightly out-of-date ham.

She waves at me from one of the many upstairs windows, and moments later opens the front door wearing a babydoll nightie: skimpy, pink satin, with lace, and her boobs pushed up to the gods. Brilliant, she looks eighteen and with my pug PJs, I'm gonna look eight.

I can hear Drake blasting out from somewhere inside.

'Hey!' she says.

I smile, give her a big hug and say, 'Happy birthday!' and give her my handmade card, an Indiana P. Raye original drawing of her surrounded by all her favourite things: her fluffball cats, her phone and Ed Sheeran.

'Wow, Indi, this is literally incredible! I never knew you could draw so good!? Thanks!' gushes Grace, and it makes me beam to see how much she likes it.

'Oh my GGGGG . . .' screams a voice from around the corner. 'This must be THE Indi Raye that I've heard about! Come on in, darlin'. I'm Alison but you can call me Ally! What we drinking? OJ? Coke? Lemonade? I've got a bit of voddy if you like?'

Grace looks a bit embarrassed but *WOWZERS*, her mum is STUNNING, wearing skin-tight mint green leggings and a matching crop top. Her blonde hair is piled on top of her head in a bun and she dances to

Drake as she approaches the front door. She could be Grace's sister, instead of her mum.

I think about Tubs in her green work tunic, yellow rubber gloves and anti-bac spray in hand. Tubs would NEVER offer us alcohol. Also, she wouldn't know who Drake is if he stood in front of her and said, 'Hi, I'm Drake.'

'Nice to meet you,' I say to Ally, before Grace says, 'OK, that's enough chatter, Mum. Go back in the kitchen now,' and leads me away feeling a bit rude that we didn't converse more. She seems really cool.

Grace pulls me by my hand down a long corridor and I sneak a peek into the rooms we pass: the living room . . . dining room . . . study . . .

Everything inside this house is white.

White sofas, white worktops, white walls, white birthday balloons, all marble and mirrors.

This would be a terrible place for me to start my period, I think. *Urgh, what is wrong with me, why would my brain even think that . . .*

'Hey, go upstairs, my bedroom is the one at the back past the big gold mirror. Nisha's there. I'll be up in a sec, gonna grab us some birthday cake,' she says, before bouncing back to the kitchen.

I climb the staircase – it's one of those super-posh ones which splits into two at the top so you can head to the west wing or the east wing of the house . . .

I go via the bathroom 'cause that weeing cherub has made me need a pee. Can hear guitar chords blasting out from down the corridor.

Ah, that'll be Oliver. Forgot he'd be here.

I line the toilet bowl with loo roll, so that when I tinkle, it doesn't echo and he hears. That would be mad embarrassing. I pee gently, clocking the fact the sink has GOLD TAPS IN THE SHAPE OF SWANS before washing my hands with this luxury soap that smells like orange. So bougie. Then I slope off back down the hallway, travelling at a snail's pace and lingering outside Oliver's slightly open door.

Wowzers he is super unreal.

Although Johnny Hotpants would still win in a Sexiness Competition.

Just say hi, just say hi, just say hi . . .

'Yo, yo, yo,' I say. (*WHY!?!?!?!*)

Oliver stops strumming and says 'Alright?'

It smells like boy in here. A bit smelly, truth be told.

Also it's a tip; his single bed is unmade, there's *stuff* all over the floor and I spot a couple of plates which really need to go downstairs and get washed. Doesn't really match the vibe of the rest of the immaculate house. His bedroom wall is covered in posters: Nirvana and Foo Fighters and Iron Maiden, and I feel bad for laughing at his band name now, because, actually, it looks like me and Oliver have a lot in common.

'I like bands,' I state, putting my hands on my hips.

'What?'

'Yeah, I like bands. Like, music wise. Like, I'd rather *die* than listen to Lewis Capaldi.'

'OK . . .'

It goes awks so I lie and say, 'I can play the drums.'

Oliver goes, 'Oh yeah?' and he points to the drumkit behind him which I DID NOT SEE. 'Go on then, show us what you got.'

I freeze. *You really know how to throw yourself under the bus, Indi Raye.*

'Errrrr . . . oh, I can't right now. Gotta go hang out with your sis. The ol' birthday girl. I just . . . I . . . can't, soz, SEE YOU, THEN,' I shout much too loudly then leg it out before I make myself look any more stupid.

These lies have got to stop, I swear to god.

7.26 p.m.

'Knock, knock,' I say at Grace's bedroom door, pushing it open to reveal what I sort of imagine heaven looks like. Soft lilac walls, light flowing curtains, and a floral duvet spread that sprawls across a king-size bed. She has a massive TV affixed to the wall and a sheepskin rug which is currently occupied by Roger or Dodger. Not sure which is which but either way my nose starts to itch. Bloody allergies.

Nisha is lying on her stomach, flicking through Netflix.

'Hey. How was training?' I ask.

'Not the best. Conceded three goals. Megan went mad at me saying I need to up my game, even though she didn't score a single goal.'

'Speaking of which, assume they're not coming tonight . . .'

'Ugh, they were never gonna come.'

She begins to whisper in case Grace walks in on us. Roger or Dodger sidles up towards me and I shoo him away before I start sneezing during this Very Important Chat.

'I hate them lot, y'know. Grace was bullied by those girls. They were *so* mean to her. She *really* wanted to be in their group, so she'd turn up every day at school and try to impress them. But they knew that, so they made her "earn" her place, like they'd make her buy chocolate for them, and if she brought it into school, she'd be welcomed into their gang, but if she didn't, they would act like she didn't exist.'

'That's . . . that's really sad,' I whisper. 'I had no idea.'

'Well, Grace would never say.'

We hear footsteps approaching us.

'Don't tell her I told you, will you?'

'No way!' I whisper.

'Right, who's for chocolate cake!?' calls Grace, balancing three paper plates in her hands and pushing the door open with her shoulder.

'Thanks, Gracie. Cheers!' says Nisha, raising her slice, and we all 'cheers' it.

'Happy birthday, Grace!' I smile.

9.29 p.m.

We've just finished a film with a sex scene in it – it's soooooooooo cringe when people do it on TV! Honestly, if it's like that, it's putting me right off. Maybe I never will do it and I'll be perfectly happy about it. For now, I'm happy concentrating on necking.

'OK, SNOG, MARRY AVOID!' says Grace. 'Indi, you're up first. OK . . . Mr Basi, that P.E. teacher, you know, Mr Graham? Orrrrrr . . . Mr Frederick!?' asks Grace.

'Ewwwwww, why did you have to start with teachers,

GROSS!' I squeal.

'Oh please, Mr Graham is boyfriend goals,' says Grace mischievously.

'Yeah, but he's also got *huge* pecs. He's got bigger boobs than I HAVE!' I reply.

'Come on, you have to chooooooose . . .'

'OK, avoid Mr Frederick, OBVIOUSLY. Can you imagine necking on with him!?!!?!'

'Stop it, I'll vomit,' says Nisha, breathing in deeply through her nose and clutching her throat.

'I'd marry Mr Basi, because he's good with numbers and would do all the banking and stuff in the house, you know I'm no good with maths . . .'

'Very practical.' Nisha replies.

'And yes, I'd neck on with Mr Graham. ONLY if I have to though!' I conclude.

'I think I'd probably have to agree with that. Right, do me!' says Grace.

'OK,' says Nisha. 'That lad from town the other week, the one who hasn't texted you back?'

'Ohhhhh don't remind me. Urgh, he was unreal . . .'

'. . . Oh what's his name? Spider-Man. Tom Holland! . . .'

'Oh my GGGGG, yes, and?'

'Alan from the chippy!'

We screech with laughter.

'Awww, I'd love to marry Alan, he needs a good wife! But I *need* to marry Tom. Alan would understand, wouldn't he!?'

'Don't explain yourself to me, Grace. It's Alan you have to apologise to!' I say.

'Right, Nisha, your turn. Charlie Grenburg, Marcus Jones orrrrr . . . Potwash Will!'

Nisha pauses and says 'Um . . .'

She looks embarrassed. Her face has gone red and she avoids our eyes which are looking at her for an answer.

'URGH, NISHA, JUST PLAY THE GAME FOR ONCE,' sighs Grace exasperatedly.

'What if I don't fancy any of them?' she asks.

'You have to pick! That's the game!' I chime in.

'Yeah, come on, Nisha, it's just a game! Who're you picking? Start with who you'd neck first. Which boy would you, Nisha Chowdhury, like to lock lips with?'

'Er . . .'

The doorbell rings, interrupting the awkwardness.

'Oooh, that'll be the boys!' gasps Grace.

'I'll get it, babes!' shouts Ally.

'LEAVE IT, MUM! DON'T YOU *DARE* ANSWER, GO BACK IN THE KITCHEN, NOW!' screams Grace.

We scurry downstairs and Grace sultrily opens the door saying, 'Oh, hey, boys!' in her sexiest voice.

They're *Year 10s*. Mason Daniels, Evan *Something-Something* (he has a double-barrelled name, like *Farquhar-Peterson* or something) and . . .

OH MY GOD, JOHNNY HOTPANTS IS ON GRACE'S DOORSTEP.

JOHNNY HOTPANTS IS IN FRONT OF ME AND I'M WEARING THE PUG PJS OF AN INFANT.

'GRACIE!' he says, grabbing her for a hug. He squeezes her tight and she beams. 'Ow, Josh, get off!'

Josh. What a great name.

'You alright?' he smiles as he releases her.

'Yeah, you?' she simpers back.

Oh my G, they're flirting. He's totally checking her out.

'Listen, we can't stay, yeah?' says Evan. 'Some of the boys from footie are doing a FIFA tournament so . . .'

'Ohhh,' pouts Grace, sticking her bottom lip out.

I watch this interaction like I'm watching exotic animals on an Attenborough documentary. I can hear Sir David's voice in my head: *'The females are attracted by the scent of the males – most likely Hugo Boss – and they will do whatever they can, to impress them and ensure he slides into her DMs . . .'*

'Yoooo, are you the one who bought the lizard, yeah?' someone asks. I realise they're talking to me, and it's Mason asking the question.

'Er, yeah,' I reply, wishing I had more to say.

'That's mad, you know . . .' Mason says.

'No, it's not . . .' I giggle, taking a leaf out of Grace's book and, AND . . . playfully punch him on the arm.

WHAT A MISTRESS OF SEDUCTION I AM. I'M GONNA HAVE TO HAVE A LONG SHOWER AND SAY SEVERAL PRAYERS AFTER THIS.

I catch Josh watching me for a moment. It catches me off guard and my stomach twists with butterflies so I look away, avoiding eye contact.

I can tell Grace is devastated they're not stopping over.

In a desperate last-ditch attempt to persuade them to hang out she touches Josh's arm and says, 'You don't really have to go, do you? '

'Ahhh, soz, can't stay,' he says. 'Have a great night, ladies, yeah?'

He says it while looking directly at me, but Grace answers, grinning: 'Oh, we will. See you later, babes!'

Evan, Mason and Josh say, 'See ya,' in unison. And we stand watching them pass the weeing cherub and mooch off down the street.

Grace sighs and closes the door.

'Don't go there, Grace . . .' says Nisha from the staircase.

'WHAT!?' Grace replies indignantly.

'Yeah, don't go there with what?' I ask.

'They've got history, ennit . . .' sighs Nisha. 'Their mums both do Pilates together every week. Grace and Joshua Wood have known each other . . . how long?'

Grace laughs, 'Since I was four. Went to the same primary school.'

Nisha puts her arm around Grace. 'Problem is' – she gestures towards where Josh had just been standing at the front door – 'Josh never used to be so stunnin'. He was just Grace's childhood friend. But NOW . . . now Josh is *total* boyfriend goals and Grace is *in love*.'

'NO. I'M. NOT. Nisha, stop. You can't *fancy* someone you grew up with; it's literally like fancying your brother or something . . .' Grace insists, but her smile is giving her away.

'OK, but admit it, Grace . . . he is soooo boyf goals?' I offer.

She pauses for a second before admitting: '. . . oh god, like, SUPER BOYF GOALS. Do you want to hear something so cringey? Our mums used to let us run around in the back garden in just our pants on hot days in the summer when we were little, with the hosepipe on! Josh Wood has literally seen me nakey, guys!'

We all SCREAM with laughter.

SUNDAY DEC 6th
1.01 a.m.

The three of us are curled up close together even though there's loads of room in Grace's king-size bed. The girls are both asleep and Nisha is snoring gently into the darkness. I really do feel like I've hit the jackpot. I've managed to find the two best girls in the world to be my besties. I cannot mess this up.

1.03 a.m.

Oh, and I managed to get the tea on Josh. Turns out he's called Joshua *Albert* Wood. He's so good at football, they reckon he might get into Stockport's youth academy next year which is HUGE news. Everyone thinks he's brilliant. Grace thinks he's brilliant. I think he's brilliant.

9.08 a.m

'So, how was it?' asks Tubs the next morning, whilst hurriedly making us a cup of tea. She's late for work whilst I doodle the letter J surrounded by hearts on my science homework.

'Oh my G, you should have seen it. The downstairs loo, right, it was TWICE the size of our entire living room. The floor was all shiny and they had a GRANDFATHER clock. Oh yeah, and there's a cherub statue which pees on the lawn!'

'Wow. Do they need a cleaner at all? Yer must ask your Grace's mother, alright?'

'Will do . . .' I lie as she scoots out of the door.

NOT IN A MILLION GAZILLION YEARS, TUBS.

Can you imagine the sheer embarrassment of *my* mum cleaning *Grace's* house?

At the moment, I've done a pretty good job at keeping the girls away from my home life. They don't know about Number 64 – about how small and shabby it is. Reece has been a real mate too and kept his mouth zipped. They have no idea that Tubs is a cleaner and they genuinely believe Dad's off living his best life, travelling across the world.

It feels like we're all equal and I like it that way, thank you very much.

9.10 a.m

The other day, Tubs physically winced at the checkout at the supermarket as the lady scanned our tomatoes, sausages and potato waffles. We can't even afford potato waffles and yet Grace has gold taps.

I head into my room, reach into my schoolbag and pull out a tenner from my chippy wages before heading back into the kitchen and popping the cash into Tubs's money tin.

FRIDAY DEC 11th
8.05 p.m.

Christmas is just a few weeks away. I'm planning to spend this weekend making Christmas cards for Grace, Nisha, Alan and Reece. Maybe Miss Addo too. I've got red and green glitter everywhere, all stuck in the fibres of my manky beige carpet. Tubs is gonna pop off. I keep thinking that I suppose I should count myself lucky to have had Christmas with Dad for fourteen whole years. To expect a fifteenth was probs asking too much.

I mean, he *might* turn up on Christmas morning at Number 64 . . .

Tubs would be trying her hardest at making a turkey dinner (she's not the best chef.)

I'd be watching the film *Home Alone* on the sofa with Gary; it's about this boy called Kevin who gets left all by himself at Christmas. He loves it at first, watching 18+ movies and ordering pizza but then it all goes a bit wrong and these two burglars show up and Kevin gets proper violent for an eight-year-old boy: he chucks paint cans at them and he even sets a guy's head on fire with a blowtorch.

Actually, when you think about it, I'm not sure why Tubs allows me to watch this every year. Sounds more like a horror film.

This is why she won't win any 'Mum of the Year' awards.

Anyway, there'd be a knock at Number 64 and Tubs would say: 'Who on earth could that be? It's Christmas Day! Are yer expecting the girls round, Indi?'

And I would say:

'No, who could it be?'

And we'd scoot excitedly down the hallway and open the door and Dad would be there, with his big smile and his arms full of presents. He'd grab Tubs and give her a big kiss and he'd ruffle my hair and do that proper annoying thing where he tickles me right in the crevice of my neck which makes my head and my shoulder snap together like a clam.

And then we'd spend the best day together. Dad would put on his records, The Rolling Stones followed by some Pink Floyd. I'd request Slade's 'Merry Christmas Everybody', which I love 'cause of that bit that goes '*IT'S CHRIIIIIIIIIIIIIISSSSTMAS!!!!*'

Tubs would have the biggest smile on her face all day long, we'd be pulling crackers and playing Monopoly and Dad would fall asleep in front of the TV.

Nobody would ask any questions about the last few months, we'd just continue as normal, one blissful family.

Perfect.

WEDNESDAY DEC 30th
11.05 a.m.

Spoiler alert: none of that happened.

Tubs managed to burn the tiny joint of turkey she bought from ASDA, which, considering it was frozen, was quite the achievement. Then we watched re-runs of *Mrs Brown's Boys* and a hideous episode of *EastEnders* where Phil's ex-wife turned up at the door, shouting, 'Ah'm the muvva of your baby Phil!' or something.

But never mind, 'cause *uh-oh, I did a thing* . . .

I, Indi P. Raye, have become an online sensation!

'indi14_xoxo' has hit the online world! I even added a cartoon avatar of myself . . . designed by me, of course. Captioned my profile:

just a normal girl

manchester

14

love music

part-time model

The last bit is a lie, obvs, but that's the internet for you; it's *so much easier* to fib online.

A world of lying awaits!

It's catfish o'clock.

Followed the girls, obvs.

Grace is soooo popular online – she's got over 1000 followers 'cause she doesn't lock her profile.

Added Josh, who has been living rent-free in my mind since Grace's sleepover. Found him via Grace's profile. No follow back . . . yet.

I did, however, get followed by someone called 'biscuitlover9583' and a DM flew straight into my inbox.

biscuitlover9583: hey
indi14_xoxo: hey
biscuitlover9583: whats up

indi14_xoxo: good you?

biscuitlover9583: how old are you?

indi14_xoxo: 14 – you?

biscuitlover9583: 18

Uh oh. He's 18. I've never spoken to an eighteen-year-old before.

indi14_xoxo: kk

biscuitlover9583: what do you look like?

indi14_xoxo: look at my profile pic

biscuitlover9583: ye but thats a cartoon i mean IRL

indi14_xoxo: just normal really altho people do say i am exceedingly beautiful and tall and look a bit like Selena Gomez . . .

All lies. Obvs. *Wowzers, this is sooooooo easy.*

biscuitlover9583: saw you love music me too

im in a band

you should come see us play one day

we do all the rock hits

indi_xoxo: kk whos your faves? i like old stuff like foo fighters and blink 182 and stuff my dad got me into them

biscuitlover9583: yeah same

OH MY GGGGGGGG AN EIGHTEEN-YEAR-OLD
WHO LIKES THE SAME MUSIC AS ME. THIS IS
AMAZING.

biscuitlover9583: you r really sexy

UH OH, THIS IS GETTING OUT OF HAND NOW . . .

indi_xoxo: thx but you're probs a bit too old for me
biscuitlover9583: aw dont say that!
indi_xoxo: you are tho!
biscuitlover9583: kk what if i told you . . .

Oh no. Where's this going.

biscuitlover9583: . . . that im actually not 18?

Oh god oh god oh god.

indi_xoxo: how old r you then?

It takes a while for him to reply.

biscuitlover9583: . . .
biscuitlover9583: . . .
biscuitlover9583: . . .

biscuitlover9583: im 11.

WHAT!?!?! ELEVEN-YEAR-OLDS AREN'T EVEN SUPPOSED TO BE ON HERE!

I click on his profile and sure enough, there he is. His profile reads:

hughie

year 7

single n lookin for luv

MORTIFIED.

CHAPTER 11

WE'D BE EGGSCELLENT TOGETHER

MONDAY JAN 4th

12.44 p.m.

Have just seen Charlie Grenburg knock back a whole bag of Quavers and then gulp a can of Fanta, mixing it all up together like a washing machine inside his mouth, before swallowing.

Why are the general public so hideous!?

12.46 p.m.

My excitement at being back at school this morning is slowly being destroyed by this limp salad from the canteen for my lunch. It tastes like water and I think I'm gonna have to put some of Reece's chips on top to make it more bearable.

His brow is furrowed.

'What I don't get is *why* you were talking to someone you thought was eighteen anyway,' he says, swirling his chips in a pool of ketchup.

I've just regaled him with my story about Hughie the internet faker.

'I dunno, just a bit of a laugh, I guess. I wouldn't have gone and met him or anything, would I, I'm not stupid. I dunno. It feels like the next step for me is, like, a boyfriend or something.'

'Er, OK. But you could, like, talk to someone your own age, couldn't you?'

'Well, I'm talking to you aren't I, divhead . . .'

'Yeah, but not like . . . that. You know, you're not, like . . . flirting with me, are you . . .' he mutters, pushing the last chip around his plate before shoving it in his mouth. And just like that, a heaviness descends in the air around us.

'Ha, er, no, no way! I mean, not that I . . . it's just different, 'cause . . . I mean . . .'

Oh bloody hell, I don't know what to say . . .

'. . . older boys are just *maturer*, that's all. Grace says older boys know how to treat a girl.'

'Grace Walkden also said she once saw an alien at the end of the school field. Indi, she's hardly Einstein, is she?'

He seems proper irritated.

'OK, chill out! Why are you getting annoyed?' I ask, half-smiling so it's not too cringe.

'I'm not.'

'You are.'

'I'm not.'

'You are.'

'Shut up now.'

I throw a salad leaf at him. 'You shut up.'

He's smiling again now, biting into his apple and I'm happy the cringey vibes have disappeared.

But I think it's pretty clear . . . that Reece is jealous. *Oh god, maybe the girls are right, maybe he DOES fancy me? I was SO sure they were wrong, but the way he's being now . . . oh I dunno, this is too confusing. I'll have to swerve him over the next few days at least to make sure his sheer THIRST for me eases.*

This is like what they say about buses, isn't it?

When you're waiting ages for one, two will come along at once.

Two whole boys in less than 24 hours, lusting after little old me!

Although one is my mate and the other is basically still using the potty so . . . not great options.

And neither of them are Josh Wood . . .

3.36 p.m.

My phone vibrates in my pocket.

> Nisha: hey bestie wya bet you're with reece

> chippy. 20 mins. GRACE HAS NEWS

4.07 p.m.

We're sitting in the window at The Jolly Fryer.

It's become 'Our Table': perfect for spying on passing school mates (slash potential boyfs), but private enough for important chats like this one. Grace sits across from us as we listen, goggle-eyed with anticipation.

Nisha sucks on a straw dunked in a can of Dr Pepper. 'Come on then,' She raises one eyebrow and leans over the table. 'What's the tea?'

'SO . . . he's called Sam and he came to Mum and Dad's New Year's Eve *soiree*. His dad has started working with Daddy at the office or something, they've moved here from Birmingham I think and *anyway* he invited him and his wife round for the party and they brought his son and he's literally UNREAL . . . aaaaaaaaaand . . .'

She pauses for dramatic effect. She is LOVING dragging this out, all the attention on her.

'AND?' me and Nisha ask in unison.

'. . . and it's time for an entry in *The Doing Bits Book*!'

'ARRRRGGGHHH!' Nisha screams, a bit of her fizzy pop dribbling down her chin.

'Flamin' 'eck, girls!' shushes Alan. 'Keep it down, will yer? You'll scare all me flamin' customers away!'

'So come on then,' Nisha whispers. 'What bits, Gracie, tell all?'

'OK, so, it's only a tiny little thing but it was SOOOOO romantic. Basically, he said, "Shall we go for a private chat?" so we end up in the utility room where Mum keeps Roger and Dodger's cat food and THEN he said, "Fancy doing some necking on then?" and even though the smell of the Whiskas was making me feel a bit sick, I went for it and we had a full-on neck for, I'd say, seven seconds!'

'OH MY GGGGGGG, it's going straight in the *Book*!' shrieks Nisha.

'Sorry,' I interupt. 'What's *The Doing Bits Book* . . . dare I ask?'

'OK, so, it's this little purple diary that Nisha keeps tucked away in a shoebox in the back of her wardrobe so her mum can't find it. Every time me or Nisha – usually me, though – has any kind of romantic encounter, it gets jotted down, along with extra notes like, I dunno . . . *"Smelled nice"* or *"Nice lips"*. And they also get a rating out of ten.'

'And what's the scores for Sam, would you say?' asks Nisha.

'Hmmmm ... Sam gets a solid 8/10. *Only* losing points 'cause he'd eaten pickled onion Monster Munch crisps pre-neck ...' She giggles. 'Listen, practice makes perfect. And I intend on doing LOTS of practising with him!'

We all laugh.

'So, look, now we're all officially besties, what about you, Indi? We need to get you in *The Doing Bits Book*, ennit!?' says Nisha.

'Yeah! Come on, Ind – tell all!' goads Grace.

I can feel the back of my neck starting to heat up. You could crack an egg on it and it'd fry. In fact, it's hotter than Alan's deep fat fryers. I get the feeling they both know that I have done *No Bits* but want to put me through some weird torture of having to tell them so.

I mean, surely Nisha hasn't gone very far? I mean, no offence to her, but she's ... y'know ... she's not exactly swamped with male attention, is she? She can barely even talk about boys!

'See, I think it's only fair that we hear about Nish's *Doing Bits* history first?' I say, rallying it back like I'm in a tennis match. 'You are a founding member, after all ...'

Come on, Nisha. Just say you haven't ever done anything and then I won't have to do one of my Big Fat Lies. End of convo.

'Indi . . . I went to The Love Shed,' Nisha says, putting her hands together in prayer, a bit like a priest at a Sunday service and Grace squeals with laughter.

Grace winks. 'Listen, you might think Nisha's all innocent, Indi, but last year, after school, she would have regular meet-ups in the HOCKEY SHED with a MYSTERY LOVER. Oi, is that who you were texting at Oliver's gig??? Oh my G it is, isn't it?'

'Nooooo, stop, enough now. And actually, can we stop calling it "The Love Shed" now though? It sounds dodgy. It wasn't dodgy, Indi – it's just nice and warm in there . . .'

'IMAGINE HAVIN' IT OFF NEXT TO A LOAD OF SMELLY SHINPADS!' cackles Grace. 'Oooh, maybe it's Marcus Jones?'

'Ew, NO! Also, do you really think my mother would let me date Marcus Jones? Do you really think my mother would let me date at all?'

'Good point.'

'Anyyyyyywayyyyyy,' laughs Nisha. 'Enough about me. Indiana, spit it out.'

Don't lie. Don't lie. Don't lie, Indi. You don't have to. Just be honest. For the first time in your life, just BE HONEST. Tell them the truth. TELL THE TRUTH.

'OK, so . . . er . . . I haven't . . . I haven't really, you know . . .'

I can see the sides of Grace's mouth curling up into a snigger.

I continue. 'You know, it's like, 'cause of, like, travelling the world and that, like, I never really . . .'

'But what about your Spanish boyfriend, the one that fell off the horse?'

'Well, we just never really . . .'

'OH. MY. G,' shouts Grace. 'YOU'VE NEVER BEEN NECKED?'

'OK, can we not shout so loud 'cause—' I can feel heat spreading from my neck round on to my face. My cheeks are turning red, I know it.

'Nowt at ALL, Indi?' Nisha laughs, with a hint of pity.

'Er, nope . . .'

'But . . . but what am I gonna write in *The Book*?' she sniggers.

'Just put a "B" . . .' replies Grace. '. . . for beginner!'

They both honk with laughter.

'Er, right, I'm gonna have to get myself home. Told Tubs I'd be back at five to . . . water the plants . . . so,

I'll see you tomorrow, yeah?'

'Oh Indi, we're only joking!' says Nisha.

'Yeah, I know! No, it's fine! I know you are. It's funny! Anyway. See you tomorrow . . .'

I clang out of the chippy before they see my stupid eyes filling up with wet.

5.26 p.m.

I'm going to bed. YES I KNOW IT'S EARLY BUT I DON'T CARE! Tubs just asked if I want dinner so I told her to MIND HER OWN BLOODY BUSINESS!

5.31 p.m.

URGH, WHAT DID THEY EXPECT?

That I was some kind of Necking Goddess, seducing boys without mercy?

NO. OBVS NOT.

Boys don't go for girls like me: girls with chests flatter than a pancake on Pancake Day. They go for girls like the Graces and Megans and Amelias and all those girls who basically look like *Dua bloody Lipa*!

I thought me, Nisha and Grace were starting to be real friends but maybe not. They *loved* seeing me squirm. Maybe they're just keeping me around to laugh at me for my lack of make-up and my lack of experience and the fact I smelt like chicken nuggets that ONE TIME.

5.33 p.m.
Mmm, chicken nuggets.

Seriously, though, it's your own stupid fault, Indi.

You're the world's best liar.

Why didn't you just say that a boy called Pierre took you up the Eiffel Tower for a ten-course meal and proposed to you on one knee with a rose in his mouth before giving you a big, fat, juicy neck right on the lips?

That would have shut them up.

Ugh, this is the last time I EVER try and be truthful!!!!!

WEDNESDAY JAN 13th
10.20 a.m.
Mr Miller is making us read a whole scene of *Romeo and Juliet* for our English homework, which I can't be dealing with 'cause it's all 'thou' this and 'thee' that. Apparently, Juliet was only thirteen in this play and she was doing loads of necking on with Romeo.

I'm SO behind schedule.

12.20 p.m.

Reece just scribbled 'lunch?' on my German textbook while we were translating sentences like, *'Wo ist meine gelbe banane?'*

I scribble back:

'Can't – pottery class' even though such a thing does not exist at St Cath's.

I'm feeling totally confused about our so-called friendship. *Friends* don't buy other friends love-berets. *Friends* don't get jealous about online chats and *friends* don't *always* have to go to lunch with each other.

12.21 p.m.

... but on the flipside, I really need to get necking, it's now a national emergency.

12.22 p.m.

Here's a thought.

Maybe Juliet just necked on with Romeo so she could get her first kiss over and done with?

I could just shut my eyes proper tight and imagine someone like ...someone like, I dunno, a *Love Island* boy or something ... *mmm, yeah* – and get a little neck done and dusted with Reece. Just to impress the girls, like.

And then, ta-da, I'm in *The Doing Bits Book* and Reece gets a cheeky little necking out of it – OH, I DUNNO WHAT I'M SAYING!

12.23 p.m.
This must be what happens when you turn fourteen. Those hormones be flyin' around like no one's business.

12.24 p.m.
What I would give to just . . . I dunno, neck on with someone like Josh Wood.

12.25 p.m.
BTW HE'S WELL OUT OF MY LEAGUE; like, I'm not saying that like I *could*. Plus Grace has a thing for him, hasn't she, so . . .

But what I mean is, wouldn't it be amazing?

12.29 p.m.

Dear God and Jesus,
Just poking my head in. If you are listening, PLEASE
can you sort me out with just ONE neck?
     Just so I can say I've done it. I don't want anything
else from you I swear!

*Oh, apart from the request for some boobs: that
is important that one, so don't forget it, but also if
we can add the necking as well, that would be great.*

*Actually thinking about it, if you give me the big
melons, it might help out with the necking?*

*Bit of a 2-for-1 deal, like. Just some food for
thought, big guy.*

*I've got to go to lunch now, but I'll leave it with
you, amen.*

SATURDAY JAN 30th
9.22 a.m

'WELL, the last thing we heard was that he was
travelling around Peru somewhere,' I say to Alan.

Alan's so nice. Always checks in to see how me and
Tubs are getting on.

'Super-bad phone signal up the mountains there,
but the gifts just keep on coming and coming; he
sent me a scarf made from ... get this ... alpaca
wool!' I lie, whilst chewing down some post-shift
chips at the chippy.

Dad's also 'supposedly' sent me a digeridoo from
Australia in the last couple of months. Nisha was
super excited about that one because she's always
wanted to have a blast on one.

It's funny, when I first started lying, I was really worried about getting found out. But I've been doing it so much now, for so many months, and NOBODY has noticed a thing. Here's a few zingers I've told Tubs recently:

1. She thinks I used a fiver the other day to buy a proper lunch. I didn't. I just bought six bags of smokey bacon crisps and ate them all in one go.

2. She thinks I go to sleep straight away when my bedside light goes off. I don't — I stay awake, sometimes until gone one a.m., thinking about how to neck on with boys.

3. She thinks I had a stomach ache last week. I didn't — I just wanted to stay home and watch *Homes Under the Hammer.*

4. She thinks I hang up all my clothes after she's ironed them. I don't — I shove 'em at the bottom of the wardrobe. For easy access. I am a busy woman. I do not have time for clothes hangers.

5. She thinks there's a ghost in Number 64. There isn't — I just told her I see a headless man sitting on the couch in the living room and move her mug around when she's not looking to freak her out.

I swear to G, instead of being an illustrator one day, maybe I should be an actor? Might arrange a meeting with Mr Frederick next week to discuss being the lead role in the school play this year.

SATURDAY FEB 6th
1.33 p.m.
THE WORST MOMENT OF MY ACTUAL LIFE ACTUALLY JUST OCCURRED.

There I was, minding my own business, shovelling lunches on to chip shop paper and rolling it up. I've gotten really quick at it, y'know – I can pack loads of chips in really nice and tight so they keep nice and warm for people ferrying them home.

I glanced at the queue which snaked out the door – busy day – and when I looked back to the customers in front of me, there he was.

Johnny Hotpants. Josh Wood.

'Scampi and chips, please, Indi,' he said, grinning.

Oh my G, he knows my name.

'Wasn't sure it was you underneath that hat. You look like a dinner lady,' he joked.

I'm like a deer in headlights. I smile at him. But I don't know what to say. My heart is beating so fast I'm scared he can see it through my apron. My whole face must be about 100 degrees Celsius thanks to the hot fish in front of me combined with my sheer self-consciousness. My mind is whirring, trying to find something witty or intelligent to say, so I suddenly blurt out:

'SCAMPIS ARE ACTUALLY PRAWN TAILS.'

He looked at me, bemused, and it was so random and cringe that I just . . . ran away. Dropped the chip shovel and flew off, leaving Alan shouting after me.

And here I am locked in the customer toilets, silently screaming into a bog roll, wondering how Josh Wood is ever gonna neck me when I'm such a hideous weirdo.

SATURDAY FEB 13th
6.31 p.m.

Alan had me on tills all afternoon and my brain went proper dead from all the fish-maths and then when I got home, there was no hot water for a shower and to make things EVEN WORSE, Tubs is now singing another Adele song but this time it's a more up-tempo one and she's crooning along in a sort of joyful, warbly kind of way.

Hmmm, she sounds happy, this is suspicious.

I follow the crooning to her bedroom. She's trying on dresses again, but not in a bummed-out way like before. She pulls up the straps, and shimmies in front of the mirror.

'Ah, Indi . . . you can sort your tea out tonight, yeah? I'm heading out tonight!' she trills.

'Oh yes, shift at the hospital, is it?' I say, deadpan, knowing full well it's not.

'Don't be silly. Yer never gonna believe this,' she says, flushing with excitement. 'I've got meself a date!'

WHAT. THE. HELL.

'You can't just go out on a date, Tubs. You're an old woman and—'

'Errrr, I am NOT old, Indiana, thank you very much. *Jonathan* says—'

'JONATHAN!? THE CREEPER FROM ACROSS THE HALLWAY!?'

'He's not a creeper!' Tubs does air-quotes as she says 'creeper'. 'He's a lovely man and *he says* I'm actually in the prime of my life, me urges are currently at their highest and—'

'OK, NO, CAN WE PLEASE NOT TALK ABOUT YOUR URGES, TUBS!!!! FOR GOD'S SAKE.'

'Look, Indi. I know it's a bit strange for yer, but it's just a drink at the local pub.'

'OH YEAH, JUST A DRINK IS IT? On February 13th? A likely story!' I scoff.

'What's February 13th got to do with it?'

'IT'S VALENTINE'S TOMORROW, DUH.'

'That hadn't even crossed me mind!'

'Yeah, right. Anyway, you can't go out 'cause there's been an emergency.'

'This better be a real emergency, Indiana Raye . . .'

'It is.'

'Well, spit it out!'

'Well, dunno if you've checked the bathroom as yet . . .'

She looks at me sharply. 'What's happened? I haven't done me teeth yet—'

'THE GEESE ARE BACK.'

'Oh, Indiana.' She sighs, grabbing her lipstick.

'IT'S TRUE! AN INFESTATION OF THEM. AT LEAST ELEVEN, MAYBE TWELVE. GEESING ABOUT IN THERE! ONE OF THEM LICKED THE SOAP, TUBS. GOOSE LICK ALL OVER IT!'

'Indiana, stop. You really think that I believe that twelve geese walked all the way up to the top of this block of flats, opened the door and started lickin' the soap? I don't know where yer get your imagination from sometimes. Look, Jonathan just seems nice, that is all. I haven't really made any friends here as yet . . .'

I feel sorry for her for a second. That was, until she said:

'. . . I mean we both have to accept that yer dad's not coming to get us, is he, so—'

I explode. Like a box of fireworks.

'Errrrrrr, I think you'll find he's not coming to get *YOU*!' I roar. 'HE'S GONNA COME AND GET *ME*. AND SOON, I BET. I TEXTED HIM. AND HE'S PROBS READING IT NOW AND BOOKING HIS TRIP TO MANCHESTER AS WE SPEAK.'

'Er, where did you get his number, Indiana Raye!?'

'ENJOY YOUR *DATE*,' I shout.

And then I say something soooo bad.

'*Thou shalt not commit adultery?* Hopefully that almighty GOD you claim you worship won't think you're a BIG OLD SLAG!'

Her face falls and I storm out, slamming her bedroom door. I stick The Prodigy on the record player and crank it up LOUD. Gary appears to use his hands to cover his gecko-ears.

My poor father's not even cold yet and she's DATING other men.

(I appreciate that makes it sounds like Dad's dead and he isn't, but Tubs is basically treating him like he is and quite frankly, I think it's HIDEOUS.)

A rotten end to a rotten day.

And I mean that literally: I found a rotten fish in the chippy freezer earlier and Alan said I had to clear it up and it slipped out of my hand and fell on to my shoe.

7.02 p.m.

I know what you're thinking.

You're thinking I should feel bad.

Well, guess what?

I don't.

OK, I do a bit, a tiny little bit, but mainly I don't, so THERE.

MONDAY FEB 15th

8.59 a.m.

Oh my G. Just opened my locker. There is a RED ENVELOPE inside. <u>The day after Valentine's Day</u>.

It's probs a mistake. It doesn't even have my name on it. It's probs for someone else that got put in the wrong locker.

Nevertheless, I frantically rip it open and pull out the card inside.

On the front there are two goggle-eyed cartoon eggs with love hearts all around them and it says: We'd be EggSCELLENT together.

Inside it reads: Guess what? You have a secret admirer X

10.11 a.m

Can't concentrate in art, which is weird for me. Miss Addo just clicked her fingers in front of me face and said, 'Hellooooo, anyone home?' because I was so zoned out.

10.13 a.m.

Maybe my boobs HAVE started to grow after all? Maybe I've become irresistible!?

10.16 a.m.

Gonna ask the girls what they think.

10.53 a.m.

'Oh, come on, Indi' says Nisha, as we walk down the corridor to our next lessons. 'Of course you know who it's from.'

'Why are you playing dumb?' asks Grace.

'Reece didn't send this. I'm telling you now. It's a step too far,' I say, reading it again.

I really don't want it to be from Reece because:

A) If it is from Reece, our entire friendship as we know it is over, surely?

B) I'd much prefer it to be from Josh Wood.

'I'm willing to put money on it that he did,' says Nisha. 'But if you really want to be sure, you know what you need to do?'

'What?'

'Compare the handwriting,' she calls, as she walks off to R.E.

TUESDAY FEB 16th
14.54 p.m.

In German. Reece is sitting next to me as usual. Feel super awks.

OK, Indi. All you need to do is lean over and have a good look at Reece's textbook. Particularly interested in how he draws his 'g's'. My Secret Admirer's 'g' is all curly like this:

g

'Pssst, Reece,' I whisper to Reece. 'Erm. How do you spell *guten tag* again?'

'Are you kidding?' he asks, confused.

'No, I forgot. Can you write it down for me?'

'Well, it's obviously "g" . . .' He starts to scribble, but after that first letter, I pay him no attention.

guten tag

Curly g's all round.

OH NO!!!!

CHAPTER 12

ZO, 'ARRY, DO YOU 'AVE A — WHAT ZE FRENCH SAY — LA PETITE AMIE?

THURSDAY MAR 11ᵗʰ
1.21 p.m.

This weekend is St Cath's Spring Fête. A major date in the school calendar. Alan's even given me and Nisha the day off for it which is great because I want to spend the entire morning washing my hair to make sure there's no hint of chippy about me. When I bump into Josh, I want him to forget he ever saw me in that bloody white hat.

'It's very, very, VERY important that you come looking proper stunnin',' Grace says over lunch. 'Think like . . . Ariana Grande crossed with school fête chic. Think red-carpet Rihanna crossed with tombola vibes.'

'That makes no sense. What does that mean?! What are you wearing?'

'Oh, I don't know yet actually, I haven't decided . . .'

Sometimes I think Grace DOES know, she just doesn't tell me on purpose, 'cause she likes to look the prettiest. She's like an evil magician who never shares her secrets.

'It just hits differently,' she continues '. . . being at school on a Saturday. It *sort of* feels like school . . . but it *doesn't* feel like school? Y'know what I mean? And also, duh, it's open to the public so who *knows* who might show up! The love of your life might literally walk through the school gates. You might finally get necked. Got. To look. Your best,' she says, flicking my nose.

Sometimes I think she'd make an excellent matron from Victorian times.

One that whips orphans.

She's right though.

It could be the perfect place for my first kiss, tucked away behind the dodgems. Ideally with Josh Wood . . .

'Hey, maybe we could come to yours first, Indi, and have lunch?' ventures Nisha. She's already expecting me to make up an excuse, I know it.

'Ah can't. Tubs has got all her mates coming round. You know she's bezzies with Tess and Claudia from *Strictly Come Dancing*?' I lie.

Again.

SATURDAY MAR 13th

2.34 p.m.

Grace made it sound like St Cath's playing fields were gonna be transformed into Disneyland, and while it's not *quite* like that . . . it is quite cool!

There's a Big Wheel and the game where you hook a duck on a fishing rod and a van selling burgers and candy floss and stuff! Spring has sprung and the sun is peeking through the clouds. Loads of families of the students have come too and little kids run around with Spider-Man face paint and there's the sound of people screaming as they ride the waltzer.

It's weird seeing teachers here; they're on hosting duty but they've been allowed to wear their *leisurewear* 'cause it's a Saturday; Mrs Angus is sporting a purple floral kaftan, Mr Frederick has ditched his shabby grey suit for a shabby grey tracksuit and Mrs Jenkinson trots by in a quite cute floral dress but still in full headteacher mode saying, 'Afternoon, ladies, best behaviour today, yes?' and we all trill back: 'Yes, miss!'

Little does Jenko know, Grace has other plans.

'This way!' Grace says sneakily, running off down the alleyway near the bike sheds. She's giddy with excitement and we follow her. 'I've got a surprise for you both . . .' She looks around shiftily and from inside her pink coat she pulls out a luminous pink bottle, her eyes wide. 'Ta-daaaa! Nicked it from me mum!'

'What is that?' I ask, face scrunched up.

'Not sure, let's see . . .' She reads the label. 'It says, "VK Watermelon with alcohol and fruit juice." Mum's had this in her drinks cabinet for *years*, think it was a Christmas gift from my nan . . .' she says, unscrewing the cap.

Uh oh.

I've never drunk alcohol before. When I was younger, Tubs used to take me to church and everyone was drinking wine from the priest out of this little cup. But then someone said it was the 'blood of Christ', which was very confusing. The thought of having a bit of Jesus blood used to make me feel proper gippy so right then and there, I decided that if turning an innocent church congregation into a bunch of bloodsucking vampires every Sunday morning was a thing, religion NOR wine was gonna be for me.

'Right, open wide, Indi. I'm gonna pour it straight in, OK?'

Tubs would kill me if she knew what I was doing. But I can't exactly say no, can I?

'Er, OK, just a bit though, 'cause, you know, I need to cut back . . .' I lie.

'Cut back?'

'Yeeeeeeeeah . . . 'cause of all the church wine I've had over the years.'

I'm questioning, once again, why I make up lies like this.

These ones aren't even fun, they make me sound SO stupid, but before I can get too deep, Grace is pouring it down my throat . . .

. . . and *OH GOD IT IS HIDEOUS!*

No wonder her mum doesn't like it! Watermelon flavour!? As if!

It's sharp and burns my mouth but it's also sweet – but not sweet in a nice way: it tastes like hand sanitiser. URGH! I want to spit it out straight away, but I force it down, grimacing as I swallow it. I cannot BELIEVE people drink this for fun!

Grace necks some and then so does Nisha.

'Wheeeew!' chokes Nisha. 'That is gross!'

'Right, Nish, will you carry it in your backpack? What shall we do first!?' yelps Grace.

'Waltzers?' replies Nisha, taking another swig and then shoving the bottle deep into her bag.

If we get caught with this, we'll get excluded

immediately and Tubs would probs ground me for the rest of my life ... but I can't lie, it feels proper exhilarating to be breaking the rules.

3.01 p.m.

We spin around and around and we're laughing and laughing. This hideous 90s dance song is played at treble speed; it's so terrible, but we sing along anyway.

We shout at Waltzer Boy to make us go faster and I watch my friends' joyful faces, everything going blurry behind them. Whatever's going on outside this waltzer cart doesn't matter to me now. I only care about us.

I wonder whether we'll be friends forever?

I reckon we'll go to university together and meet three boys in a nightclub who are *also* best friends and we'll all hang out.

And then maybe one day we'll get a flat and the boys will get a flat opposite us.

And one day, maybe each one of us will get married to *each one of them* and we'll have babies and our kids will grow up being best friends ... and then our husbands will ultimately die, but that's OK because it'll just be us three again in the retirement home, popping off, like we are right now.

We jump off the ride, all dizzy and disorientated and it takes us a few minutes to compose ourselves.

Miss Reynolds from P.E. walks by and says 'hello' and we say 'hello' back, maybe a bit *too* enthusiastically, possibly because of the rush from the waltzers . . . possibly because of that disgusting drink.

We start walking across the grass when Grace stops dead in her tracks. 'Oh my G, it's him. It's Sam . . .' gasps Grace.

'Who?' asks Nisha.

'Sam. Sam, my situationship-Sam.'

'Ohhhh, Monster Munch lips!' I say.

Nisha giggles.

'OH MY G, don't call him that! He doesn't know I told you that story! I invited him today but wasn't sure if he'd come . . .'

She looks completely doe-eyed. Besotted. He *is* good-looking to be fair. He wears black jeans and Air Force 1s with a white T-shirt and a coral-pink shirt over the top. Defo not in the same year as us . . .

He catches her eye and winks at her and right then and there, it looks like she might physically melt. She's all jelly, like a big flan.

'Oh my G, I'm stressed, do I look OK?' she says, turning to face us. 'How's my lipstick?'

'You look unreal,' I reply. She smiles, takes a deep breath, turns on her heel and saunters towards him.

She goes from nervous schoolgirl to ultimate babe in a heartbeat.

'How does she do it?' I ask Nisha.

'I have no idea. I guess it's just talent . . . Hey, don't you think . . . he looks a bit—'

'Old?'

'Yeah! I thought he was our age?'

'No way!' I exclaim. 'He looks ancient!'

'Hmmm,' says Nisha, looking a bit concerned, before taking another secret slurp of VK and grabbing my arm. 'Right, where next!?'

We spend the afternoon eating hot dogs and riding the Big Wheel and eating more hot dogs and Nisha wins a teddy bear on the Strongman game.

'Smack it, Nisha! Hard as you can!' I shout.

'OK, ready!?' She raises the mallet above her head and BANG – the puck races right to the top, making the bell ring out across the fête.

'YESSSSSS!'

'Oh my G, you are freakishly strong, Nisha Chowdhury . . .'

'I. AM. WOMAN. FEEL MY WRATH!' she says, drumming her chest like a gorilla. 'I do need a wee, though. Be right back.'

3.14 p.m.

Pretending to be on my phone so nobody thinks I'm a super-basic loser, standing all by myself by the candyfloss stand. Megan and the hockey girls stroll by, on the prowl for Year 11 boys to chat up. Maya sneers at me as she passes even though I've literally DONE NOTHING EXCEPT EXIST . . . so I sneer back. Feel braver standing up to them now I have Grace and Nisha on my side. Charlie comes over and asks how Gary the Gecko is getting on and I say, 'Yeah, he's good,' and use my hands to show how big he'd grown and I chat with Mr Graham, the P.E. teacher, and decide that he's actually quite attractive for a teacher . . . even with his big pecs.

No idea where Nisha's disappeared to and I haven't got time to waste. Today is the best opportunity I've got to land a first neck. I need to think like a sniper in the army, ready to pick off a victim . . . with my lips. ANYONE WILL DO.

3.30 p.m.
Target locked and loaded.

Harry Foxton. Seen him on my bus a few times. Year 10. Blond. Medium height. Not too tall. Not too small. Likes playing *Fortnite* and rugby. Not handsome but not ugly either. Never spoken to him before . . .

4.11 p.m.
HAVE MANAGED TO CONVINCE HIM I'M FROM FRANCE BY PUTTING ON A DODGY FRENCH ACCENT. *Hahahaha, oh wowzers, I am a hoot!* Pretending to be other people is one of my new favourite ways to lie 'cause it involves making up a whole new persona. I'm a great actor, you know – I should probably look at a career in Hollywood after I'm finished up here in East Manchester.

'Hey, Indi! You. Want. To. Come. On. The. Big Wheel?' he says, super slowly, so 'us Frenchies' can understand. *'La Grande . . .* er . . . Wheel?' he says again, pointing at it.

'Oh oui, oui!' I reply.

We have a right French laugh up La Grande Wheel then we head off and buy sugary doughnuts.

5.05 p.m.
Sitting on the steps that lead up to the geography huts.

My doughnut is glazed with pink icing and hundreds and thousands. Harry's is straight up jam, and he laughs when he bites into it and it leaks through the hole at the end.

I try to make myself look as stunnin' as possible, using my thumb and forefinger to pick at the doughnut and popping it delicately into my mouth (even though I just want to shove the whole lot in and gobble it like a big, hungry doughnut-swine).

I giggle softly at his jokes rather than letting him hear my real honking laugh and I've heard if you say the word 'prunes' it makes your lips look all pouty so I say it in my head and make my lips create the puckering shape.

'Zo, 'Arry, do you 'ave a – what ze French say – *la petite amie*?' I ask.

'What's that?'

'A *girlfriend*?' I say, pouting again and whispering 'prunes'.

It goes silent for a second and he glances at my prune-lips and I think *YES, YES, NECK ME, DO IT HARRY, NECK ME!!!!* and I SO think he was gonna! . . . until a couple of his mates bounce round the corner asking if he's gonna go on the Twister ride.

OH BLOODY HELL.

'Er, see you later, Indi . . .' he says, getting up from the step.

'Yeah, whatever, timewaster,' I mumble, back in my normal English accent.

'What?' he asks.

'I said, "*Oui, bon voyage* . . .",' rolling my eyes at him. *Wowzers this VK is making me sassy.*

BACK TO SQUARE BLOODY *UN*.

5.31 p.m.
Oh my G. Josh and Evan are throwing balls at coconuts. *God that's sexy.*

I slow my pace to the speed of a sloth, skulking past, locking my eyes on Josh's. I try to *saunter* like Grace does; a sort of slow, alluring walk, but I get the feeling I look like a slow-motion squid. I also prepare my best Frisky Eyes and start mouthing 'prune' over and over again.

Turn around, turn around, turn around . . .

Evan lobs a long ball at Josh, who tries to jog backwards to catch it, but it's gone too far . . . and it lands right at my feet.

HALLELUJAH! IF THIS ISN'T A SIGN FROM GOD, I DON'T KNOW WHAT IS. THANK YOU, JESUS, FOR THIS WAYWARD COCONUT!!!

I bend down to pick it up, in a sultry manner. Frisky Eyes are in full force, blinking away so much they might fall clean off.

'You OK? Got something in your eye, Indi?' asks Evan.

'Alright, Evan?' I say. 'No, I'm fine!' and throw him the ball.

'How's ya night, babe?' Josh says.

OH MY G, HE CALLED ME BABE.

'Yeah, it's cool.'

'Here, come take a shot for me.' Josh grabs me by the hand and pulls me towards the coconut shy. *OMG.*

'You're letting *Indi* go for you? Remember we've got a fiver on this, Josh.' Evan snickers.

'Right, girl, let's see what you got. Aim for the middle one, I reckon.' says Josh.

This is it, Indi. Don't mess it up! All you have to do is knock the coconut off its little stand and Josh will think you're the most amazing girl that ever lived. Let's go.

I take the ball from his hand into mine. First time I've ever touched him and it's electric. I turn slightly to the right and squint one eye to help me aim. *Three, two, one . . . THROW!*

5.40 p.m.

Have run away because I managed to make contact
NOT with the coconut, but the bald head of the man
running the stalls.

6 p.m.

Spot Reece near the merry-go-round. He catches my
eye and beckons me over to him.

'Reece!' I cry, wrapping my arms around his
neck.

When I pull away, he looks genuinely disturbed
by my behaviour. I've been giving him the cold
shoulder for weeks since the 'curly g's' incident.
We've barely spoken. When we've had to, in German,
it's been pleasant. Formal. I know he's been feeling
really confused . . . and he looks even more confused
now.

'Indiana Raye. What's going on?' His arms are limp
at his side, refusing to hug back. The sounds of
people squealing in the Haunted House rings out
around us.

I pull away. 'Nothing, Officer,' I reply, saluting him
with two fingers at my forehead.

'Hmm, nothing? Yeah, sure. Just out of interest,
how much alcohol has Nisha consumed this
evening?'

Reece grabs my shoulders and turns me ninety degrees. Nish is on the carousel. Backwards. Singing at the top of her lungs. 'Let It Go' from *Frozen*. A small crowd is gathering and filming her on their phones. She's defo gonna end up on socials in the next few minutes . . .

'Er, just a tiny, little bit. She's just a bit crunk, you know crazy-drunk,' I laugh, showing him what tiny is using my finger and my thumb. 'I swear she had the smallest amount, the amount a mouse would have . . . if a mouse enjoyed VK Watermelon, ahahaha!'

Reece turns me back to face him. 'Look, Indi, I don't want to be a killjoy but if you lot get caught, you know you're gonna be in so much trouble . . .'

'Reece,' I say, grabbing his face so that it's square with mine. 'If you don't want to be a killjoy, don't be a killjoy! You don't have to worry all the time.'

I feel his arms relax a little. Our faces are incredibly close and I see him look from my eyes to my lips. He's holding his breath, I can tell. Turns out, so I am.

Are WE about to neck on!?!??

Just as I begin pruning-up again, I hear Nisha yelling one of their hockey chants: 'EVERYBODY! REPEAT

AFTER ME! OGGY, OGGY, OGGY! OI, OI, OI!'

'OK, we need to get her home NOW,' says Reece, pushing me away from him. He's gone into full 'Dr Reece' mode.

'Er, yeah, actually you're probs right,' I mumble. 'Her parents are proper strict, apparently.'

'See, this is what I mean! It's—'

'Yeah, OK Doctor Know It All, you've made your point . . .'

Reece has this way of always being right. It's so irritating.

I call Grace and when she picks up, I can hear laughing at the end of the phone.

'Heyyyy, you OK, babe? . . . *OH MY GOD, SAM, STOP!*' she screeches.

'Grace, where you at, we've got a bit of an emergency!' I shout over the cheery organ music that soundtracks the carousel.

'Sorry, Indi. Sam keeps TICKLING ME. SAM, GET OFF!!!'

'Grace, I'm serious, I need your help, meet me by the merry-go-round?'

'URGH, FINE. Be there in a sec.'

6.13 p.m.

Alice Welby has had the good sense to get Nisha off the ride and has given her a blueberry Slush Puppie, which she's holding, like a three-year-old, with two hands. Grace finds us and we run over, prompting Nisha to stand up, unsteady on her feet, dropping her drink and reaching her hands out to us. *God, she's SO like a giant baby.* She grabs my hand and shoves it in Grace's hand. And then both *our* hands into hers, so we're standing in a triangle. Feels a bit like being in a cult.

'Guys. GUYS. I need to say something. Thank god for the chippy, for it has brought us together. You girls are my friends for life, ennit. We're like . . . like . . . a pack of bumblebees, we work as a team . . .' she slurs.

'You don't get "packs" of bees, Nisha! You get swarms or, like, beehives.' I laugh.

'OK, then WE are The Beehive, ennit! To be in The Beehive is to *be* in The Beehive. You won't ever get ANYWHERE in life . . . without The Beehive', she says, deeply and sincerely. 'OK?'

I nod.

'OK.' Grace laughs.

Nisha nods . . . then immediately vomits bright blue slush down herself. Behind her, the hockey girls hoot with laughter with Amelia screeching 'Urgggggh!'

'OH GOD!' screams Grace. 'For god's sake, Nisha!'

'I shall put her in the recovery position! Mind out, everyone!' shouts Dr Reece.

'Urgh, let's just get her out of here. Come on, Nish, let's go!' I shout, wedging myself under her shoulders, ready to carry her home.

CHAPTER 13

WE ARE THE BEEHIVE

7.06 p.m.

We have to physically draaaaaaaaaag Nisha home. It's bloody miles away and it's starting to get a bit chilly and we're going SO slowly. We have to stop multiple times for various reasons: one minute she 'fancies a little sit down', the next minute she 'thinks she saw a dog' and the next minute she's shouting at some oncoming traffic.

'You should have never brought that watermelon stuff, Grace!' I groan.

'What!? It's not my fault she can't handle it!' retorts Grace.

'Oh god, is the bottle still in her bag?' I panic.

'Oh yeah, it is! Quick, get rid of it!'

'Mum's gon' kill me . . .' mumbles Nisha.

'No, she's not, Nisha, 'cause she's never gonna find out! I just need you to stand up straight for me and walk home nice and steady, OK?' I say, chucking the bottle in the nearby bin. It clangs and smashes. Evidence destroyed.

'Are we there yet?' moans Reece. 'Dad's gonna start wondering where I am . . .'

'Hey youuuuu. Reece. Reecey. What's goin' on, eh? You and Indi . . . I just think . . . you should get married . . .'

'Nisha, shut up.' I snap.

'. . . I just think . . .'

'STOP IT,' I hiss.

Reece keeps his eyes to the ground, embarrassed.

After what feels like A MILLION HOURS, we reach a row of eight terraced houses, tucked away behind the local shop, and stop outside a dark green front door. I turn to The Giant Baby and say:

'OK, Nisha, we need to sneak you inside, OK?'

'SSSSHHH!' she shouts. Then, whispering: 'Mum's in the living room, she'll see me!'

'OK, back door?' Grace asked.

'Nope. Locked. BACK WINDOW,' says Nisha, eyes wide and mischievous. With a speed I didn't expect, she runs off around the back of the house. We follow her, through some overgrown shrubbery, and she kicks a broken fence panel so we can squeeze into the back yard.

'You've godda help me geddup there . . .' she slurs, pointing at her bedroom window. I *mean, in theory,* she *could* climb up on to the kitchen window sill, pull herself up on to the porch roof, and then shimmy up to her bedroom. It *would* actually be doable . . . if she wasn't a total mess.

'Nisha, no, you can't—'

'Don' have a choice . . .' she laughs. 'Give me a leg up. C'mon, Reece.'

'No way, it's dangerou—'

'Reece, just do it, quick,' I snap.

Just then, a voice appears from a window above us. 'Yo, what's going on?'

'Not now, Arun!' hisses Nisha. 'Sozguys . . . tha's my brother . . .'

Arun is Nisha's eldest brother. He has a bit of a furry moustache above his top lip and he's wearing a gaming headset.

'I'm telling Mum . . .' he taunts.

'If you tell Mum, you'll regretit, ennit . . .'

'Oh yeah, what you gonna do?' he replies.

Nisha thinks and somehow zings back with: 'Show Mum your internet history . . .'

His eyes widen, scared, and he shuts his window promptly, retreating back to his XBox.

As quietly as we can – Nisha keeps yelping – Reece interlocks his fingers so she can use it as a launch pad up on to window ledge. She balances herself and grabs the porch roof with both hands. From underneath, we push her feet up until she can swing her left leg up on to the roof. One final heave aaaaaaaannnnndd – *she's up!*

'Wahey! DID IT, GUYS!' she hisses and punches the air . . . right before a tile from beneath her left foot slips out of place, falling to the ground below and smashing. We freeze. It sounds loud, *extra loud* at this time of the evening. The dog next door barks and a light flicks on at the back of the house.

'UH OH!' says Nisha, panicking.

'Quick, hide!' squeaks Grace, pulling the rest of us behind an old, dilapidated shed.

Nisha's unsure whether to leap for the bedroom window or to stay where she is. She goes to move but her balance is off and she slips. She falls on to her back and rattles down the roof, *bom-bom-bom-bom-bom-bom*. She makes a grab to try and hold on to the gutter but it's too late and she tragically flops off, hitting the grass below with a thud.

'MY GOD, WHAT IS HAPPENING, NISHA?' Nisha's mum yells, pulling her cream silk dressing gown tighter around her waist.

Nisha springs to her feet. 'Nothin' to be worried about, Mum, it's—'

'YOU'VE BEEN DOING DRUGS.'

'NO!'

She sniffs Nisha's face. 'Alcohol. Even worse.'

'Mum, alcohol is NOT worse than drugs,' says Nisha, rolling her eyes.

'Well, that depends. Alcohol *is* technically a drug,' mumbles Reece from the shed.

'Not now, Reece!' I hiss.

Mrs Chowdhury spots us. 'Get inside, Nisha. And you, you lot . . . come,' she says.

We creep out through the grass, Grace pushing me first.

'Ah, Grace!' she says, smiling. 'How is your mother?'

Grace's face lights up, thinking she's out of troubled waters. 'Ah, she's fine, Mrs Chowdhury. Thanks for asking!'

'Good. Tell her I'll be calling her about you tomorrow,' she snaps.

Grace's face falls.

'And you two, who are you?'

'Reece Williams, ma'am,' he said, bowing to her like she's royalty. I look at him incredulously.

'And you?'

'Erm. Claire . . .' I lie.

Grace shoots me a look so I say: 'I mean, Indi. Indi Raye.'

Nisha's mum shakes her head. 'How are you getting home?'

'Oh, don't worry, my dad will fetch us!' says Reece, pulling out his phone to send a text.

'Good. Go wait out the front. And YOU!' she yelled at Nisha. 'Get inside . . .'

Nisha suddenly seems sober, and follows her mum, mouthing 'sorry' to us. Arun leans out and laughs at her from his bedroom window.

We exit in an orderly fashion via the garden gate rather than the broken fence . . . and burst into hysterics.

'Oh my G, she's scary!' I gasp.

'I've known that woman since I was three years old and she *still* doesn't like me! I don't know what to do!' laughs Grace.

'Hahahaha, your face when you thought you'd gotten away with it!'

'I know!! I can't believe she turned on me like that!'

'And YOU, Reece!' I roar.

'What?' he replied, innocently. He knows what.

'You, with the whole "the name's Reece, ma'am",' Grace teases, in a phony American accent.

'Reece, you bowed, like she was the Queen!'

'I panicked!' retorted Reece and we all crack up.

Reece passes me a little secret smile, one just between us, and I smile back. Maybe it's the Watermelon VK talking . . . but I have really missed him.

7.43 p.m.
Reece's dad pulls up, none the wiser about the events of the day, and we pile into the backseat of the Audi. *Wish it was MY dad picking us all up . . .*

'Good day was it, gang?' asks Tony. 'Right, what's your postcode for the sat-nav, Indi?'

Oh my G, I hadn't planned for this. I thought I'd be getting the bus home tonight! Oh god, GRACE is gonna find out where I live!!! And she'll definitely tell Nish too as soon as she gets the chance. I've been doing such a good job at keeping Number 64 a secret from them but now I've blown it! I blame the VK Watermelon.

I mumble my address and can't speak a word until we pull up to the flats. Grace unwinds her window and peers out.

'Oh,' she says, quietly.

I know what 'Oh' means.
It means, 'Oh, well, THIS isn't exactly The Ritz.'
It's, 'Oh, I thought you lived in a massive penthouse?'

It's, 'Oh, no weeing cherubs round here' . . . although there is a high-key chance of seeing an *actual* person relieving themselves against the bins, so . . . almost the same.

Reece and Tony don't blink an eye though.

'Let me walk you in, Indi,' says Tony, his niceness suddenly standing stark against the absence of my own dad.

'Nah, it's OK, Tony. I'm fine. Thanks, though,' I say to him.

'You sure, babe?' says Grace. 'I can come in, if you like?'

'NO, NO. It's fine, don't get out. Text you when I'm in. See you Monday, guys,' I say, leaping out of the car as fast as possible.

7.58 p.m.

I wander up to the block. What a bizarre day. Not your usual Chippy Saturday.

Can't wait to brush my teeth – my mouth feels rotten from that hideous drink.

Oh look, there's Hawkeye in her kitchen. She appears to be dancing around the kitchen with Mr Biggles in arms, wearing a bedsheet as a cape.

I head up two flights of stairs – nine more to go – when suddenly the hallway light pings on and a man makes his way down the steps towards me. He offers a friendly smile as he passes. I continue my journey upwards, and then I hear him call out:

'Scuse me, sorry, hi. Are you . . . Indiana?'

'No,' I lie, as I turn around on the stairs.

'Yes, you're Joy's daughter, aren't you? I've seen your photo around the flat! I live just opposite.'

Ah. Jonathan.

'Ah. Jonathan,' I said to him. 'It is true, I am Indiana P. Raye.'

'Yes. Nice to meet you,' he says, climbing the stairs to meet me and sticking out a hand. I shake it, with great reluctance.

Jonathan looks like he wants to start a conversation but I say, 'Well, I'm off now. My mum wouldn't be happy about me talking to STRANGE MEN at this late hour.'

'Your mother would be quite right!' he laughs. 'Right, cheerio. See you soon, Indiana. Say hello to Joyful Joy for me,' and he walks back down the hall.

Hm. Jonathan seems nice. Too nice.

I'm gasping for a drink, so sneak into the kitchen, turn

the tap on and guzzle straight from the tap.

The Beehive.

We are The Beehive.

I'm just not ready to tell them the whole truth yet.

CHAPTER 14

REAL-LIFE WOMEN'S PROBLEMS!

MONDAY MAR 15th

9.21 a.m.

The videos of Nisha being a hot mess are circulating online but an unspoken secret code is created between every student at St Cath's. Tête-à-têtes about the fête-a-fête are whispered and sent via WhatsApp and scribbled on notes passed in class, a communal effort to keep what happened at the fête, stay at the fête.

Unfortunately, grown-ups are cleverer than they look.

2.36 p.m.

Our last lesson today – geography for me – has been cancelled because an emergency assembly has been called and we all know what it's gonna be about.

A cloak of dread descends on everybody across the school as we take our seats in the school hall.

Nisha's a ball of anxiety; she keeps saying, jiggling her leg next to me: 'I bet my mum's called the school, I BET it's MY mum who's called the school . . .' She prepares herself for the national shame of having The Mum Who Dobbed Everyone In.

'Shut up, Nisha, you're making me anxious,' snaps Grace. 'It's gonna be fine.'

3.05 p.m.
'REPORTS OF ALCOHOLIC BEVERAGES'

'EXTREMELY DUBIOUS BEHAVIOUR'

'GIVING THE SCHOOL A BAD REPUTATION'

'YOUR PARENTS WILL BE INFORMED'

'POLICE MAY BE INVOLVED'

'NEXT YEAR'S SPRING FÊTE MAY BE CANCELLED'

Just some of the words used by Jenko, who's completely popping off. She's so angry, you can occasionally see bits of spit escape her mouth, flying across the hall stage, dancing in the sunlight.

4.17 p.m.

When I get in, Tubs is slamming pots around the kitchen.

'Hiiiii, Mummy,' I squeak.

'Anythin' yer wanna share, Indiana?'

'Psssst, Indi, tell her you saw a meteor,' seems to whisper the fridge magnet on the fridge door. It's a fridge magnet of a frog. We got it from a trip to Tenerife one year with Dad, but its right eye chipped off in the suitcase on the way home, so now it looks like it's winking.

'Oh Fridge Frog, I can't, I'm in too much troubl—'

'DO IIIITTTTTTTT!!!!!' it screams.

'Erm, yes, I do have something to share, actually. I saw what appeared to be a meteor, or perhaps you may know them as comets, this morning, streaming through the sky—'

'Pack it in with the lies, Indiana! Less than six months and I've got the school callin' me, naming you as one of the girls who caused a scene and consumed alcohol. You SPECIFICALLY.'

Tubs faces away from me and pours a large glass of wine.

OK, she's right to be mad. I get it. I really do. But isn't it kinda ironic that Tubs is currently standing against the kitchen counter WITH A GLASS OF ALCOHOL IN HER HAND?

'You're drinking . . .' I mutter.

Well, that makes her pop right off, doesn't it.

'I'M ALLOWED TO DRINK! I AM AN ADULT. YOU ARE A CHILD AND THEREFORE IT IS ILLEGAL!' she erupts. 'YER GROUNDED, INDIANA RAYE. The school said they're not gonna to suspend yer because it was an out-of-school event, BUT YOU HAD BETTER COUNT YOUR BLESSINGS, SO HELP ME GOD.'

There's a moment of tense silence which gets punctuated by an *unexpected* slurp. I look over at the kitchen table.

Jonathan's been sitting there like an awkward turtle this whole time.

'Hello!' he says gawkily, cup of tea in hand.

I turn back to face Tubs. 'Why's he here, by the way?'

'GO TO YER ROOM,' Tubs shouts, as she pours herself some more wine.

5.34 p.m.

I've let Gary sit on my shoulder whilst I FaceTime the girls.

'I'm grounded,' I say.

'Grounded,' echoes Nisha.

'Grounded,' replies Grace. 'Well, sort of. Ally will

probably let me off tomorrow. She's just been in my room asking if I fancy having dinner down the pub this evening.'

'Urgh, you're SO lucky that your mum is cool, Grace,' I moan.

Grace smiles, whilst Nisha seems exceedingly stressed out. She's moving around her room at speed, and watching her truck about is making me feel seasick. Then she drops her phone before propping it up on her windowsill.

'Girls, I think the police might be watching my every move so I'm gonna use code words, 'kay? You know the PINK FLAMINGO we drank. I MEAN MET – you know the pink flamingo we MET *that time*? I don't think we should *meet that flamingo* again.'

'What are you on about?' asks Grace, filing her nails.

'I said, you know THE PINK FLAMINGO?' Nisha winks, exaggeratedly. 'He was bad news. He's caused a lot of trouble . . .'

'If you're talking about the pink vodka Nisha, yes, we get it, we're all in deep doo-doo.'

'OH GOD!' Nisha howls, worried that the Greater Manchester Po-Po are gonna descend on her house at any moment.

Grace hasn't mentioned what happened on Saturday seeing where I live in all its glory. And I assume she hasn't told Nisha, because Nisha doesn't mention it either, which I should be grateful for, but I can't help but think *why not*?

I suppose, I didn't let Grace inside? . . . maybe she still thinks there really is a posh flat lurking at the top of the high rise? No. It's too obvious from the exterior.

Maybe they think it'll embarrass me if they bring it up? I mean, they'd be right.

Maybe they're making a list, one by one, of every lie I've ever told, and one day they're going to stand up in assembly and reveal all my deceits and falsehoods to the entire school???

God, I hope not.

I go to sleep that night trying not to overthink it.

SATURDAY MARCH 20th

3.01 p.m.

Today at the chippy, a pigeon walked in. Bold as brass! Just strutted in. Turns out, Alan's terrified of them.

'Indiana, Nishaaaaaaaa!' he squealed in the shrillest voice I've ever heard omitted by a grown man. 'Gerrit out!'

Well, we ran around with the broom, shooing this way and cooing that way and then it did a poo on the floor and that's when Alan really lost his nut.

'I'LL GIVE YOU BOTH A TWENTY POUND

BONUS TODAY IF YOU GET IT OUT!' he screamed and guess what? WE DID, by making a trail of chips out of the door, back on to the pavement.

Forget dolphin training as a future career, I AM THE PIGEON WHISPERER.

THURSDAY MAR 25th
1.23 p.m.
'Wait up, Indi,' says a voice behind me in the history corridor, causing me to spin around.

Oh my actual G – it's Josh.

His tie is loose at his neck; if Jenko sees him, he'll get done for that. *I just wanna reach out my hands and adjust it for him . . .*

'Hey, was mint to hang out the other day. Oh man, when you smacked that bloke on the head with the ball. Dead funny, that,' he laughs.

'Ha, I don't think throwing is one of my best talents. I'm a great catcher though.'

'Who needs talent, when you're proper unreal, eh . . .'

MY EYES ALMOST POP OUT OF MY SKULL.

DID JOSH WOOD JUST CALL ME UNREAL?

'Oh, hey, you guys,' says Grace, walking towards us and interrupting us at JUST the wrong time. 'What you two chatting about?' she asks, coming to a standstill. Her arms are crossed firmly across her chest and her smile is plastic.

Oh my god, did she just hear what he said??

'Ah, hey, Grace. Nothing,' says Josh, looking straight at me. I feel myself getting hotter.

Is he giving me Frisky Eyes?!

'Well, you must be talking about something?' Grace pushes. She's not happy. Not one bit. 100% giving shade.

'Just chit-chat. Right I'm off, gotta go see Mrs Jenkinson for one of my weekly telling-offs . . .' says Josh laughing. 'See you guys later.'

He slopes off down the corridor, leaving a proper weird vibe hanging in the air between me and Grace.

'So . . .' I start to try and break the ice

'I've got to go to class,' she mutters. 'I'll see you in a bit.'

TUESDAY APR 6th
5 p.m.
Round Nisha's with Grace doing maths homework. Was scared to come over after our last run-in with Mrs Chowdhury, but turns out she's working late. PHEW.

230

Nisha's house is so cosy. Everything is warm: rusty-red sofas, with blankets and cushions thrown across them. Heavy curtains. Old ornate-looking rugs. Knick-knacks everywhere, little ornaments and keepsakes. Shelves and mantelpieces FULL of photo frames, containing the pictures of Nisha's brothers and aunties, cousins and grandparents.

We're sprawled out on the living room carpet. Grace has taken control of my phone and we're having to listen to some horrific boyband. NO idea what they're called, and frankly, I don't want to know. They're making my ears burn. I dare not say anything though; what with the whole flat thing and then Josh in the corridor last week, I think I'm skating on thin ice.

Suddenly Grace squeals and grabs Nisha's neck. 'OH MY G, WHAT IS THIS?' she hollers, pulling on a gold chain necklace with a little gold heart pendant.

'Nothin'!' says Nisha defensively, slapping her hand and tucking the necklace down inside her shirt. Her face is burning a deep plummy colour.

'Oh my G! You're going all red! Why you so embarrassed, Nisha?' I tease.

'I'm not,' she grumbles.

'You literally NEVER wear jewellery, Nisha Chowdhury. Where'd you get it?'

'Nowhere! I mean, my brother got it me.'

'Oh pur-lease. I've known Arun basically all my life. He wouldn't buy you a necklace. He'd rather spend his pocket money on video games. No offence, like.'

I sidle up to Nish. 'UGH, OH, COME ON, NISHA! Who's your boyfriend!?' I tease. 'Or girlfriend . . . could be a girl.'

Nisha gives us a sarcastic smile and says, 'Right, time for you two to get yourselves home now, lovely to see ya, safe journey, ennit!' before basically shoving us out the door.

Very sus, indeed. Not that I'm one to talk about secrets . . .

TUESDAY APR 13th
11.34 p.m.
Ugh. Jasmine bloody Singh is talking SUPER LOUDLY about how her dad proposed to her mum at the weekend. Apparently now's 'THE TIME' and Jasmine is gonna walk down the aisle as a bridesmaid in a lavender dress and she's gonna get her hair and make-up done professionally.

'So then, my dad literally GOT DOWN ON ONE KNEE and was like, "Will you marry me?" and I was like, cringggggggggggge, but also it was quite sweet. They might get married at a castle you know and—'

I mean, why does she have to speak so loudly? The WHOLE class can hear her wanging on about how fire she thinks she's going to look in purple.

I stare down at the maths equation in front of me.

$$3(6x+4)=2x$$

Can't be bothered with this.

I raise my hand. 'I need the loo, Mr Basi!'

He sighs.

'Indi, can you have a go at a few of the questions on your worksheet first, please. Then I'll let you go.'

'Can't, sir. Women's problems . . .' I say.

Every girl knows that if you tell Mr Basi you have women's problems, his face sets on fire with embarrassment and he'll release you straight away. It's the oldest trick in the book. And today is no exception.

I meander along the hallway at a super leisurely pace, in no hurry to get back. I pull out my phone; background is currently of Gary with a cricket in his mouth looking like a happy dog with a bone.

Mr Frederick comes down the corridor and barks, 'Phone away, Indiaaaaaaana! Shouldn't you be in maths?' and I reply that I'm going to the toilet and pull my phone out again once he's out of sight. Make my way into one of the cubicles and decide I can probs waste about ten minutes in here before I have to head back. Time for a nice, long wee.

I will never understand why some people's lives are so bloody amazing and meanwhile mine is so bloody hideous. While the Singhs are playing happy families, *it's been over six months now since I saw my dad. Six months without even a text. Have occasionally asked Tubs if she's heard anything, but no. My stupid dad never even proposed to Tubs. I was born out of wedlock. I'll never get to be a bridesmaid.* Not to mention stupid Jonathan has been knocking about more than usual AND I can't stop worrying about how I'm gonna get a neck on. I may as well go and die in a hole.

I grab some toilet roll to wipe and that's when I see it, lurking in my pants.

Blood.

HELLO YOU!

OH MY G, IT WAS WOMEN'S PROBLEMS! ACTUAL, REAL-LIFE WOMEN'S PROBLEMS! I WASN'T EVEN

LYING TO MR BASI. Wowzers, this is a really momentous day for Indi P. Raye.

It's not what I was expecting. I always thought having a period would be a proper massacre in my knickers, like there'd been a zombie apocalypse down there or something. But really, it's no more than a smudge of reddish goo. I didn't even feel it coming. I mean, I had a little stomach ache yesterday but I thought that was from the tuna I ate. Turns out I was having period cramps! Who knew!

That being said, the thought of heading back to class with damp pants, no period pad to hand and Jasmine banging on and on and on about her perfect life is too much for little old Indi Raye today. I have had enough for one Tuesday. So instead I take a deep breath, unlock the door and then dramatically splay myself out on the toilet floor, clutching my stomach. And I scream:

'HEEEEEEEEEEEELLLLLLLLPPPPPPPPPPP PPPPPP!'

Within moments, Mrs Angus rushes in and calls out in her Scottish accent: 'Everything OK? What's happened?'

'I've had an accident!' I call out.

'What kind of accident?'

I go silent, pretending I've blacked out, for extra drama.

OK, I know what you're thinking; nobody should lie about being seriously ill. I understand, I really do. But this Dad stuff is really stressing me out; this kind of thing could give me a heart attack and it's important I'm in a hospital where I'm being looked after by professionals . . . right?

Within about ten minutes (*proper* quick, I note, thank you NHS!) two paramedics have arrived. They push the door inwards, and squeeze me out, picking me up by my armpits. We stagger down the maths corridor and the faces of Year 7s and 8s peer out to see what all the commotion is about and I really have to lay on some of my best acting. I implement a hobble for added effect, look up at the Boy Paramedic and, with big, mournful eyes, and in my best *dying-hero-in-action-movie* voice, I ask him: 'Am I dyin', doctor?'

'No, you're gonna be fine, we're just gonna take to the hospital for a check-up,' he replies.

Suddenly Reece bursts out of nowhere, running to my side and grabbing my hand.

'Oh hell, are you OK, Ind?' he asks, panicked.

So many eyes are watching me right now. Don't want Josh to find out me and Reece held hands . . .

I snatch it back and hiss, 'I'm fine, don't make a scene . . .'

'Where are you taking her, Manchester Royal?' he asks the paramedic. 'Great hospital, don't worry, you'll be in safe hands there, I'll message you later!'

'Yeah, cool, bye,' I reply and hobble off. I'm outttttaaaaaaa heeeeeereeee!

11.58 a.m.
Never been in an ambulance before! I lie down on a bed and I'm strapped in. Make a mental note to tell Tubs that the long car journeys to see Auntie Cass would be ten times better if cars had beds in them.

I spot one of those masks used to give people oxygen.

'I think I'm gonna need a puff on that ...' I say, pretending to wheeze.

Girl Paramedic looks at me sceptically and says, 'You should be fine without it.'

Hope they put the blue lights on and sound the ambulance siren. How cool would that be? All those cars having to pull over, out of our way, to let us pass. I pull out my phone and tell the paramedics that I'm texting Tubs, when in fact I take a grinning selfie and send it on the group chat to Grace and Nisha.

> Grace: you k????

> Nisha: whats happened???

> Nisha: dont mention the pink flamingo else theyll be onto us!!!

Think she's confused the ambulance service with the police.

12.16 p.m.

Ugh, taken to the *children's* A&E, which is a bit annoying 'cause, actually, HELLO!? I have a period in my pants which means I am a woman now! I should be on the grown-up ward!

12.57 p.m.

Tubs arrives in a flap, wearing her uniform. Her journey was short; we're at the hospital she cleans at and she's literally been scrubbing away just two floors below.

'OH, THANK GOD!' Tubs says to me, grabbing my hand. 'How are you, baby?'

'Mama, it's hurts!' I say.

God I'm good at this hahahahaa.

'Apologies for your wait today,' says the doctor,

drawing the cubicle curtain back. 'Alright, Joy?' she says to Tubs. 'I'm Dr Flanaghan, Indi. OK if I take a quick look at you?'

I nod.

'We just want to check it's not appendicitis,' she says, lifting my top and starting to poke around my stomach. Dr Flan has cold hands. I've heard about appendicitis. Apparently it's when your appendix bursts. Bluergh. That's *obviously* not what I've got . . .

'Does it hurt here?' she asks, pushing the right side of my abdomen. I yelp in response.

'Hmm, OK. How about here?' she asks, prodding the left side. I yelp again.

'And now?' she asks, pushing a little lower, which makes me want to wee. I yelp and add a 'Oh yeah, that *really* hurts,' for dramatic effect.

'OK . . .' she says, with a tone of suspicion in her voice. 'And how about this?'

She pokes my lower arm this time and I make the same noises. The same when she pokes my knee. *Yelp yelp yelp, keep yelping.* She casts a side-eye to Tubs. I know that look. It's the look that says, 'We've got ourselves a faker on our hands'.

'And have you had any other symptoms, Indi? Any fever? Loss of appetite?'

'No, she were perfectly fine when she left for school this morning,' says Tubs.

'I do have one other symptom, actually,' I say. 'Bleeding. I'm bleeding.'

Tubs leans in and looks even more concerned, picking up my hand.

Dr Flan looks at me over her glasses. 'Bleeding, you say? Whereabouts, Indi?'

'Erm, well, you know,' I say, using my eyes to gesture at my crotch. 'Downstairs. I think I might need one of those, erm, tampon things.'

Dr Flan looks confused for a moment. Tubs drops my hand.

'So, sorry, just to confirm then . . . *are* you in pain? It's important I know if you have pain or not, Indi.'

'Yes.'

'OK, well, we'll get you into surgery as soon as possible, open you up, have a dig around . . .' she says.

Uh oh. This was all a bit of fun; last thing I want is being chopped up on an operating table!

'I mean no!' I reply, shaking my head. 'No pain, no.'

Starting to look a bit silly now, after my big Oscar-winning performance. I glance at Tubs who's glaring at me with gritted teeth.

'Okaaaaaaaaaay, so no pain, but you've noticed some blood in your underwear, is that right?'

'Yep.'

'Have you ever had blood in your underwear before Indi?'

'Nope.'

Dr Flan squeezes her lips together. 'OK. I think, Indiana, what's happened is that you've started your period,' she tells me.

As if I didn't already know.

'Really, I think this is just a very normal start to the menstruation process that most young women experience. No need for ambulances or hospitals. I can get you a leaflet about your cycle.'

Tubs glares at me. 'I'm so sorry, Doctor. She knows all about periods, we've chatted about them at home, and she had talks in school. I dunno why she's done this . . .'

'It's not a problem,' Dr Flan forces herself to say. 'I'll get the nurse to bring in some period pads along with that leaflet, OK?'

She pulls the curtain behind her as she leaves.

'WHAT ON EARTH IS ALL THIS ABOUT!?' hisses Tubs. 'EMBARRASING ME LIKE THIS IN MY WORKPLACE?'

'Erm, aren't you gonna congratulate me?' I ask.

'Congratulate yer for what??'

'Becoming a woman!' I beam.

'Congratulations!' Tubs says. 'You get to spend yer first week of womanhood grounded. AGAIN. Like a little girl. How about that!?'

She storms off for a cup of coffee and I reach down, lift my hospital blanket and whisper 'thanks' to my vagina for getting me out of maths and Jasmine Singh's hideous parents story.

3.45 p.m.

Nisha and Grace arrive, tumbling in loudly.

'Oh my G, are you OK?' Grace asks, hanging her bag on the chair. 'What happened?'

'Oh god, is it serious? Must have been serious for them to call an ambulance!' Nisha says.

I'm SO touched that they've come along to check I'm OK!

'It's all good, guys, I'm fine!' I say, grinning ear-to-ear, 'You're gonna laugh so hard.'

Nish and Grace look at each other then back to me.

'SO, we were doing a test in maths and I was like, "I can't do this question, it's too hard," so . . . so . . .' I laugh. '. . . so, I go to the toilet and there's my period, right, so I thought, "Why not pretend I've had an accident and make them call an ambulance, so I don't have to do the questions!"'

There I am, hooting away . . . but Nisha and Grace aren't laughing with me.

Nisha sits in the hospital chair and Grace perches on the arm. 'Eh? So, let me get this straight . . .' says Nisha. 'You couldn't be bothered with maths today, so you faked a serious injury to get out of it?'

'YES!' I shriek, absolutely popping off with laughter. 'Plus Jasmine was wanging on about something soooooo borin—'

'Indi, that's SO not cool,' says Grace, cutting me off.

'No, it is – it's just a joke, like,' I insist. 'Like, just a bit of fun!'

Tubs comes back in clasping a paper cup of coffee.

'Oh, girls! You must be Nisha and Grace? Well, listen I'm very sorry yer've come all this way for no reason . . .'

'That's OK,' says Nisha, through gritted teeth.

Oh god, they're furious with me.

'I'm sure she's told yer,' continues Tubs. '. . . but things have been a little bit tough for us since we arrived . . .'

'OK, Tubs, no need to tell them our life story!' I say, panicked.

'. . . it's all very unsettling, and y'know, with her dad being *god-knows-where*, we've just had to make do and, well, she's always been somewhat difficult at the best of times, y'know . . .'

'Tubs, don't—'

'Yeah, we heard. He's in Australia, is it?' asks Grace.

'AUSTRALIA!' hoots Tubs. 'Pah, I doubt that! No, love. Sixteen years we were together and we only went to Tenerife once! No love, no idea where he is and quite frankly, I don't care! We've split up. Can I get an amen, sisters?'

The girls glare at me.

I avoid their eyes and we all reply back, monotone:

'Amen . . .'

'Well,' says Grace curtly, making to leave. 'It was lovely to meet you, Mrs Raye, but I am supposed to be meeting up with Sam after school and instead I'm here worrying about this one for nowt so I'm gonna head off . . .'

Nisha stands up. 'Yeah, me too. It's been an *interesting* visit, Indi. Let's catch up soon, shall we?' she says, in a way that's a bit sinister. 'Come on, Grace, let's go.'

'Feel better, Indi,' says Grace, sarcastically, shutting the green hospital curtain behind them and possibly shutting the curtain on our friendship forever. It feels

like the end of a play, when the curtain comes down.
Except there's no applause.

Great, Indi, so that's:

Grace livid ✓

Nisha livid ✓

Tubs livid ✓

Grace stomps back in again and grabs her handbag she's forgotten, before storming back out again, scowling.

End scene.

6.22 p.m.
Back home. Got a message from Nisha:

Emergency meeting. Tomorrow
after school. Chippy.

'This is gonna be bad, Gary,' I say.
'Hmm. Good luck, sunshine,' he seems to reply.

WEDNESDAY APR 14th

4.13 p.m.

'Sorrylwastedyourtime,' I mumble, swirling the vinegar bottle between my fingers. We're sitting at Our Table in the window, and the sun shines on my face.

'Hmm? What was that? Little louder for the people at the back, please, Indiana . . .' demands Grace.

'I said, sorry I wasted your time yesterday. It was stupid.'

'It's nothing to do with wasted time, Indi, it's about you lying. We have noticed, you know! We're not idiots,' says Nisha, sipping on a can of Coke.

'Noticed what?' I ask, with faux innocence.

'Grace told me about your flat. And we knew your dad wasn't just off travelling. I mean, no offence, but did you really think we believed that he sent you a digeridoo?' says Nisha.

'And the thing about your Spanish boyfriend falling off the horse, I mean, come on . . .' says Grace.

'AND Tess and Claudia being best mates with your mum!!'

I pick at the vinegar bottle label.

God I'm embarrassed.

All along, they've known what I've been up to. Wish the ground would open up and swallow me whole.

'So, I'm guessing that's it for us then,' I mumble.

'It's fine, like, I totally get it. I wouldn't want to be mates with a liar either to be fair. It's just . . . well, Tubs was right. It has been a bit weird without my dad and that. Just feels like everyone else's life is just perfect and mine's just . . . rubbish. But yeah, I totally understand if we wanna just call it a day, y'know, with The Beehive.'

Nisha rolls her eyes.

'Don't be stupid. Course we're still The Beehive, you div,' says Nisha, sympathetically. 'Just don't lie to us. That's not what mates do, OK?'

'OK,' I squeak, trying not to cry with relief. *Phew.*

'Beehive forever,' says Grace. 'I do have one question, though. And you have to answer honestly.'

'I will, promise,' I reply.

And I really mean that.

Indiana P. Raye will no longer tell lies.

From here on in, I will tell the truth, the whole truth and nothing but the truth, so help me God.

'Do you like Josh?' she asks inquisitively. 'I've seen you staring at him . . .'.

My heart races in my chest.

A lump forms in my throat.

And it takes me approximately 2.3 seconds to reply:

'No.'

CHAPTER 15

I QUITE LIKE MY DAMP PATCHES, THANK YOU VERY MUCH

MONDAY MAY 3rd

1.12 p.m.

'OH. MY. GEEEEEEEEE!' screams Grace running into the canteen. Dinner Lady glances at her like something might be wrong, but there's nothing wrong. Grace just gets this loud when she's proper giddy.

'Daisy Rowling is having a house party at the end of the month! WE HAVE TO GO!'

'She's Megan's sister, Grace. She's literally never gonna invite us . . .' I say.

'You *actually* don't know that, Indi, don't be a Negative Nancy.'

'I'm not, I'm being a . . . Realist . . . Rachel. Who's going to this party anyway?' I ask coyly. What I mean is: *Do you think Josh might be there?*

'Look at her,' she says, glancing over to Daisy

Rowling at the opposite side of the canteen. 'Imagine being that cool.'

Daisy Rowling *is* cool. Even cooler than her sister. She's not got a single spot in sight. I bet she drinks eight pints of water a day and never eats chips. I'd love Daisy's skin. I'm aware that sounds creepy, like the thoughts of a serial killer, but it's true. She has chestnut-brown hair and rosy cheeks and she's tall and has the most perfect boobs; big, but not too big. Once she came into school on Dress Down Friday wearing a floral dress and *Doc Martens* and a denim jacket. She wasn't even trying to be sexy, but she was. Oh, and she has a nose piercing!

'Look,' says Grace. 'All we need to do is get on her radar. We're *obvs* never gonna get an invite to a YEAR ELEVEN PARTY if she doesn't know we exist.'

'And how to you suppose we do that?' asks Nisha.

'What did you say that time, Nisha?' Grace asks me. *'To be in The Beehive is to be in The Beehive. You won't get ANYWHERE in life . . . without The Beehive.* Well, my little bumblebees, you just leave this one to me. I'll sort us out.'

She stands up, the metal legs of her chair screeching on the floor, and struts over in Daisy's direction. She's about to take one for the team . . .

'Oh no . . .' I moan.

'Despo times, despo measures . . .' says Nisha, watching her creep up to Daisy and the gaggle of equally stunnin' Year 11 girls on her table. They're laughing at something on one of the girl's phones.

'Hahahahaha . . .' laughs Grace.

They all turn around to see who's enjoying their private joke with them.

'Ahhhh, *I* know something that's funny . . .'

'Er, do you?' Daisy asks, looking up from beneath her eyelashes, which are heavy with mascara.

'So *apparently* Mr Frederick . . . has got no knees! His legs are just, like, one long bone. Oh my god, can you BELIEVE IT!?'

Grace kills herself laughing while the Year 11 girls look at her blankly.

'Erm, yeah, that's literally impossible. Like, medically impossible,' says Daisy flatly, putting an abrupt end to Grace's amusement.

You can actually see Grace shrivelling up and DYING inside.

First, the blood drains out of her face and she goes white as a sheet.

Her beaming smile falls into a frown and her wide, gleeful eyes turn into pure fear.

Her straight posture buckles and slumps and then

she gulps, her mouth now desert dry.

'Oh, right. Yeah, I knew that. Er . . . yeah. See you later, Daisy. See ya, girls . . .'

IT'S SO SUPER CRINGE.

She scurries back to our table, redder than beetroot.

'Well, that went well . . .' I murmur.

'Shut up, Indi,' she hisses.

'Where on EARTH did you hear the leg thing??? That is THE stupidest rumour I've ever heard!' says Nisha incredulously.

'Oh my G, what if she never invites me to any of her parties ever again!?' whines Grace.

'Well, you'll have to go to your own parties. Party for one . . .' Nisha says gravely, trying not to laugh.

'Grace is NEVER GONNA BE INVITED TO A PARTY EVER AGAIN – *it's literally impossible. Like, medically impossible,*' I join in, quoting Daisy's now infamous burn.

Grace wails and hides her face under her blazer.

It's probably best that we don't go anyway. After everything that happened after the hospital, I'm on my best behaviour right now. The girls were really good, they let bygones be bygones. I made a mistake. But we're The Beehive and that's what friends do.

Forgive each other. I also think they felt a bit sorry for me after what blabbermouth Tubs revealed about Dad.

'Do you wanna talk about your dad or anything?' asked Nisha in the chippy the other weekend, whilst we were doing the leftover dishes. Potwash Will had clocked off early, said he was off to an underground rave in Leeds or something.

　'There's nothing really to say,' I replied. 'I don't think he's coming back. Thanks, though.'

　'Anytime, sis.'

THURSDAY MAY 6th
7.32 p.m.

Lying on my bed, headphones in, minding my own business listening to music, when there's a knock on the door. Three jazzy but firm knocks, *rat-tat-tat-ta-tat*. It isn't Tubs (Tubs doesn't knock, rude) so I know it must be—

　'Only me, Indi!' calls a cheery voice.

　Jonathan. Jonny Boy. The Big J. Ugh, what does he want?

　He's been coming over more and more recently. Started with the odd cup of tea and has slowly built up to more and more evenings round ours, having candlelit dinners in the kitchen and watching Netflix with Tubs.

I get up from my bed and open the door, peeking half a face out.

'Can I help you?' I ask coldly, positioning one headphone away from my ear.

'May I pop my head in? Your mum says there's a couple of damp patches on the walls in here, just wanna take a glance . . .'

I open the door tentatively and he slides himself in.

'Coooooool! Love what you've done with the room!' he says, scanning around, looking at my band posters and Disco Girl drawings, and giving me a smiley thumbs up.

Oh my G, he's sooooo cringe, it's painful . . .

'What you listening to?' he asks, leaning jauntily against my desk, which is MOST unwelcome.

'Fleetwood Mac,' I muttered. 'My DAD got me into them.'

I proper emphasise the word 'DAD' to let him know that his intrusion is getting on my nerves. 'Dad and my mum used to dance around the kitchen to "Everywhere". You know that song?'

'Oh yes, top band. Stevie Nicks, isn't it?'

I'm a bit aghast that he knows them but even more aghast that my mention of Dad doesn't perturb him one bit.

'Erm, yeah. Well, anyway, it's very much *their* song. Forever and ever. 'Til death do 'em part!'

He looks at me and smiles.

'Show me where this damp patch is, then?'

I reveal it by pulling down a great cartoon of Disco Girl in an intense battle with a robodog. He touches it with his hand.

'Hmm, feels cold. Maybe there's a leaky pipe somewhere . . .'

He takes a photo of it with his phone.

'Right, leave it with me. I'll pop a call in with the council tomorrow, get someone proper to come and have a look. Someone needs to sort out the boiler anyway, so I'll get them to check this out too.'

'Er, no thank you, Jonathan.'

'Pardon?'

'I quite like my damp patches, thank you very much,' I say.

'Indiana, we can't leave it; no, it's not good for your health, love. Or your gecko's, for that matter', he says, peering into the tank.

'Me and Gary find the damp very refreshing actually.'

Jonathan looks exasperated. 'Indiana, can I just say . . . I know it's a bit . . . you know, difficult at the minute. You've both got a lot going on an' that. And with your mum, I just thought I'd give her a hand with stuff—'

'Are you in love then?'

He laughs. 'I mean, she's a lovely woman, Indi, but blimey! I mean, I dunno, it's quite early, we've only known each other a few months! Tell you what. If I start to . . . you know . . . fall in love with your mother, I'll keep you posted, shall I?'

'That would be very much appreciated, Jonathan, thank you.' I reply curtly.

'OK. Hey, if you like Fleetwood Mac, you should check out a band called The Beatles. They made some really top tunes back in their day,' he says, leaving my room.

BLOODY HELL. I KNOW WHO THE BEATLES ARE, JONATHAN!

THURSDAY MAY 13th
2.40 p.m.
Sitting in history losing my mind with boredom when my phone buzzes in my blazer pocket:

> BEEHIVE ASSEMBLE!!!!! chippy after school wahooooooooooo
> 🐝🐝🐝🐝🐝🐝🐝🐝
> 🐝🐝🐝🐝🐝

Thirteen bumblebee emojis. Excessive, even for Grace.

4.08 p.m.
I arrive at The Jolly Fryer and spot Grace dancing though the window, a mixture of shimmying and kicking.

I walk in, give Alan a quick wave and turn my attention to Grace, who gives us a showgirl-esque point of her shoe with every word.

'GUESS. WHAT. GRACE. HAS. DOOOOOOOONE!'

'I'm willing to guess it's something to do with Daisy's party?' says Nisha, chewing chips from a cone.

'MIGHT. BE . . .'

'Oh bloody hell, Grace, spit it out . . .'

Her kicky-dance has now turned into the can-can.

'I'VE. GOT. US. A. WAY. IN . . .'

'Shut the front door?' Nisha says. 'How? OH MY G, this is amazing!!?'

'Er, I thought you weren't bothered, Nish!?' I ask.

'Well, I'm not, really, but—'

'So, turns out . . .' Grace says, '. . . that Daisy Rowling's second cousin who lives in Weaste, yeah, his best mate Nathan, yeah, *he's* best mates wiiiiiiith . . . drumroll, please . . .'

Me and Nisha sigh and tap our fingers on the tabletop.

'. . . he's best friends with *my* Sam!'

'"*My Sam*", urgh! Don't call him that . . .' says Nisha.

'Well, he is, and *he's* got us an invite so he's my Sam, he's your Sam, he's *everyone's* Sam now!'

I'm THRILLED. I start can-canning too. *A house party with Year 11s? It's so . . . adulty!?*

'Hahaaaaa, in your FACE, Megan!' Oh my G, we're gonna be inside Megan's house, how weird is that?' says Nisha.

'There's gonna be boys and music and OH MY GGGGGG, IT'S GONNA BE AMAZING! OK. Right. Plan of action, I'm gonna get Mum to book me a blow-dry, and Indi, no offence, but you're gonna have to buy something to wear because you CANNOT turn up wearing, you know, those old hoodies you usually tramp around in—'

'*Tramp around*?!' I protest, putting an end to my can-can.

'NO OFFENCE, I SAID. If I say, "No offence", I mean *no offence* so you shouldn't take offence!'

'Saying "No offence" doesn't mean it's not offensive, Grace!' laughs Nisha and we both roll our eyes at the same time.

'Whatever. And while we're at it,' she says in a sarky way, '. . . will you be washing your hair for the occasion, Nisha, or turning up looking like you've been dragged backwards through a bush?'

Nisha laughs again: 'Errrrrr, savage!'

Grace laughs. 'Sorry, that was too far.'

6.12 p.m.

'Indi?' calls Tubs as I kick off my shoes in the hallway. 'That you?'

'URGH' I shout, heading straight into my bedroom, slamming the door and flopping on to my bed.

Tramping around!? Is that really what everyone thinks of me?

'What do you think, Gary?' I ask, staring at the pile of clothes on my floor.

'Well, let's be honest, love . . . you've had some of this tat since you were a kid. You're a grown woman now, dahling! You've blossomed! You need to level up! Show them what you've got! Wow them! TRES CHIC!'

6.15 p.m.

Tubs bursts in. Told you she doesn't knock. 'What's up?'

'I'm fine,' I grunt.

'No, you're not. What's up?'

'It's nothing.'

'Come on . . .' she says, perching on my bed.

I've tried not to moan since we moved up here, I really have. I do know she's working really hard. But Tubs has NO idea what it's like being a teenager. We need *things*. We need *stuff*.

'I'm . . . I'm just SICK TO DEATH of all my bloody clothes. I hate them all. They all make me look like, like . . . Mrs Twit. You know, the smelly woman from the Roald Dahl books.'

She looks uncomfortable and I feel a bit bad.

'It's just . . . when Dad was here, I didn't feel . . . *like this*. Y'know?'

'I know. Things have changed, eh? Yer dad used to take care of everything. But, Indi, that's not the way it should have ever been. I should have grown me own vegetable patch.'

'Yeah, no offence Tubs, but I don't think a career in farming is gonna help us . . .'

'NO, I mean it metaphorically!' she laughs. 'I mean I was never self-sufficient. But what? You think I haven't got a plan? Oh Indi, Indi, Indi . . .' and she jumps up, hands on her hips.

'Plan A is to become that Jay Z's secret wife, so that Beyoncé divorces him and then I can have all his money instead.'

'Could happen . . .'

'Exactly, but you know, everyone needs a Plan B, and mine is to do one of those – what do you call them now? – Open University courses.'

'No way, in what?'

'Sport and fitness,' she says, deadpan.

I smile at her. She's funny, Tubs. Must be where I get it from.

'I was thinking of doing law, actually. You do it six years part-time, so I can still do my cleaning work at the same time.'

SIX YEARS!

SIX YEARS OF BEING DEPRIVED?

So, basically, the rest of my teenage years and then some. Great, BLOODY GREAT . . .

'Good for you, Tubs.' I smile supportively.

'Thanks, Ind. Now. This clothes situation . . . I agree, yer've got some very old things in here. Grab a binbag, let's get rid of some of them.'

We go through my wardrobe, pulling out old bobbly jumpers and T-shirts I've had since I was ten. Socks with holes and shoes with flapping soles. If there's still life in them, they'll go to charity, and if they're unusable, it's off to recycling.

'One time, Grace said she gave her dress to charity and then she saw it in the window of the charity shop. It was a proper expensive dress dress, though – not sure why she got rid of it, to be honest . . .' I say, holding up a baby blue T-shirt I love in front of me.

This one's sticking put. I'll pretend it's vintage.

'Must be strange with Grace sometimes . . .' says Tubs.

'How come?'

'Well, her parents are filthy rich, aren't they?'

'Ha, yeah. It's funny, though: sometimes she says stuff and doesn't realise what a princess she sounds like,' I laugh. 'She's nice though. Her heart's in the right place . . . most of the time. Oh yeah, she's got us an invite to this party . . .'

'Whose?' Tubs asks, whilst heading out to the hallway. I can hear her fumbling in her handbag.

'Oh, just this girl from school. Her parents will be there, so it's all fine an' that,' I lie.

I have no idea if her parents will be there.

She comes back with two crunched-up twenty-pound notes in her hand.

'Right, you can have this, *if* you also take forty pounds out of yer chippy savings. That's eighty pounds total. I want you to buy proper stuff, though, Indi: socks, knickers, a pair of jeans, and a couple of jumpers if y'can. Don't just spend it all on one dress, OK?'

OMG?

'No, look, it's fine . . . you just . . . keep that.' I say, but I don't mean it. I want it.

'Have it.'

'No . . .'

I am a blessed angel. I am saying no to forty whole English pounds. If there is a heaven, I'm going straight there on the back of a unicorn.

'Indiana . . . take it. We'll call it a back-payment on pocket money.'

'OK. Thanks.' I smile. 'Erm, Tubs, there's been something I've been meaning to ask . . .'

'Go on . . .'

'So, y'know how . . . Dad . . . used to call you Tubs and now I call you Tubs? Would you . . . would you like me to just call you Mum or something?'

'Now why would I want that?'

I fumble around the sentence. 'Well 'cause I remember you were saying, like, you were worried you were overweight and like—'

'Indi, yer dad gave me that name when I was pregnant with you. I got this little Tellytubby belly and he would come home and kiss the bump and then kiss me and say, "Hello, Tubs."'

'I didn't know that,' I say, smiling.

'Yep. And listen, as for the fat thing, listen hard now: I were being stupid. LOOK at this body. Look at all these CURVES, baby!' she says, running her hands up and down her hips. 'We get one body and it keeps us alive, we need to be kind to it and I weren't being kind to it that night, y'understand?'

'Yeah. It's hard, though, sometimes, isn't it? Like . . . y'know, boys and stuff. They like all the skinny-but-curvy girls at school. They LOVE Grace.'

'I'm sure they love you too.'

HAHA, HOW WRONG YOU ARE, TUBS.

'Oh, don't forget, Jonathan's taking us out for dinner Saturday night.'

HE'S WHAT NOW?

'Oh, OK, have fun,' I say.

'No, he's taking US out for dinner. All three of us.'

Oh great.

'So things are getting pretty serious between you two then, is it?'

'Oh, erm. I dunno really. Feels a bit strange y'know . . .' says Tubs, twiddling her silver necklace.

She's like a girly schoolgirl, all nervous.

'Just play it cool, Tubs. Nisha told me that the worst thing you can do is beg it.'

'What's "beg it"?'

'Begging it. Like, being despo.'

'Play it cool, yeah?'

'Play it cool.'

CHAPTER 16
YEAH, YOU'RE RIGHT, PRAWNS!

SATURDAY MAY 15th
14.43 p.m.

The chippy is proper busy today. The sun's out and it feels like the first day of proper summer, which is nice, but it makes me feel sorry for Alan who's spinning plates now that me and Nisha have clocked off. This lunchtime a party of TWELVE came in all at the same time – never seen so many cods being cooked at the same time, the deep fat fryer looked like a very tragic aquarium. Also Alice Welby and Marcus Jones came in together which makes me speculate whether they're dating . . .

We're currently fuelling ourselves with chips and battered sausages, ready for the hard afternoon of shopping.

'OK, we have to think carefully because eighty quid won't actually get you *that* far,' says Grace, in a tone that's a little bit *too* condescending for me today, but

I'll let it slide 'cause she's helping me out.

'You need, like . . .' says Nisha, thinking out loud, '. . . I dunno . . . an aesthetic, Indi. Something that tells people who YOU are. And stuff you feel comfortable in, obvs.'

'Ugh, but I feel comfortable in leggings and a hoodie, isn't that enough?'

'OK, so what do YOU think an old pair of leggings and a hoodie says about you, Indi?' asks Grace, pointedly.

'I dunno, it says . . . it says laidback. Yeah, it says I'm laidback. Cool.'

'It says you're a pig,' laughs Grace, without a breath.

'Graaaaaacie, that's a bit harsh, come on now . . .' snorts Nisha. 'I dunno, maybe you just look a little bit slobby.'

'Look,' Grace says. 'Like it or lump it, we live in a world where the drip is *everything*. I mean, do you think they're EVER gonna let ugly people on *Love Island*? Er, no!'

'Yeah, they might be super attractive, but they're all so shallow, Grace!' I protest.

'No, they're not! They do all these really good causes like . . . like teeth whitening!'

'And how's that a good cause?' scoffs Nisha.

'Well, people need nice teeth, don't they?'

Nisha rolls her eyes at me.

'Nisha, how much have you made in tips at the chippy, say, in the last month?' says Grace.

'Er, I dunno, five, six quid?'

'Exactly. Maybe if you smiled a bit more, you'd make a bit more.'

'This doesn't sound very feminist, Grace . . .' I say.

'ALL I'M TRYING TO SAY IS THIS: *I* think being attractive is an advantage.'

'Well, *I* think it all sounds like hard work,' Nisha says. 'Like, I don't wanna sound like an inspirational quote, but . . . shouldn't we all just be ourselves? 'Cause y'know, everyone else is already taken? OH GOD, I *DO* SOUND LIKE AN INSPIRATIONAL QUOTE, DON'T ANSWER THAT, I JUST MADE MYSELF CRINGE.' Nisha laughs.

'I just want you to be the *best* version of you, OK?' says Grace.

'Just do you,' says Nisha.

WAIT, WHAT? I AM SO CONFUSED.

They're right about one thing, though, and that's having to spend my money wisely today. Grey hoodies in Primark cost seven pounds. But as soon as something's got a little branded logo on it the size of a FLY, *shops want an extra forty quid for it?* YEAH, FINE, NO WORRIES. TAKE MY MONEY. DOESN'T SOUND LIKE A RIP OFF AT ALL! It's so annoying but the general vibe at St Cath's is that branded stuff is good and unbranded is ... well, cringe. I mean, what's the point in brands anyway? Isn't fast fashion bad? OH I DUNNO, WHAT'S WRONG WITH LEGGINGS ANYWAY?

'I think I've got a solution,' offers Nisha. 'So you know how you like old music and bands and stuff, yeah? Well what about that cute, grungey look? You know, like cute dresses with ripped tights and choker necklaces and chunky boots. But not like brand new, you literally get everything second-hand. Vintage!'

'Yesssssss,' says Grace. 'It's perfect; it's ... it's classic Olivia Rodrigo, without paying full price. Nisha, you're a genius!'

'Drink up, girls, we've got bargains to find,' I grin.

I usually find shopping tedious. I feel overwhelmed by the number of T-shirts and skirts and jumpers, blouses and shirts (what's even the difference?) and trousers in skinny fit, high waist, mom style, straight and flared. It's all too much for my little mind.

270

But with a little bit of help from The Beehive, after digging around a load of Oldham Street's finest thrift stores, I'm all sorted with ripped jeans, an unreal denim dress and fishnet tights and a jumper with, like, the shoulders cut out of them. In retrospect I've essentially bought a load of stuff with holes in it, but it's too late now, Tubs will just have to deal with it. I even managed to get some knock-off Dr Martens.

We're about to go jump back on to the tram, when Grace stops us.

'Woah, woah, we missed something,' she says, with a sneaky grin on her face. 'What does every girl-in-a-band have?'

'Er, I dunno? A guitar? I've only got £5.40 left and I'm not sure it'll stretch—'

'A PIERCING!' screams Grace, pulling up her top, reminding us of her own bejewelled belly-button.

4.56 p.m.
Twenty minutes – and a whole lot of blagging about our age – later, I find myself lying down on a bed like the type you get at the dentist. It smells the same in here too: *antiseptic*. The walls are adorned with prints of the various tattoos: skulls and tribal ones and big fish and even nudey ladies, if that's your kind of thing. Grace handed over forty quid for us ('my treat' she

said) and here we are; Nisha is lying on a bed adjacent to mine, and we're holding hands.

'Right, feeling OK?' says a man who has so much jewellery in his face, he'd struggle in Mrs Arkwright's physics class about magnets. Or going through those metal detectors at airports.

I don't feel OK. I feel like I'm gonna gip. But I lie and reply cheerily that I'm fine.

'OK, deep breath for me', says Metalface. '. . . and breath out.'

As I exhale, I feel a searing hot pain through my stomach. It feels like someone is stabbing me with a knife. A knife that is on FIRE. I have to bite my lip and make a 'hmmhppph' sound.

'Sssh, sssh, it's almost theeeeeeere . . .' coos Grace, as Metalface fiddles around. '. . . aaaaand it's done! Oh my G, it literally looks SO GOOD, Ind!'

I'm scared to look down in case it makes me go giptastic, but when I do, I see this little blue gemstone hanging from my bellybutton and Grace is right.

'Oh, I love it!' I gasp. 'Right your turn, Nish. Don't worry, you basically don't feel a thing. Nish . . . Nish?'

Nisha has passed out. 'For god's sake . . .' grumbles Metalface, while another member of staff fetches some water. 'Come on, kid, wakey wakey . . .'

'Bleurgh, I feel sick . . .' she says when she comes to.

'Ahhh, don't worry, it'll pass. Right, lift your top up . . .' I say.

'Not happening,' she murmurs.

'But, but! We made a Beehive pact!' I protest. 'You get one, I get one!'

'Sorry . . .'

I proper love these girls, but I'm beginning to think that The Beehive pact is about as useful as boobs on a nun.

7.51 p.m.

Bored. Making a swan using my napkin. Looks more like a duck.

Been a while since I spoke to Reece. He doesn't even sit next to me in German anymore; he's moved next to Alice instead. Decide to message him underneath the dining table, punching out the words:

> hey long time no speak

> did a thing tubs gonna kill me

He replies immediately:

> now what?

'Indi, phone away, please. It's rude,' snaps Tubs. She sits up straighter and looks at Jonathan with love-heart eyes.

Urgh.

We're sitting at a small table at the back of an Italian restaurant in town called Mario's. It's kinda run down and I wish we'd just gone to Prezzo or something but Tubs says Mario's is charming. It's full of couples on Saturday night dates and I feel like a third wheel between Jonathan and Tubs.

I'm trying to be supportive, I SO am. But Jonathan. Jonathan!

Mr Nice Guy.

Mr 'Have-You-Listened-To-The-Beatles'.

Mr 'I'll-Fix-Your-Damp-Patches'.

Can't be that much of a nice guy if you're splitting up a relationship . . .

He butters a piece of bread and feeds it to Tubs, which I feel is high-key unnecessary.

Dad would hate this, he'd be popping off with anger.

I glare at them both with contempt as they chat about how warm it is outside. The waiter brings over our food; Tubs has chosen a risotto that looks like chewed-up-and-spewed-out baby food, Jonathan has a big margarita pizza (borin') and I've gone for prawns in spaghetti, which is one of my favourite foods.

Did you know lots of people are allergic to prawns?

They make people get itchy sometimes and can make their tongues swell up and they can even die. Imagine that, a little crustacean being the reason you snuff it.

What an annoying way to go.

Some of the prawns on my plate still have their heads on, their little beady black eyes looking up at me through the tomato sauce.

'Are you thinking what I'm thinking, Indi?' one of them seems to whisper at me.

'You know what to do . . .' says another prawn, winking at me.

'I can't, guys, Tubs will pop right off! She's trying to play it cool!'

'If he wants to be your new dad, let's put him to the test!'

'Yeah, yeah, you're right, prawns!'

I smirk to myself and then use my fork to wind up a mouthful of spaghetti, stabbing a prawn on the end and shoving it into my mouth. I chew it down and swallow. And then grab my throat and cough a couple of times.

'Everything OK, Indi?' asks Jonathan, concerned.

'Oh no!' I gasp, coughing again. 'I think . . . *cough cough* . . . I think I'm allergic! My throat, it feels like it's closing up!'

Jonathan panics and looks at Tubs.

'She doesn't have a shellfish allergy, does she!?'

'No, no, she don't,' says Tubs, deadpan.

'*Hrrrrk! Hrrrrkk*, help me, *hrrrrk*!' I splutter.

Tables of diners around us are looking over now. It should be embarrassing, but it spurs me on even more.

'Jonathaaaaan . . . hrrrrk!' I choke, reaching my hand out to him like I'm dying.

'*Now fall off your chair!*' yells one of the prawns from my plate.

'*Yeah, roll on the floor, Indi!*'

So I do, pulling the tablecloth as I go down, spilling the drinks, and all the waiters come rushing around to see if I'm OK.

'She's fine, she's fine!' shouts Tubs. 'Get. Up. Now. Indiana.'

'Urgh, fine,' I say, using the table to drag myself up reluctantly.

Then I hear her *scream*. Not like a cry – a bloodcurdling *scream*. Right in the middle of the restaurant. My top has risen up during my rolling around, and Tubs is staring at my midriff, eyes wide.

'WHAT IN THE GOOD LORD'S NAME IS THAT!?' she hollers.

'Nothing,' I lie, hastily tugging my jumper down again.

'Lemme see!'

I lift it up gingerly. My new piercing is leaking a bit . . .

'Oh my god, it's real, it's real!' She looks away and starts praying . . . '*Hail Mary, full of grace, the Lord is with thee . . .*'

'Now calm down, Joy, let's take a breath and try not to overreact . . .' says Jonathan.

'Try not to overreact!? Me daughter has mutilated herself!' she wails. 'You tell me the name of the piercing shop right now, Indiana Raye. There's gonna be hell t'pay tomorrow!'

'I mean, you should have asked your mother's permission, Indi,' says Jonathan. '. . . but I'm not gonna lie to ya, I think it looks preeeeeeeeeettty trendy.'

TRENDY!? OH MY G, HE'S SUCKING UP TO ME.

'Yeah, well, THANKS, JONATHAN, but no one asked your opinion!'

'OK. Can we get this food to go, actually?' says Jonathan to a passing waiter.

8.18 p.m.
I sit in silence in the back of Jonathan's car, proper furious, wondering if Tubs will consider ringing her local priest to do some form of exorcism on me.

I stare at Jonathan in the rear-view mirror.
TRENDY.

Who does he think he is?

*He can stop right now with this 'I'm a cool stepdad'
business, it's proper cringe.*

*A real dad would ground me for my fake prawn allergy
antics, not tell me I'm TRENDY. Pah.*

Are we living in the medieval times?

Who even says 'trendy'?

Such a dullard thing to say.

*Although it's been EIGHT MONTHS since I heard
anything from my actual dad, so he's not gonna win
'Father of the Year' either . . .*

11.51 p.m.

I struggle to sleep, running through all the things I did
wrong, accounting for each one, and why it might have
made Dad get sick of me. Trying to make it all add up.
But it just doesn't.

How could he leave me and Tubs with stupid
Jonathan?

CHAPTER 17

HE EVEN LOOKS GOOD
IN BATHWEAR

SATURDAY MAY 29th

7.06 p.m.

The three of us are crammed into the toilets at the chippy, an entanglement of arms, legs and laughter. I've got on my new-but-old vintage black denim skirt, a pink lace top, fishnet tights and the rip-off Doc Martens which are a bit big, but I've stuffed the toes with kitchen roll and worn two pairs of socks. I'll have blisters by the end of the night, but I don't mind. I am also the proud owner of a leather jacket. SO ready for Glasto!

'Do I look OK?' pouts Grace. She's gone for a pair of flared lilac trousers, crop top and a furry multi-coloured jacket. If I'm death warmed up, she's sunshine and rainbows.

'You look stunnin', Grace. Love the tie-dye crop, Nisha Chowdhury!' I say.

'Thaaaaanks, was half-price actually!' she replies.

'Guys, I don't wanna be big-headed . . . but we look unnnnnnnnreaaaaaaal tonight! Also, we smell nice.'

'I washed my hair and double-conditioned,' I reply.

We spray on some of Grace's perfume, which was proper expensive but actually stinks a bit of a car air freshener. It'll have to do. We've had to get ready at the stinky ol' Jolly Fryer so our parents don't find out we're off to an unsupervised _YEAR 11_ party.

Praying Josh is going: I really want him to see the new-and-improved Indi Raye.

'Tonight, Indi's gonna have her first neck on, I'm gonna "wow" Sam and Nisha's gonna try not to end up falling off a roof,' says Grace. 'Let's do this!'

'The Beehive is GO!' I shout, and we fumble out of the loos making a bumblebee buzzing noise, right into the path of Alan.

'And where'd yer think yer off to then?' he says suspiciously.

'Nandos,' we all say in unison. We've practised our cover story.

'Oh yeah, dressed like that?'

'It's a party,' we all trill.

'REALLY? And what time does it start?'

'Half-past seven,' we say, in complete harmony.

He squints at us. He's knows we're up to no good but he's on our side tonight.

'Go on with yer . . .' he says, nodding at the door. 'Just make sure yer behave yerselfs! And get home in time for yer parents!'

'LOVE YOU, AL-DOG!' shouts Nisha and we fly outside.

7.29 p.m.
You know in movies, when the most popular girl in school walks down the corridor? And she takes her sunglasses off and flicks her hair behind her shoulder, and everything's in slow-motion. And watching it, you're like, 'Wowzers, she must be sooooo cool 'cause she's moving in slow-mo!'?

That's how we feel sashaying up Daisy's driveway.

My boots crunch on the gravel and I wave with tinkly fingers to a boy I don't even know. Grace winks at some Year 10 lads and Nisha blows a kiss like a film star. Three absolute 10/10s, on our way to a YEAR 11 party, the magic of our entrance only broken when Charlie Grenburg hangs out of the bathroom window and shouts:

'ALRIGHT, LADIES. BRAS OFF ELSE IT'S NO ENTRY!'

'Shut up, Charlie, you perv!' yells Nisha. 'Come on, girls.'

Dance music pounds from the living room; there's a bunch of people gathered round an iPhone plugged into a sound system, lining up tracks on Spotify to play next. Megan, Maya, Amelia and Jas have all come wearing the *tiniest* of mini-dresses. They dance on the sofas, shrieking, trying not to fall off. *Can't wait to try and sneak into Megan's room later, see what it's like.* The kitchen is strewn with bottles and cans. Daisy is sitting on the worktop, her boyfriend Ryan standing in front of her, with his arms around her.

Aw, they look SO in love. Must be amazing to have a boyfriend.

She's noticed us and says, 'Oh, hey. Er, welcome?'

She clearly wasn't expecting us.

She looks Grace up and down.

'Hey, Daisy. Thanks for having us,' says Grace, slightly more sheepish that usual. I'm guessing she's still mortified by what happened in the canteen. 'Erm, have you seen my BOYFRIEND, Sam?'

'Sam Nelson? Er, yeah, in the garden, I think.'

'Cool, thanks.'

'Are you two . . .?'

'Dating? Yes. We are. Two weeks I think it's been now?' She says it casually, as if she's not sure. But she knows. I bet she knows down to the hour!

'You're going out with Sam now!?' I hiss as we head

outside. We spot Sam in the distance. Grace is staring at him and may as well be drooling.

'Oh yeah, did I not mention it?' she replies, her eyes glazed.

'NO, GRACE. NO, YOU DIDN'T MENTION IT. Why do you always have to be so—'

'Enthralling? Mystical? Alluring?'

'ANNOYING! You're so annoying! Why didn't you just tell us?' says Nisha.

'Well, that's a bit rich coming from you, Nisha Chowdhury,' retorts Grace.

'And did we get to the bottom of his *actual* age, Grace Walkden?'

'Well, it doesn't matter, 'cause he thinks I'm seventeen so . . .'

'YOU TOLD HIM YOU WERE SEVENTEEN?' roars Nisha.

'Yes, but sssssshhh—'

'And once again Grace, I ask, how old is he?'

'Also seventeen,' she says.

'Oh my god, that's ancient, you may as well go out with Alan!' jokes Nisha.

'Don't be ridiculous'

'Is that even legal!?' asks Nisha.

'It's fine, as long as we don't . . . you know . . . *do anything*.'

'Ugh. Look. It's your decision, but . . . I dunno, are you sure, he's . . . like . . . is he nice?' I ask.

She's beaming. 'Guys, he's literally *so* nice. And even though it's only been two weeks, one day and fifteen hours, right, yesterday – get this – he told me *he thinks he could fall in love with a girl like me*.

'With a girl LIKE you, or . . . you? 'Cause there's a difference . . .' says Nisha bluntly.

I smack her in her side.

Grace rolls her eyes. 'Right. I'm gonna go say hello TO MY BOYFRIEND. Be back in a bit.'

And off she goes. The boys he's with all cheer when she arrives. Every single one of them checks her out.

8.22 p.m.

While Grace is off playing grown-ups, we wander through the house watching everyone get sillier and sillier. A boy smashes an ornamental plate off the wall and buries the broken pieces in a plant pot. A girl we don't know is kicking off 'cause she said someone's nicked her drink. Charlie's on a mission to neck on with ten girls. He's done three so far and seems proper chuffed with himself.

We laugh at the photo on the mantelpiece of

Daisy and Megan's dad in full horse-riding gear, helmet, jodhpurs, EVERYTHING. Somebody's squirted shampoo in some lad's hair and now everyone's calling him 'John Frieda'. A couple in Year 11 are having an argument in the driveway. We hear that when he got in a taxi, she went running down the road after him screaming, 'Khaaaaaaaalllid!'

Apparently it was proper undignified.

My phone buzzes.

> hey im here! meet me outside?

It's Reece.

Oh.

Didn't know he was coming.

I was kinda hoping to try and secretly find Josh tonight.

Really don't need Reece as my wingman *for that* . . .

I didn't think we were talking anyway?

I head out through the increasing chaos of the party – someone's using a mattress as a slide down the staircase – leaving Nisha to find us some punch to drink. I find Reece standing by the gates, wearing a shirt and – get this – a tie. He looks truly out of his depth, like one of those baby zebras who've been separated from the herd.

'Why are you here!?' I say, admittedly with a bit more sting in my voice than is necessary.

'Oh, and hello to you too,' he replies. 'Are you gonna get me in then?'

'Yeah, course . . .' I say. There's a weird reluctance in my voice and Reece can hear it.

'Ohhhhh, don't worry, Indi. Marcus is coming in a bit, I'm not just gonna leech on to you . . .' he says, exasperated. He looks me up and down. 'Anyway, what happened, mate? Funeral, was it?'

'What?'

'You're dressed like a dead crow.'

'Oh yeah, er, we went shopping. Check this out . . .' I lift my top ever so slightly so he can see my belly-button piercing.

'Grace's idea, was it? I presume she told you to get a piercing . . .'

I cross my arms defensively.

'No, Reece, I make up my own mind. But please enlighten me further. I mean I didn't know I was being detained by *the fashion police*, but you seem to have a lot to say, so spit it out, let's go!'

'You just, you don't look like you tonight, that's all! You've changed.'

'What are you TALKING about? What do you mean I've "changed"?'

'I just mean—'

'Do you know what, Reece? What I do is NONE of your business! I can walk around half-naked if I want, or I can wear a duvet, it has nothing to do with you. I mean for god's sake, are you IN LOVE WITH ME OR SOMETHING? GOOD DAY!' I shout, before stomping back down the gravel driveway in my oversized boots.

I'm not sure why I shouted 'good day' like I'm from the nineteenth century, but it seemed like a good thing to say to end the conversation.

Stupid Reece. Every time I give him an inch – send him a little text or whatever – next minute he's ALL OVER ME. That's it now. No more. We had a good run, but I think it's safe to say, when he's being like that, we can't be friends. It's over.

I stomp into the garden and ask Grace if she's seen Nisha. Of course she hasn't, she's way too busy being in love. I decide to check upstairs and start clomping up the steps. I'm watching my feet on the plush carpet – it's a royal blue colour with gold diamonds on it – when I feel someone grab my arm.

'Hey!'

'Oh hey!' I smile.

OH MY GEE, JOSH IS HERE!

'Having a good night?' he says, brushing his hair back from across his face. He's wearing a white T-shirt and blue jeans.

Unreal.

'Er, yeah, it's mint. Grace's boyfriend got us in . . . he's old . . . hey, erm, have you seen Nisha?'

'Nah, sorry . . .'

'OK. Well, see you in a bit.'

'Yeah, see ya . . .' he says. 'Hey, I like your jacket, by the way. Do you wanna go for a chat, like, just you and me?'

My eyes pop out of my head.

My heart starts banging in my chest.

My palms instantly perspire.

If Josh is after a sweaty girlfriend, I'm his gal.

'But we're chatting, just you and me, right now . . .'

'You know what I mean, Indi! You know, just us, so we can chat properly! C'mon . . .'

OH.
MY.
G.

We head up the remaining staircase to the bathroom. He locks the door behind us, dulling the sound of the thudding music and the screams from the dining room where an energetic game of beer pong is being played. I perch on the toilet lid while Josh climbs into the bathtub. He pulls an aqua green shower cap on, which makes me laugh.

GOD, HE EVEN LOOKS GOOD IN BATHWEAR.

It's kinda awks, just me and him, alone. I don't really know what to say, so I make up a lie to fill the silence.

'You wanna know something cool?' I start.

'What?'

'This leather jacket is vintage and it used to be worn by Sid Vicious,' I lie.

'Who?'

'Who's Sid Vicious!?' I am appalled. 'He was the bassist in the Sex Pistols.'

'SEX PISTOLS!? Yo, you can't call a band that, who picked that name? It sounds like a man's widgie, is what it sounds like, Indi.'

I laugh. 'What's a widgie?'

Josh looks a bit confused about how we've gotten to this point already and, to be fair, I don't blame him.

'A widgie . . . is . . . well it's what we called our bits growing up in our house,' laughs Josh.

'A WIDGIE!!!' I scream.

'Alright, alright, Indiana Raye, calm it,' he says, chucking a sponge at me.

He climbs out of the bath. 'So, like, I've been meaning to ask you, yeah . . .'

OMG . . .

'. . . do you fancy . . .'

Yes, I DO FANCY YOU (I say in my head – I'm not a complete weirdo).

'. . . meeting up? Like, outside of school? Just us? Cinema or somethin', I dunno.'

OMG. OMG. OMG. THIS CAN'T BE HAPPENING, AM I DREAMING? THIS IS A JOKE.

'Oh, shut up, Josh. Why would you wanna go out with me . . .' I mumble, staring at the moss-green bathroom tiles.

'Becaaaaause . . .' he says, moving down the bathtub so he's sitting closer to me. He rests his head on the side and looks up at me with *those eyes*. 'Because I think you're funny and a bit weird and pretty.'

290

'Shut up . . .'

'I do! So, come on then? We goin' out or what?'

OH MY G! SO THIS IS WHAT IT'S LIKE TO GET ASKED ON A DATE!

I bite my lip. My mind immediately thinks of Grace. She'll go crazy if I say yes. But then I remember her comment about me 'tramping' around in my hoodies and the fact that she's out in the garden necking on with Sam right now and how she can't have him AND Josh and find myself saying: 'OK,' my face doing a hideous job at hiding how ecstatic I am.

He grins, reaches into his back pocket and pulls out his phone, unlocks it and hands it to me to put my number in. My hands are trembling as I type and I worry that he can see me quivering.

Just at that moment, someone starts banging on the bathroom door.

'WHATEVER'S GOING ON IN THERE, CAN YOU STOP, BECAUSE I NEED A WEE!' says a distant voice.

Josh jumps up and unlocks the door, opening it for me, so I can lead the way out.

'Next Saturday then?'

OH MY G. I'M GOING ON A DATE WITH JOSHUA
ALBERT WOOD.

9.43 p.m.
I scurry off to find Nisha. Everything's gone foggy. My
memory is going into overdrive, despo trying to store
every little piece of what happened into my brain
forever. It's like my mind can't deal with it all: his
beautiful big eyes, the sponge, Sid Vicious . . .

There's too much amazingness floating around and
it all starts to swim away and makes me think . . . DID
IT EVEN HAPPEN?

I pinch my arm discreetly.

I read once that you're supposed to pinch yourself
if you're worried you might be dreaming, 'cause the
pinch will wake you up if you are. But I'm wide awake,
it seems!

Alice Welby tries to catch my eye and I give her a
courteous 'Hey . . .' before steaming past her into the
back room, where everyone's gathered around a pool
table. I hang at the back.

'OK, so, Truth or Dare, Nisha? Your pick.'

'I'm not playing . . .'

'OH, COME ON, DON'T BE BORING!'

'I've got a Truth for her,' pipes up Megan Rowling.

'Are you a lesbian 'cause Maya said she caught you staring at her boobs when we were getting changed for P.E. . . .'

The whole room bursts into laughter. Megan looks pleased with herself.

'Come on, Nisha! You've got to tell the truth, that's the game . . .' someone taunts.

'Is it hot in here, because she's turning the colour of a tomato,' someone else jeers.

Nisha swipes at a drink on the pool table, drenching Megan and a few of the lads beside her.

'Pathetic?!' cries Megan.

'Yes, yes, you are . . . AND you're homophobic!' Nisha zings back, turns on her heel and walks out.

THAT'S MY GIRL!

I run to catch up with her.

'Nisha . . . Nish!' I call out to her in the hallway.

She turns back to me and says, dismayed, 'Can we go home now?'

I've never seen Nisha upset; she's always so confident and loud and *unashamedly Nisha*.

'Yeah, course,' I say, grabbing her hand. 'Let's find Grace and get out of here.'

10.31 p.m.

We find ourselves back at the chippy, on Our Table.

'That was an . . . interesting night,' I offer, glancing at Nisha to see if she wants to talk about what happened at the pool table. She doesn't.

'Hmm,' she says. 'Hey, did you hear that Mason Daniels and Jasmine Singh were apparently getting up to all sorts in the downstairs cupboard?'

'That's gross, get some dignity . . .' says Grace.

'Ennit.'

'How was your night with Sam?' I ask coyly, munching on a chip.

'Ahhh, amazing. I don't want to get ahead of myself, girls. But it's, like, when you know, you know . . . you know? I can just *feel* that he was the person I was supposed to meet. Does that make sense?'

'Yeah, totally!' I say, supportively. Knowing Grace is knee-deep in Sam will make everything a lot easier. 'True love, do you think?'

'I think so. *OH MY G, I'M IN LOVE* !' she shouts. 'It's amazing. You'll get there one day, girls.'

Well, thanks to that little dig, now I can't help myself, can I? I have to tell all.

'Well, speaking of boys – and by the way, I am in no way comparing this to you and Sam—' I start.

'Oh my G, have you got tea to spill, Indi!?' asks Nisha.

'Well, sort of—'

'It's Reece, isn't it. Reece was there, wasn't he? Did you neck on with Reece!? I KNEW there was something going on between you two! Nisha, get *The Doing Bits Book* ready . . .!' Grace says with excitement.

I feel a flutter of nerves in my stomach. 'Nooooo, no, it's not Reece . . .'

'WHO THEN!?' says Grace and Nisha at the same time.

I pause. They're defo gonna think I'm lying about this one . . .

'Josh.' I say quietly.

'WHAAAAAAAAAAAAAAAAAAT!?' screams Nisha.

'Ssssssh, keep your voice down. It's late!'

'So, what happened then? Thought you said you didn't like him?' asks Grace abruptly. Her face is like thunder.

I begin to babble. 'Well, we just were chatting in the bathroom and he's actually quite nice, isn't he, for one of the lads, and—'

'So what? So you had a chat and . . .? No offence, Indi, but that's not exactly news, is it?' She laughs mockingly.

'Well, actually, he's asked me if I fancy the cinema next week so . . .'

Silence falls on us and it's so awks, super awks, more awks than it's ever been awked before.

'Oh right. Cool,' says Grace sharply.

Nisha senses the bad vibes and dives in to save the day.

'So, did you also hear that Amelia had a massive argument with Maya about cats . . .'

And we carry on chatting about the night, but with a newfound discomfort between me and Grace.

That night, tucked up in a sleeping bag on her bedroom floor, I'm overcome with the worst feeling of guilt.

I barely sleep a wink.

CHAPTER 18

I SHOULD HAVE GONE HOME

TUESDAY JUNE 1st

1.25 p.m.

Grace has left me on read for three whole days now.

At first, Nisha was making excuses, like, 'Oh, she's busy, she's got extra homework to do 'cause she's behind in science' and stuff. But as the days have passed by, it's obvs she's avoiding me.

No reply to my WhatsApps.

I put nice comments and heart emojis on her posts, but nothing.

Yesterday we literally walked right towards each other down the English corridor and I shouted, 'Hey, Grace!' but she put her flat palm right up to my face and walked past.

Brutal.

'I just don't understand why she's so mad, Nish! I haven't bloody DONE anything!' I say, sitting on the steps outside the back of the science block. 'She fancied Josh once. Now she's got a boyfriend. She can't have ALL the boyfriends,' I moan.

'I know what you're saying, I do. But, you know, they had this on-and-off thing going on. I just think, maybe, *she thinks* you're not being a very good member of The Beehive. You're supposed to be her friend, and you know all of this is obviously making her upset but you're going ahead with the date anyway. I agree, she can't say who you can and can't go out with. But is it worth it, if it's making your best mate feel bad?'

'But—'

She gets up from the steps, grabbing her backpack and says: 'Listen, I've gotta go hockey practice. You two need to chat. I don't wanna be the messenger. And I don't wanna get stuck in the middle.'

I watch her walk off to her next lesson and slump against the wall. Time for The Smiths. Whenever things get miserable, I listen to The Smiths. Which is stupid really because it makes me even more miserable. I pop my headphones in.

I can't bloody win. I've lied about having a boyfriend, admitted I've never been necked on with and I've got NOTHING for The Doing Bits Book.

Now I have a genuine, real opportunity to fix all of that and . . . and they won't let me have it!

It's alright for Grace.

She's confident and fun and pretty but it's not like that for the rest of us!

Nobody has ever fancied me.

Ever.

And the one time a boy actually likes me, everyone starts being selfish about it!

'Don't do this, Indi. Don't do that, Indi. It's a bad idea, Indi . . . '

Why is everyone else allowed to be happy but not me?

Why is everyone treating me like I don't know what I'm doing?

I pull out my sketchbook – which currently has a greyscale sketch of my own left hand on the page – and start to make a pros and cons list.

GOING ON A DATE WITH J.W.

PROS

✓ He's proper boyfriend goals

✓ I will have my first date <u>ever</u>

✓ I might get my first neck (maybe with tongues!?)

✓ Did I mention he's proper boyfriend goals!?

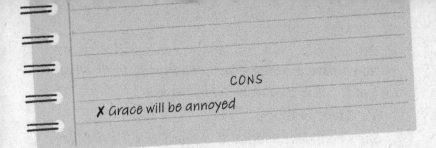

CONS

✗ Grace will be annoyed

ARGH!

She doesn't even want Josh!

She's got a boyfriend!

SHE'S. GOT. A. BOYFRIEND!

WEDNESDAY JUNE 2nd
8.06 p.m.

Trying to do my art homework. Usually super easy for me. We have to draw a Cubist interpretation of a household item, so I chose Jonathan, making him look really bizarre, swapping his eyes and ears around – but I can't concentrate.

Today in assembly, Jenko announced the Lower-School Prom.

We weren't sure if it would go ahead this year after the abomination of the Spring Fête, but Jenko knows it's a date in everyone's social calendars that everyone's looking forward to after the end-of-year tests.

She's pretty savage sometimes, Jenko, but she's not savage enough to deny us our big party.

I'm *despo* to chat to the girls about it; to decide whose house we'll get ready at (or if it'll be a chippy loos classic) and what we'll wear and which songs we'll be popping off to.

But it's dawning on me that if I go on a date with Josh, that won't happen.

Grace and Nish will both hate me.

It'll be the end of us.

Beehive destroyed.

I feel like messaging Reece and asking his advice, but we haven't really spoken since Daisy's party. I don't even know if he got in or not.

Feel a bit bad about that, looking back.

THURSDAY JUNE 3rd
6.59 p.m.

Got a face mask on. Bought it from Poundland for a bargain 99p.

It's says it will 'refine my pores', whatever that means. It's got clay in it and it clings to my face, all sticky and brown and smells like earth.

Actually, now that I think about it, maybe I've just been sold some super-expensive mud? Anyway, it's on now, and it's starting to dry, making it super hard for me to complain to Tubs.

'She'z god a BOYFWEND, Tubz,' I say, barely able to open my mouth.

'I understand but—'

'No, you DON'D UNDERSAND! She'z bin so mean aboud id!' I try to yell.

Tubs purses her lips together, literally zipping her mouth shut to stop herself telling me it's a bad idea and that I should stay at home Saturday night. She knows that would be the wrong approach and would have me sneaking out of Number 64 anyway whilst she's at work.

'Indi . . .'

No reply.

'Indi, can I offer yer some advice?'

'Rarver you dint, bud doubd dat's gonna stob you . . .'

'Look, I know you think I'm too old and past it, but I do understand, y'know? I did have boyfriends once! I mean, if you think about it, I've sorta got a boyfriend now . . .'

She laughs, referring to He Who Shall Not Be Named (Jonathan). 'A woman of my age, with a boyfriend, how funny!'

'Hilariouz,' I mutter.

'Look, I know yer all settled now at school. But

y'need to know – and I say this from experience – *they will come and they will go*. That is just how lads are. But *girl friends*, Indi . . . well, that's an entirely different thing. D'you understand what I'm tryin' to say?'

'Um-hm.' I mumble.

'Are yer listening?'

'YES, I AM. FANX FOR DE CONCERN, BUT ME 'N' DE GIRLZ ARE JUZ FINE.'

I storm off to wash my mud-face off.

FRIDAY JUNE 4th
10.57 a.m.

Tubs's words have been played around in my head so much I couldn't sleep last night.

Tried counting sheep; that's supposed to make you drop off, isn't it, but it didn't; if anything it made me more awake and thinking about how hot sheep must get in the summer underneath all that wool.

Tomorrow is the night.

I should be the happiest girl alive. But I may as well die in a hole.

I've just felt so torn about everything and I can't think about anything else, it's started to make my brain physically hurt.

The last time my brain hurt this bad was when we learned about how the Egyptians built those mahoosive pyramids in history.

Not willing to accept that humans did it.

Must have been aliens.

What I'm trying to say is that I've got a full migraine about all this, so this morning, I've decided it's time to put an end to it.

'Grace?' I call, to no avail. She passes me in the English corridor, continuing her campaign to ignore me. 'Grace, seriously, wait.'

'What do you want, traitor?'

'I just wanted to say . . . I'm not gonna go tomorrow. I – I changed my mind. I just don't think we're, y'know, compatible.'

'Well, obviously,' says Grace haughtily.

'So, yeah. Just, er, wanted to let you know.'

'OK,' she says. 'Good! So Nisha's coming round mine at, like, seven thirty tomorrow. Come over too. Bring PJs if you wanna sleep over,' and off she trots down the corridor to her drama class.

And just like that, we're friends again.

Water under the bridge.

Back to normal.

Just like that . . .

12.54 p.m.
Sitting near the lockers trying out one of Grace's new lipsticks – it's called Sultry Feline and it's a deep burgundy colour. Grace laughs when it smudges up my cheek and uses her thumb to wipe it away. We chat about all the necking her and Sam have been doing and Nisha seems sooooooo relieved that we're back being friends again, and we all joke about together like nothing's happened.

But it has.

And I can't seem to shake it off.

4.08 p.m.
Walking back to Number 64.

Absolutely furious.

Look, on the one hand I am so relieved that Grace isn't mad at me any more. I hated that feeling of The Beehive being all broken.

But on the other hand, I can't get over the speed that she went from ignoring me for days on end, to suddenly acting like everything's OK!?

She dropped me like a stone, and now JUST BECAUSE I've done what SHE WANTS, she's picking me back up again. *ARGH, I'M SO ANGRY I NEED TO KICK SOMETHING.*

I boot a bit of grass shooting up from between the cracks in the pavement. Very ineffective. Has not relieved my wrath.

My phone vibrates in my pocket.

> Josh: still on for tomorrow? 😊

I take a deep breath to steel myself.

    I know what I'm about to do next is gonna be the worst thing in the world.

    That the consequences will be disastrous.

    But I can't help myself.

    I message Grace with The Biggest Lie I've ever told her.

> Soz just realised cant make it to yours tomorrow – gotta stay in and have dinner with Tubs and Jonathan. see you monday x

And I reply to Josh with:

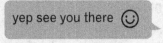

yep see you there 😊

SATURDAY JUNE 5th
10.14 a.m.
No Nisha at the chippy today. She's got a big hockey match over in Liverpool. Good job as well – don't want her asking questions about tonight.

Feel weird. Stomach is doing somersaults and it's only ten in the morning.

Thinking about some of my most recent lies to try and make myself feel better.

1. I told Alan that I was suddenly allergic to fish. Being that he runs a FISH and chip shop, this was a problem and he said he'd have to let me go. I backtracked and told him I wasn't allergic to fish, it was just a joke. Alan was confused.

2. Told the priest at Tubs's church that I'd met actual Jesus in Tesco buying a Meal Deal. She told me it wasn't funny to make up lies and that Jesus was watching.

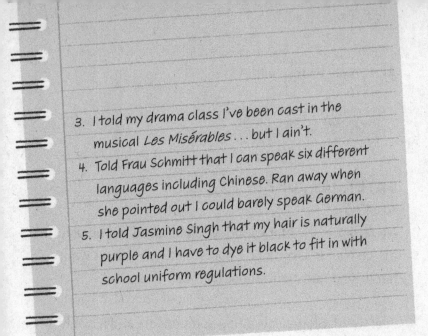

3. I told my drama class I've been cast in the musical *Les Misérables*... but I ain't.
4. Told Frau Schmitt that I can speak six different languages including Chinese. Ran away when she pointed out I could barely speak German.
5. I told Jasmine Singh that my hair is naturally purple and I have to dye it black to fit in with school uniform regulations.

6.31 p.m.

Painted my nails, watched a load of YouTube tutorials explaining how to do winged eyeliner, spent at least half an hour trying to get my fringe to sit right, and turned my wardrobe upside down and inside out, finally opting for the denim dress again, this time over a grey T-shirt and the trusty oversized boots, which I thought was a 10/10 fit until Tubs walked in with a pair of black tights.

'Ohhhhh, really?' I huffed, rolling my eyes as far back into my head as they can go.

'Really,' she replied firmly, handing them to me. 'So, what's the plan tonight then, hm? Grace's house, yeah?' she asks.

'Yep . . .' I mutter, pulling them on, tugging the seam of the toes into place.

She raises an eyebrow.

She knows full well I'm lying.

She kisses me on the head and pulls the door closed behind her, calling, 'Just be back for nine o'clock, OK?'

As soon as I hear her clanging about in the kitchen, I pull the tights back off again and shove them under my mattress, apply one last lick of pink lip gloss and leg it out of Number 64.

My phone pings.

Reece:

> hey just wanted to say im soz about
> daisys party can we be mates again?

Then another message.

> someone said you're goin out with josh tonight?

And then another.

just wanted to say its up to you but think it wud be better if u didnt go? heard hes a bit of a lad

I don't bother messaging him back. I'm too rageful and I don't want to say anything I'll regret. I'm venomous, like one of those snakes on nature programmes, all coiled up, ready to bite someone right in the leg with my fangs.

I'd bite them hard and say 'FANGS very much' and then sort of snake off.

Nobody understands.

Nobody!

And it's starting to get right on my nerves!

I pass Hawkeye on the way out.

'Oh, hi, Hawkeye,' I mumble.

She says nothing, but turns to me and shrieks 'BEWARE!' like some kind of witch.

Weird.

I have to run for the tram, which pootles up the road towards me.

It's raining and I regret wearing my leather jacket. Should have brought a coat with a hood.

Even the beret from Reece would have been useful right now.

I take my headphones out and stuff them into my ears to try and block out my own thoughts but even The Strokes can't help me now, so I stick on one of those meditation apps that play whale noises to make you feel calm.

I'm feeling so furious, I'm gonna arrive at the cinema looking like an angry beaver, which isn't a good look.

Generally speaking, I'm probs a 5 out of 10 when it comes to looks, so if I arrived hot and sweaty and rainy and angry it will SO drop me down to a 3 . . .

Why DOES Josh like me? says the naughty voice in my head.

He's a solid 9/10, maybe even a 10.

Why would he go for a 3 like you?

What if this is just one big joke!?

7.14 p.m.

Arrive at the Odeon cinema. Immediately spot Josh waiting for me in the doorway, swiping away on his phone.

Eek, what if I don't know what to say?

What if I . . . I dunno . . . just start talking about something stupid like . . . like radiators or mullets or the wingspan of the golden eagle?

I make my way, shaky-legged, off the tram. He's wearing black jeans and a pink hoody and boxfresh Nike trainers, his hair brushed back, and I immediately feel like the shyest girl in the world.

But on the plus side, every other worry I've had about this evening seems to melt away.

Isn't it amazing how love can do that to you? (*I mean it's not LOVE, I don't LOVE Josh . . . but . . . well, you know what I mean.*)

'Yo!' he says, seeing me approach.

'Hey,' I reply nervously. I'm not sure whether to give him a friendly hug, kiss him on the cheeks twice like French people do or shake his hand. *What do people DO on dates!?*

'I've got our tickets, so . . . shall we go in . . .'

'Erm, yeah. OK. Cool,' I say and follow him blindly.

We sit down on a row near the back. Near the back but not the *actual* back row 'cause everyone knows the back row is where people 'do stuff' in the dark.

We share a mega box of popcorn – sweet and salted, on Josh's request – and watch the new Pixar film but to be honest, I have NO idea what it's about 'cause I can't concentrate.

It is proper weird being *so close* to him. I can smell his deodorant in the darkness.

No, actually, it's more than that: I can smell *him*, that smell that people have that you can't really describe. I guess it's a soft, milky kind of smell. Our non-popcorn hands share the armrest and occasionally his fingers brush mine and it sends my heart into overdrive. I am one hundo percent sure I'm gonna go into cardiac arrest.

Imagine that; finally get a date and then the next thing you know, it all ends in tears 'cause your heart has popped its clogs and some off-duty doctor is rushing in to give you mouth-to-mouth. That would DEFO be the worst first neck on ever.

I urge Josh to look at me, but he doesn't even give me Frisky Eyes ONCE during the whole film – *Is he feeling shy too? Is he thinking about me as much as I'm thinking about him?*

And now the credits roll and the lights are coming up in the theatre and I'm working out what to say, trying to pluck out my favourite part of the movie from my memory to re-break the ice, when out-of-the-blue he says:

'So, shall we go down the chippy for a bit?'

It takes me by complete surprise.

I imagined that when the film was done, we'd walk outside and he'd take my hand in his, and pull me towards him. He'd say something romantic like, 'I loved spending this evening with you, Indi. May I partake in a neck with you?'

And then we'd fully neck on and fireworks would explode around us and people would clap and cheer for us. Then he'd walk me to the tram and say, 'Until next time, my love' and off I'd go home.

I didn't imagine we'd go anywhere else, especially at this time ...

But nevertheless, I reply 'OK', breathlessly.

9.33 p.m.
I know I should have said 'no'. Tubs said I had to be home by nine. She'll totally pop off if I'm late.

But this might end up being The Best Night of My Life? There's still time for necking and fireworks. And I'm not about to let Tubs nor Reece nor Nish and ESPECIALLY not Grace get in the way of it.

We clang through the chippy door.

Josh heads to the counter, while I spot Alan cleaning tables.

'Ah, Indi, what you doing here? Yer out late, want some haddock?' says Alan. 'I were thinkin', y'know—'

Before he can keep going on at me, I avert my eyes and pretend I don't know him.

I bet the girls Josh usually dates work in shops like Zara and stuff, not fishy old chip shops.

I go and sit at the table right at the back, hiding behind one of the laminated menus, leaving Alan agog.

Whilst I stay hidden, Josh orders a large chips, *to share*. And we just chat.

He tells me about his little sister Eloise and how she crawls into his bed at night 'cause she gets lonely, which I think is so sweet. I tell him about my little sister Georgie who does the *exact* same thing – which is a lie, because as we all know, I don't have a sister, but I enjoy saying the things I think he wants to hear.

We talk about how he's gonna be a footballer one day and I tell him I'll come and watch him play sometime.

We chat about how I'd like to study art at university, which he thinks is 'dead sophisticated'.

He uses this app on his phone to put stupid filters on our faces; animal ears and big mouths and squeaky voices. He films us and downloads the little videos we make, rather than posting them, which I think is proper sweet.

These moments are ours, they don't belong to anyone else.

Maybe he'll post one when we're officially boyfriend and girlfriend, though?

'You're cool AF, Indi,' he says, looking at me seriously, popping a chip into his perfect mouth.

'I know,' I reply, flicking my hair back in an OTT way. I don't know how to deal with compliments so I make a joke out of them.

'For real. You're really nice and—'

Suddenly, the door clangs open, and we hear shouting.

'What you sayin', Josh?'

'Oi oi, what's going on here, you two?'

I turn back in my chair to see four lads from Year 10, I think. Different school. Seen them hanging out around the chippy a few times. Being the only girl around all these boys, I start to feel a bit . . . uneasy. I look around for Alan, for reassurance, but he must be out back. *Shouldn't have blanked him . . .*

'Alright, lads . . .' says Josh.

'Yo, where was you Saturday?' says one of the boys. 'Needed you at training, bro. Spending too much time with your girl here, was it?'

'Nah, she's not my girl,' says Josh, screwing up his face and laughing.

My stomach drops.

'Looks like she is,' says another one, sniggering.

Disappointment swells and washes over me. I'm so painfully embarrassed.

'Shut up, bruh.' Josh laughs, throwing a handful of chips at the tallest one, who retaliates by throwing some back.

Some decisions are easy.

We make hundreds of these easy kinds of decisions every single day.

Decisions like what cereal to eat for breakfast (Coco Pops) or whether Oasis or Blur are better (it's Oasis, obvs).

But some decisions – like whether to head home – are harder, especially when you're face-to-face with Josh Wood, Mr Johnny Hotpants, The Year 10 Boy of Your Dreams.

Your decision-making becomes fuzzy.

I should have gone home.

CHAPTER 19

WIR WERDEN IMMER FREUNDE SEIN

MONDAY JUNE 7th

2.47 p.m.

It's a sweltering afternoon.

I'm sitting in geography and all the windows have been thrown open to let in the breeze. Afternoons like this make the classroom fester; the boys went hard playing football at lunch and few of them have had the decency to spray some deodorant. When Charlie arrives, he stands right in front of the window, arms outstretched, using what little air there is to cool off, his rank body odour billowing into the room.

Maya Richards' make-up is sliding off in the heat, orange foundation conglomerating on her shiny nose and forehead and she tries to compensate by puffing on more and more powder; she'd have been better off not putting any make-up on at all this morning. Even Mrs Ibrahim is struggling, trying to explain the glacial process, but you can hear the weariness in her voice.

Suddenly someone's phone bleeps.

'Whose was that?' demands Mrs Ibrahim. 'Hand it over.'

It's an immediate afternoon detention if your phone goes off in class and it's a stupid mistake not to turn it on silent at the beginning of the day. Jas Singh reaches into her blazer pocket to switch it on mute – although, turns out, she needn't have bothered.

Another phone vibrates.

Then another one.

And another.

Then another bleep.

In a matter of seconds, the whole classroom sounds like some kind of techno rave, buzzing and whirring and blipping. Mrs Ibrahim becomes powerless at this point; everyone's diving into their bags and pockets to find out what treat has been sent en masse. The excitement is palpable. Whatever's been messaged around, it's gotta be good, if it's been sent to *everybody*, right!?

I know what it is.

I know exactly what it is.

Even before I check my own phone.

Maya and Amelia slowly turn around to look at me, wide-eyed, giggling and whispering, and laughter fills up the room from my other classmates too, so I grab my backpack and scoot out of the classroom, catching a glimpse of Reece's worried face as I fly past.

I pace briskly down the empty corridors, acutely aware of the squeak of my shoes on linoleum.

OH GOD, OH GOD.

I swerve into the nearest girls' toilets and beeline for the last cubicle, locking the door behind me. The back is decorated with little cartoons; someone's drawn an impressive anime cat with extra-long whiskers, and someone else has drawn a hideous sketch of a boy's widgie.

There's lipstick prints all over the door, from where girls have smacked on the lippy and planted a kiss and someone quite rightly has written **ew y wud u neck on with the door? its dirty!** Someone else has replied to that with **whatever** and there's scribbles all over that read things like **B♡K** and **P4W xoxo** – little secret admissions of love. Someone else has etched **whoever needs to see this, no matter what you're going thru, u r strong!!!** and I suspect that's a phrase I'm gonna need, because things are about to get bad.

I pull my phone out from my bag and sit on the loo

with the lid closed. I lean my forehead against the wall to cool down, 'cause I'm boiling up. I switch on my phone and wait for it to start up.

How bad is it?

I have a load of messages already but I tap straight on Nisha's.

> omg what the hell did you do!
>
> msg me asap x

I click the video that's attached, gritting my teeth. It's fourteen seconds long. I press play.

Chips *everywhere*.

Ketchup squirted up the walls.

Battered sausages, fillets of fish and pies flying left, right and centre.

Two of the boys wrestling each other. The tall one careers into one of the plastic chairs, which snaps under his weight.

Another one (Ben, I think he was called?) punches the glass on the hot counter. It shatters into pieces, big cracks all along it.

The boys all laugh and carry on their food fight, oblivious to the damage they're causing.

You can hear Alan in the background shouting, 'Indi, what's goin' on? Right, that's it, lads, I'm callin' the police!' and while it's all happening . . .

. . . me and Josh are sitting in the background on the Beehive Table. Ignoring everyone else.

Necking on.

The video ends.

My bottom lip trembles. I shove my phone back into my bag.

My eyes start stinging. I feel like I'm gonna gip. I realise that a couple of the kids from St Cath's and their parents go to the same church as Tubs. If the whole of St Cath's have seen the video, then she will too.

Tubs is gonna ground me forever. Oh god, she was so proud of me for having a job and here I am full-on blanking Alan while he tries desperately to save his pride and joy, his chippy shop.

My brain is desperately trying to work out what to do and how I'm gonna fix this, when the bathroom door creaks open.

'Indi?' says Nisha softly.

'Indi's not here,' I squeak.

Her voice gets closer. 'Open the cubicle. Which one are you in, this end one? Oh god, what were you thinking, Indi? You can't just . . .' Her voice trails off. I can tell she's angry. 'Open the door.'

I unlock it slowly and look up at Nisha's face. I've never seen someone look so disappointed.

'OK. Just tell me the truth right now. No fibs, no lies. Is that you in the video?'

Don't lie, don't lie, don't lie, Indi.

'It wasn't me. I don't know who that girl necking Josh is.'

'INDI!' she yells at me.

She's furious.

'STOP LYING! WE CAN ALL SEE IT'S YOU!'

'Nisha, hear me out! Look, the thing is, the cinema was *really* nice. I know I told Grace I wouldn't go, but . . . it was Josh. *Actual Josh Wood.* It was a mistake, I know that now, but you can see why I went, can't you? Anyway, afterwards he asked me to go to the chippy and I know I should have gone home, Nisha, 'cause Tubs said I had to be back for nine, but I was mad at her and didn't *want* to go home. So I went. But then – oh god, it went wrong, Nish. These boys from another school, they came over and just started being divs, like flicking chips off the table and that. And Alan came out and was like, 'Indi, tell your mates to pack it in,' but I pretended I didn't know him 'cause I was embarrassed, and I ignored him—'

'Oh, nice,' snaps Nisha angrily. 'Poor Alan!'

I fully look Nisha in the eyes. It feels good to get it off my chest. My eyes start filling up with wet.

'And when Alan went out to the back-room freezer, the boys started being REALLY stupid, and, like, squirting ketchup up the walls and I said, "I think this is getting a bit out of hand," and Josh was like, "It's fine, they're lads, they're just having fun," and then he just laughed and drop-kicked his Coke can across the chippy. And then he was like, "So, you gonna get off with me?" and I just remember looking around and thinking, *This isn't how I wanted my first kiss to be,* y'know? And he said, "Come on, don't be out of order. I took you on a date and everything," so then I just felt like I *had* to kiss him and now it's all been caught on camera and I look SO stupid . . .'

There's a silence.

It's hard to know what Nisha's thinking but I reckon she's thinking, *Yes, yes you are stupid*.

I take a deep breath and bite my lip, really trying not to cry.

Just then, the girls' bathroom door slams open.

'Nish, did you find her!?'

Grace.

'Yeah, she's here, Gracie!' calls Nisha.

'What the HELL, Indi!' she shouts, as she joins Nisha to stare at me in my cubicle of shame. She looks stressed; a lick of hair has fallen out of her tight ponytail and she angrily pushes it back, away from her face.

'I'm sorry!'

I consider closing the cubicle door again so I don't have to see how angry she is.

'You literally told me you weren't gonna go on a date with him. You said! And now there's a video of you eating each other's faces!'

'I know,' I say, almost crying now. 'I didn't even want to kiss Josh, Grace, I swear!'

'Oh, yeah, right! Ever heard the story of the boy who cried wolf, Indi? You're a COMPULSIVE LIAR! You need to sort yourself out! The Beehive? It's DONE.'

She storms out.

There's another disappointed silence between me and Nisha. She sighs.

'Do you hate me too, Nisha?'

'I think . . . I dunno . . . I just . . . I need some time to think. I'll see you around, OK?'

3.57 p.m.

I decide to get the 201 bus home. Too many people will be talking about me on the school bus. Best avoid. Can't stop thinking about what Grace said. Idly watching the world rush by: cars in traffic jams . . . tree . . . man on bike . . . schoolkids . . . dog walker . . .

I'm Indi Raye, The World's Biggest Liar. And I think I'm officially cancelled.

4.44 p.m.

I turn my key slowly in the lock. If I sneak into Number 64, Tubs won't hear me and I can slip in to bed unnoticed, without dinner. I let the door close with a small *clink*. It's silent when I step through into the hallway. *Tubs must be on a shift tonight. I might be in luck.*

I walk past the living room, and almost jump out of my skin when I see Tubs sitting on the sofa, legs up curled beneath her. The fan whirs, to try and shift some of this warm air around.

God, it really is hot today.

Hollyoaks is muted on the telly.

No Jonathan. Weirdly, I wouldn't have minded his support right now.

I can't look at her.

I prepare myself for the biggest telling-off of the century.

'Don't bother, Indi,' she says wearily. 'I've heard it all. I wondered why the chip shop were closed this weekend and now I know. Alan called me. He said yer fired.'

'Are you really mad at me?' I say, sitting on the floor. I cross my legs and stare at my lap, like I'm four years old.

She pauses to think. 'I don't know. Don't have the energy, to be honest. But I am disappointed. This whole ... *thing* ... it's just really hard sometimes, Indiana.'

By '*thing*', she means me.

She means bringing up her liar of a daughter alone. She probs thinks it would have been better if she'd left me in London with my dad. That way she could do that law course without having to worry about what I was getting up to, and phone calls from school and getting fired from my job.

'I'm really sorry.'

'It's not me that you need to apologise to, Indiana.' She turns the TV volume up. 'Yer've got a lot of makin' up to do.'

TUESDAY JUNE 8th

2.11 a.m.

Can't sleep. Someone has posted the video online. I keep watching it over and over and over, with the volume turned down so Tubs doesn't wake up. People have commented:

> indi and josh, whaaaaat!?

> omg r they goin out now then or wat?

> heard ppl got arrested for trashing the chippy?

> ugh y wud Josh Wood go with her

2.13 a.m.

I'm really sad.

7.11 a.m.

Can't face school. Can't do it.

'I'm not feeling well, Tubs,' I whimper.

'Yer can't avoid it, Indi . . .'

'I know, I know. But my heart keeps beating really, really fast and my palms are sweaty and I've got a knot in my stomach. I feel sick, Tubs, I really do. Please don't make me go in?'

She looks at me, concerned and says: 'OK. Just today though, OK?'

THURSDAY JUNE 10th
10.54 a.m.
Day three of avoiding school. Have watched a hefty amount of *This Morning* on TV. Funny old show, one minute they'll be talking about indigestion remedies, the next they'll be whipping up a beef hotpot.

Reece just messaged me:

> hey. hope you're alright. Youve not been in? Don't really kno what to say atm get the feelin were not mates anymore but just wanna say hope youre ok. Best wishes. x

Best wishes. So formal. He's still mad, I know it. And he's right to be.

I walk over to my wardrobe, slide the door across and start to drag out the masses of clean washing I've been avoiding hanging up. Worst job in the world, hanging up clothes, hate it. I reach deep down and feel for felt, pulling out one Debbie Harry-esque beret. My birthday present from Reece.

I take it over to my mirror and pull into on to my head, adjusting it around my ears and tipping it slightly so it sits right.

'Suits you,' says Gary.

I look back at my reflection in the mirror. He's right.

FRIDAY JUNE 11th
12.01 p.m.

Tubs has said I've got to go back into school on Monday else she'll get into trouble. I asked her if we could go back to our old home-schooling days, y'know, a bit of drawing and *Loose Women* again but she said no. And I really don't want to cause Tubs more stress after everything I've put her through.

Oh, good news, though – at least the video from the chippy's been taken down from social media. Tubs says I have Mrs Jenkinson to thank for that. Also, I've eaten about five blocks of cheese over the past few days, so it's not all bad.

SATURDAY JUNE 12ᵗʰ
12.01 p.m.

It's Saturday morning. I should be at the chippy right now. Battering fish, cleaning down tables. Having catch-ups with Grace and Nisha. I can hear Tubs on the phone. To Alan. Apologising.

'She's never behaved like this before' and 'I'm so disappointed in her' and 'Is there really no chance she can come back? No? OK, no, I understand.'

I cry my eyes out.

SUNDAY JUNE 13ᵗʰ
4.35 p.m.

My hand feels like a claw. It's all cramped. I've been drawing for 7 hours and 14 minutes, with only two toilet breaks and a brief interval for lunch.

'What do you think, Gary?' I ask my sleepy gecko, my one true friend, whilst putting the finishing touches to my comic. It's SIX pages long.

'Ooh, a bit more colouring in and we should be there! Make Disco Girl's shoes bright pink, it's very Gucci spring-summer . . .'

'OK,' I reply. It's got to be *absolutely perfect,* this.

MONDAY JUNE 14th
10.57 a.m.

Well, this is hell. First day back. Currently walking down the maths corridor after a hideous morning. Got my headphones on, The Libertines helping me keep my head down. I feel like one million eyes are on me, and a bazillion conversations are being had about me.

Megan Rowling is propped up by the lockers and I hear her say to Jas: 'I heard she's literally done *everything* with boys.' I remember back to my first day at St Cath's when I complained that no one was paying me any attention. Now, anonymity seems like a dream.

I can't find Grace or Nisha anywhere. Might hang out near the hockey field this week, see if I can catch Nisha playing. Bit psycho, I know.

They're probably moving on without me.

I am the bee who stung those around me and now I am dying a painful death.

WEDNESDAY JUNE 16th
1.16 p.m.

I've worked out that the quietest toilets to spend your lunchbreak in are the ones down the history corridor. They're tucked away, right at the back of the school, well away from the playground and canteen, which means nobody really passes by this way. Which means

I can sneak in here and eat my lunch in peace.

I've been adding some of my art skills to the cubicle door of the fourth toilet. It's already heavily decorated, but by amateurs; lots of stars and very simplistic cartoon cats and cartoon boys' widgies and smiley faces.

I've been working on a tremendous piece; I call it 'Lizard in Hat' and it's basically Gary with a fedora on, but I've done loads of detail on it: all his little speckles and everything.

THURSDAY JUNE 17th
12.43 p.m.

Someone just came in and did a massive trump, right while I was biting into my cheese sandwich.

It seems I can't hide out in here forever, can I?

FRIDAY JUNE 18th
12.42 p.m.

I walk into the bustling canteen, trying not to feel like one of those cows up for sale in a market. You know, when they parade the cow around and everyone looks at them and goes, 'Ooh, arr, I think I'll 'ave that cow fer my farm!'

Yeah, I feel like that cow. A prize bovine.

But I'm trying to be brave, and I buy myself a sausage roll, and squish up in the corner, just like I did on my first day of St Cath's. I feel like people *have* moved on, but as soon as they see me, the memory of the video flashes before their eyes.

I spot Nisha and Grace laughing together, just a few tables down from where I'm sitting. I keep low. *God I miss them.* I can see Josh too, with the lads, sharing crisps.

Why do I feel the one who's been publicly shamed, and he gets ... nothing? No guilt, no regret, no embarrassment?

I suddenly catch Nisha's eye. She stands up, the metal chair scraping along the floor as she pushes it backwards.

OMG is she coming over?

But instead of me, she walks over to Josh instead. She looks like a lion about to eat an antelope.

'Can I have a word?' she says.

Josh looks at her with contempt. 'Er, no, you can't ...'

The boys around him snigger.

Nisha puts her hands on her hips. 'You and your trash mates absolutely wrecked the chippy. Proud of yourself?'

'Aw, why's she comin' for you with this negative energy, Josh?' says Mason.

'Shut up, Mason!' shouts Nisha.

335

She looks over at me for a second. 'Listen, I'm mad at Indi, too, yeah? She knows that. You two, just necking while everything was destroyed around you.'

I feel myself huddling down even lower than I already am.

'Er, what you talking about? We weren't necking!?' laughs Josh. 'Why would I get with *her*?'

'Oh, give us a break, Josh. There's a video of it. We all saw it!'

'Yeah, OK, Nisha – I hear you, yeah . . . but she was begging it all night . . .' he retorts.

At this point, all the boys (and a few others) erupt into laughter.

I feel like I'm gonna gip.

'Ugh, Josh, that's my mate you're talking about. YOU'RE the one who's punching!'

'And YOU'RE a stupid—'

You can feel the atmosphere change all around him and everyone knows he's half a second away from calling her a horribly racist word, but Nisha pre-empts it and punches him square in the face. Her fist makes crunching contact with his nose, making him recoil.

Everyone watching gasps, laughs – some even cheer; I feel like I'm watching a pantomime at Christmas where the bad guy gets vanquished.

As Josh pulls his hands away from his face, there's blood everywhere, dripping on to his white St Cath's shirt, and for a short moment, I feel a *tiny* twinge of pity for him. Only for a moment, though, because I realise Nisha is gonna end up getting done for assault if someone doesn't intervene.

Five people have to all grab a limb to hold her back before Mr Graham arrives to escort her to Jenko's office.

Oh god, she's gonna be in SO much trouble.

The bell rings for the end of lunch and I'm despo to leg it out of the school gates and go home. It's all too much; I feel like this whole mess is never going to end, maybe it's just better if I remove myself from the equation. But then I think of Nisha and how much she always sticks up for me (even when I've been a bad mate) so I stick around. I message her:

> im so sorry. tell them its all
> my fault! Can we talk?

If the corridors weren't alive with the sound of gossip before, they certainly are now. I hear one lad in Year 10 say that it was the best right hook he'd ever seen, Anthony Joshua levels, which makes me super proud ... even though I do not condone violence, I swear.

1.01 p.m.
I walk out into the playground for some fresh air, thinking I'll go and hide out behind the art department or something. Then I see Reece, sitting on a bench, texting.

'*Guten tag*,' I say quietly, sitting down next to him.

'*Hallo*,' he mumbles. '*Was ist los?*'

'Huh?'

'What's going on?'

'Oh. You know. Everything,' I sigh.

He doesn't say anything else.

'I made you this,' I say. I pull out the comic I've been working on all week from my bag. It's coloured in with bright Sharpies and stapled together to make a book. *The Adventures of Disco Girl and Metal Boy* looks proper good, even if I do say so myself.

'You can just put it in the bin if you don't like it, or you don't wanna be friends, or whatever. I totally understand. I ... I haven't been very nice to you recently. I'm really sorry.'

He looks at it as I slide it towards him.

'It's basically about how Disco Girl gets zapped by

the Mega 3000 Ultra-Laser-Beam which makes her go evil and ditch her partner-in-crime Metal Boy and try and take over the world, but luckily Metal Boy is her best mate in the whole world so he – anyway, I won't ruin it.'

I hope he likes it. I really hope he likes it. I even drew a little black beret on Disco Girl's head.

I can feel myself getting wet eyes.

Just then, I feel a warm hand rest on mine, giving it a little squeeze. Reece doesn't look at me when he does it, which I'm glad for because I might end up bawling.
   Instead he whispers:
   'Wir werden immer freunde sein.'

It takes me a while to work out what it means in English, but when I do, I breathe a wobbly sigh of relief.

We will always be friends.

CHAPTER 20

YOU'LL NEVER GET ANYWHERE IN LIFE WITHOUT THE BEEHIVE

THURSDAY JULY 1st

10.37 a.m.

Today in drama class, we sat in a circle and every time Mr Frederick looked down to read us lines from *A Tale of Two Cities*, we'd inch our chairs backwards.

Fifteen, thirty centimetres or so.

It took him twenty minutes to realise until he said, 'For goodness' sake, how did you all get so far away? Pull your chairs back before I give you all detention!!' and we all laughed and he looked really annoyed.

That was nice.

A bit of normality.

We've got loads of assessments at St Cath's at the moment and I know I should be concentrating on them – I'm doing everything to keep myself in Tubs's

341

good books – but every inch of my brain is focused on getting The Beehive back together.

Never got a reply from Nisha after she punched Josh.

She got suspended, hasn't been in all week. Her mum would have given her HELL about it. She ghosted me too, so I guess she's still working things out.

But if The Big Fight did prove anything, it's that she still cares about me.

There's still hope.

I'm not sure Grace will ever speak to me again, though.

4.12 p.m.
I spot someone chatting to Hawkeye as I approach home. She points upwards to the flats above and the figure makes their way up the steps.

I quicken my pace to catch up.

It can't be?

He looks more dishevelled than when I last saw him.

Skinnier too.

Hair's longer.

But it is him.

He hears me approach from behind him, stops in his tracks and turns to face me.

'That my baby girl?' he says softly.

'Hi, Dad,' I manage to croak, looking up at him.

'How ya been?'

'Oh, you know. Things have been pretty quiet . . .'
I lie.

'Y'gonna show me up then?' he asks, nodding to
the flats above, and I lead the way. He chats away
merrily about a vintage David Bowie LP he picked up
in town as we climb the stairs, like nothing's ever
happened.

Like we saw each other yesterday, not *nine
months ago*.

I turn the key in the lock and open the door.

'Muuuuuum,' I call desperately.

'In the kitchen,' she calls back.

Dad gives me a big cheeky smile and pushes his
finger to his lips as if to say, 'Ssh!' and I feel nervous
that he's just walking into Number 64 like this. Nervous
but excited.

*Maybe this is it? Maybe this is the moment they'll get
back together!?!?!*

*Tubs will see him and throw her arms around him and
he'll say, 'God, I've missed you, Joy!' and we'll be one big
happy family again!*

'You're not gonna believe who's here!' I say, beckoning Dad to follow me down the hallway.

'Surprise!' I say, introducing Dad with jazz hands.

'Oh god,' replies Tubs, aghast.

She's sitting at the table.

With Jonathan.

'Oh god!' she screams. 'Oh god, oh god, Paul!' she shouts, burying her head in her hands. 'I do NOT need this right now.'

'What's goin' on, Joy?' says my dad. 'My apologies, I'm a bit unexpected, eh?'

'YER COULD HAVE BLOODY CALLED AHEAD, PAUL!' she yells.

'It's alright, Joy,' says Jonathan, trying to calm her down.

'Eyyyyyyyy, who's this?' says Dad, with a hint of sarcasm. 'The new Mr Raye, is it?'

'Nice to meet you. I'm Jonathan . . . Joy's, er . . . Joy's, err . . .'

'Joy's BOYFRIEND,' says Tubs indignantly. 'Yes, I am a dating woman now, Paul, so you can clear off!'

'Oh can't he stay, just for tea?' I beg. It's hellishly awks in this tiny kitchen of ours, but at the end of the day, I deserve to see my dad, don't I?

I can see Tubs soften slightly.

'Actually, Joy, I could do with stayin' the night, if that's OK. Don't worry, Jonjo, I'll be on the couch!' he says, winking at a super-uncomfortable Jonathan.

The two men couldn't be more different. Dad in baggy jeans, a vintage T-shirt with Pearl Jam on the front, all beardy and smelling of smoke. Versus Jonathan, with his beige pleated trousers and grey woollen jumper that looks like it itches.

'Sounds like you guys have got some stuff to sort out, so I think I'll head off . . .' says Jonathan.

'YOU BLOODY WILL NOT. Sit down, Jonathan,' demands Tubs.

Nevertheless, Jonathan gets up. 'It's alright, Joy. Just give us a call tomorrow,' he says. Tubs rises too and leans over to give him a big smacker on the lips, but Jonathan turns his face to the side and accepts a peck on the cheek.

'See you later, Indi. Nice to meet you, Paul,' and he shuffles out of the kitchen as my dad says, 'Nice to meet you too, Jonjo!'

We hear the front door shut.

THURSDAY JULY 8th
6.48 p.m.

Dad ended up staying all week.

In the evenings, he'd come into my room and we'd listen to our favourite records. We ate chippy teas together, and chatted about old memories like the time that Tubs found a huge spider in the bathtub and called for Dad to come and get it 'cause she was scared, but he saw it and *he* was scared too and in the end *I* had to catch it and throw it outside, even though I was only seven!

I really thought, *This is it. We're back. The Raye family is back.*

But then Tubs and Dad started shutting the living-room door, leaving me eating pudding on my own in the kitchen, or sending me to my bedroom with just Gary for company. I hated the noise of them arguing. I would stick my fingers in my ears and hum Fleetwood Mac songs to drown it out.

Now it's all over, it seems. I look up from my sketchpad to see Dad popping his head around the door. Can't help but notice he's got his denim jacket on, and his holdall in one hand.

'Been good seeing you, baby girl.'

'Are you off again then?'

He leans against the doorframe. 'Well, your mum's got a nice new boyfriend now, eh? So we've decided it's just better if we go our separate ways, y'know?'

'So you're not getting back together then?'

'Fraid not.'

My head is racing.

'But you've got . . . a girlfriend, right? That lady you met?' I ask.

'Ahhh, I'm afraid that ship sailed.'

He spots the concern across my face.

'I'll be fiiiiiiine, don't worry about me.'

I want to hug him goodbye, but I also want to punch him. I want to know whether he's going back to the London house, but at the same time, I don't want to know; I'm settled here now. I'm worried he's gonna be lonely, all on his own.

But then again, he didn't worry about *me* being lonely, did he? And he isn't worried whether I'm going to be lonely in the future; on my next birthday, when I do my A Levels, when I leave for university.

I feel like there's so many things I need to get off my chest so without thinking I say:

'I don't think what you did was OK, y'know. Tubs is brilliant. And you let her go. And then . . . and then you never even rang us or messaged or anything. And I love you but . . . what you did, it wasn't cool. You didn't just leave her. You left me.'

He looks at me, stung.

'I know,' he says. 'I'm ashamed, Indi. I am. I let you down. I never stopped loving you, I want you to know that. I was just . . . selfish. I'm gonna be better.'

There's a pause.

'I'm moving. To Paris, actually.'

PARIS??? . . . How on earth will things be better in PARIS?

'Paris???'

'Yeah. Fresh start. But I want you to know, I'm here for you. Any time. You can visit and I'll visit. I have your number now, don't I? My big brave girl.'

I nod, biting my lip. I don't want to get wet eyes in front him.

'It's been really nice to see you, Dad.'

'You too, baby,' he replies, coming over and kissing me on the forehead, before closing my bedroom door. A few seconds later, I hear the main door close.

And I can't help but wonder if I'll ever see him again.

FRIDAY 16th JULY
7.18 p.m.

The music from the school prom thuds from within the assembly hall. I can't quite make out what song it is, on account of currently lurking about in the carpark.

'Don't wanna go in.'

'Well, we can't just hang out round the back of the bins all night, can we, Indi?' says Reece.

I'm dressed in a black tulle prom dress in the school car park. It's actually one of Tubs's old dresses; we took it to the tailors and got them to chop off the big puffy sleeves and make the hem shorter and it's looking bloody excellent, actually. I've teamed it with my fishnet tights and my fake Docs. I actually feel quite pretty.

'Come on, what's the worst that can happen?' he continues. He does look nice. He's got a blue bow tie on with a blue shirt. Should be geeky but he looks smart.

I picture what could have been – me and the girls getting ready at the chippy, Grace doing our make-up, Alan raising a piece of plaice to toast us on our way, as we head out into the night. The Beehive, all together, like it should be.

'I shouldn't have come, I'm gonna go . . .' I say, trying to flee.

'NO, YOU ARE NOT,' Reece says, grabbing my arm. 'Come on. Don't worry, I won't link your arm or anything, I know you'll freak about being seen with me . . .'

It bothers me that Reece thinks I'm embarrassed of him. I'm not. Not anymore. He's the greatest friend I've got right now. I should never have taken him for granted. I reach into my bag and take out the beret he gave me for my birthday, a lifetime ago. I position it on my head, and he straightens it up for me.

'Looking mint, Indi Raye,' Reece smiles.

I stretch out my arm to offer it to him, smiling, and he grins back and takes it and we walk arm-in-arm round to the front of the school assembly hall, the music from the band blaring to greet us.

Megan's got a full-length gown on; it's emerald green and she's got her hair pinned up. Supermodel vibes as usual. Some of the boys have come in black tuxedos, and some have got their ties around their heads, popping off, skidding across the floor on their knees.

Reece fetches us some lemonade, and I hide in the darkest corner I can find watching my ex-best friends dance from afar. They look so on point.

Nisha is wearing a beautiful kurta. She told me the name of it once when I was being nosy, looking at the photos on her mantelpiece of her big family weddings. It's long and black with little silver jewels adorning the hem and neckline. She looks super elegant for a girl who . . . well . . . threw up blue Slush Puppie down herself.

Grace, of course, looks incredible too; the slinkiest red halter neck dress, teamed with dazzling earrings, probably some of Ally's diamonds, I bet.

8.27 p.m.
It's been an hour and I've not moved. Reece is getting restless, I can tell. Tobias and Marcus have arrived and they're raving hard to the band's mediocre cover version of 'Cotton Eye Joe'.

'You can go and dance if you want,' I mumble eventually.

'Oh, can I!?' he exclaims, relieved. 'I love this song! Will you be OK, on your own, like? You should just go and talk to Grace and Nisha. Just go and say hello.'

'I'll be fine. Go,' I say and he scurries off, straight into the arms of Alice Welby and a Dosey-Doe dance. He looks hilarious. No inhibitions whatsoever. I laugh into my lemonade.

Maybe I should just go and talk to the girls. Make the first move? Better than sitting here all alone?

I find myself standing up. My feet start walking towards the band. I stride up three steps on to the stage. It's warm up here, I start sweating immediately, and the glare of the lights is bright in my eyes; I can barely see the dancefloor below me, which is probably a good thing. *Oh god, what am I DOING, have I actually lost my MIND!?*

The band finish 'Cotton Eye Joe' and I grab the microphone from the lead singer. His shocked eyes widen from behind his glasses and he wrestles back, holding on to his precious mic with all his might.

'What are you doing??' he hisses.

'Let me sing one song,' I hiss back.

'No!'

'Look over there!' I yell, pointing behind him. He falls for it hook, line and sinker, releasing his grip and the mic is mine.

'I'll give it back, I promise!' I say.

The crowd below is now wondering what all the fuss is about and start murmuring. I whisper to the band, "Everywhere"? Fleetwood Mac?'

They know it. *Brilliant!* The drum kicks in and my mouth runs dry. *Oh god what am I doing?* But I know it's too late. This is happening.

I clear my throat and say, 'This one's for Grace and Nisha. They're the greatest friends I've ever had and I let them down and I'm trash and I've seen in movies that if people, you know, do a big gesture of love or somethin', then everyone makes friends again so here we go in five, six, seven, eight . . .'

I start warbling away, only realising just now that my voice at home, in my room, singing along to Gary, sounds MUCH better than it does now, in front of the whole school.

OH GOD I'M SINGING IN FRONT OF THE WHOLE SCHOOL.

I can see my Beehive staring back at me in disbelief. Nisha looks aghast and shakes her head at me. Grace is gleeful.

'O O H H H H H H H H H H H H H H H H H H H H , WOOOOOOOOOOOOOOOO!' I sing, really giving it some welly on the big note but that's when the heckling starts . . .

'BOOOOOOOO!'

'GET HER OFF THE STAGE!'

'INDI SOUNDS LIKE MY CAT WHEN IT'S HUNGRY!'

'MY EARS, MY POOR EARS!'

The spectacled lead singer grapples the microphone back off me with vengeance. He gestures at the braying crowd and sarcastically says, 'Probably time to go now, good effort, though, yeah?'

He's right; this has NAAAAAT gone down well . . .

I leg it down the steps, through the crowd, past the smirking Hockey Girls and towards the cloakroom to grab my coat. I pass my ticket to Miss McGregor.

'Leaving early are you, Indiana?' she says, rifling through the mess of coats and jackets.

'Er, yep . . .' I say, eyeing the door, tapping my fingers impatiently on the table.

'Number fifty-four, number fifty-four . . . ah, here it is. This leather jacket, is it?'

'Cheers, miss,' I say, snatching it from her. I run for the exit, fling myself into the cold air outside, and standing right in front of me . . . are Nisha and Grace.

'What the HELL was that?' says Grace, straight-faced.

'I, er . . . I . . .' I splutter.

'No really . . .' says Nisha.

I can barely meet their eyes.

'. . . what the HELL was THAT!? *AAAAAAAAAA AAHAHAHAHAHAHA*!' They both howl with laughter.

'Who knew you had such a TERRIBLE singing voice, Indi, I mean my GOD!' screams Grace.

'Why did you DO that? Are you insane??' says Nisha.

'Oh stop it, I can't breathe,' wheezes Grace.

And they're laughing so hard it starts to make me laugh.

'I dunno, do I? I just wanted to, I dunno, apologise!'

I admit. 'To make you notice me.'

'Oh, we noticed! EVERYONE NOTICED!' hoots Nisha and she slings her arm around my shoulders.

'You do realise that you're the most ridiculous person I've ever met, Indi,' says Grace, shaking her head. 'And . . . and we've missed you too.'

And my heart zings so hard I can't even speak.

Every time we manage to stop laughing, someone sets us off again. When we finally calm down, I grab their hands and say:

'I mean it, though. I am so sorry for everything. Chippy tomorrow? Our Table?'

SATURDAY JULY 17th
2.11 p.m.

The lunchtime rush is over, just a couple of oldies having a lazy afternoon of cod and peas at The Jolly Fryer. The smell radiating from the shop makes my stomach growl; I can't say I've eaten much these past few weeks and when I have, I've ended up on the toilet more often than I've been off it. Who knew being nervous makes you poo? It's gonna be super awks with Alan, but this is the only place for it . . .

I spot Nisha and Grace in the window, sitting at Our

Table. I get a lump in my throat. Last night really happened, but it doesn't mean things are fixed.

'No, out, yer banned remember?' states Alan firmly, as I enter. *Oh god I feel hideous.*

'I know. Alan, I'm really sorry. I just need fifteen minutes with the girls. Please?'

He thinks for a moment. He's still really, *really* angry. 'Ten minutes,' he says. 'Then I want yer gone.'

'OK. Thank you, Alan,' I squeak, feeling worse than ever.

So here we are, Indiana. Make or break time.

I mooch over, barely able to look at them, and take a seat.

'Hi.'

'Hey.'

'Hey.'

It's proper awks, it's so very super awks that I sort of want to laugh, but I don't because that wouldn't be a good start, would it?

'Grace . . .' I start.

'Right, can I just say ONE thing, right . . .'

Here we go, she's gonna lay it right into me. I brace myself.

'. . . Sam broke up with me.'

Oh?

'He said I was too immature which is a *total* joke. I'm literally the maturest person I know, *he's* the immature one. Did I tell you he's got Spongebob Squarepants socks? Ick. He's trash. Anyway, what I'm trying to say issssssss, I'm feeling high-key stressed right now and I don't need any more drama, OK, Indi?'

'Er, yeah. OK. I'm sorry he broke up with you, he seemed . . . nice.'

I look at Nisha.

'Urgh, he actually wasn't, you know. He was a bit of a weasel.'

'And he was also a bit . . .'

'—old. Yes, thank you, Nisha. Yes, he was. Also . . . LOOK AT ME. I'm way too stunnin' for him, he was lucky to be with *this*.'

'I thought you were "undateable", Grace . . .' says Nisha, mockingly.

'Nope. I'm just fine the way I am, thank you very much. Single, but fine. Anyway. That's done now. Let's talk about *all this* shall we,' she says, shifting the mood back to uncomfortable again.

'Look, can *I* just say,' I interject. 'I'm PROPER SORRY that I went out with that stupid boy – whose name I shall not repeat – it was SO stupid of me, 'cause I knew that you liked him and, like, I was reading some stuff online and it said that Rule Number One is you never go out with the person your mate likes, so I ruined The Girl Code and I'm so sorry, it wasn't even a good date, defo not worth losing you guys over and I'll never do that again, I swear—'

Grace holds her hand up to make me stop babbling.

'Ind, stop. It's OK. I mean, yeah, it was a bit crappy of you. But I don't own him, do I?'

I look down. 'Yeah, but you liked him, didn't you?'

Grace fiddles with the salt bottle. 'Yeah, but I was going out with Sam so . . . I just think . . . I was a bit jealous of you.'

My jaw physically drops at this point. So does Nisha's.

You know when your mum or dad says, 'Close your mouth or you'll catch flies'? Well, we could attract a whole nest with how agog we are.

How can someone like GRACE be jealous of someone like ME?

'How can someone like YOU be jealous of someone like ME?' I say to her, out loud, 'cause actually it's a proper good question.

'Listen, I *am* stunnin' and fun and charismatic . . .' she says, jokingly. '. . . but I also have to work *really* hard to be those things. You and Nisha, you're all of those things, but it just comes to you both so naturally . . .'

I am SHOOK. Never in a million years did I think Grace would be jealous of US. She's the one with the huge house, and the best mum and the boyfriends and the perfect boobs.

'I can *guarantee* you, it doesn't come naturally, Grace. I think . . . I think maybe we're all just faking it, aren't we?'

'Yeah. Falling in love makes people go mental, I swear . . .' says Grace.

We smile, which I think means I've made it over the first hurdle. I mean, I've been limping, tripping and stumbling *all the way* to the first hurdle, but I'm over it, nonetheless.

'We do need to talk about the kiss, though, Indi. You do know that if you don't want to kiss someone, you don't HAVE to, right?' says Grace.

'Yeah, I know that now. I just felt like he'd bought the cinema tickets and the chips and he'd hung out with me all evening. I felt sort of, obliged. It was pretty hideous. 1/10, if you want to add it to *The Doing Bits Book*.'

'Well, you're *never* obliged. And it doesn't matter if you change your mind. You're allowed to. At ANY time.'

'OK. I mean, sounds like he didn't enjoy it either to be fair. Said I was "begging it",' I mutter.

'Josh is trash. He's never seeing my paddling pool again, that's for sure! Tell you what, from now on, let's ONLY kiss people we actually want to kiss, OK?' says Grace.

'Deal,' I say.

Nisha starts twiddling the ketchup bottle. She's gone super quiet, which is super uncharacteristic for her.

'OK, just while we're on the subject of, you know, kissing and stuff . . .' says Nisha. 'I suppose I should say . . .'

Me and Grace look at her, half-knowing what's coming next.

'. . . you guys keep asking me about the boys I fancy, ennit. But . . . but I think that maybe instead of boys . . . I actually like girls,' she murmurs, her eyes fixed downwards.

I feel myself swelling with pride, so proud of my friend's bravery. I'd heard how hard coming out is and

Nish's actually gone and done it.

'Oh my GGGGG,' says Grace, almost welling up. 'Oh my G, I'm so glad you told us! And you told us *first*! I assume you told us first, right?'

'Oh yeah, still trying to figure out how to tell Mum and Dad . . .'

'Hmm, that'll be interesting . . .' I say sarcastically, smiling at her for reassurance.

'I know right?' she says. 'So, if we could just keep it between us for now, that'd be . . . useful.'

'Of course,' says Grace.

'You don't have to say anything to anyone else until you're ready,' I say.

'Oh my G, the necklace!' shrieks Grace. She looks at me. 'I've literally been trying to get it out of her for weeks, but she's STILL being stubborn.'

Nisha grins. 'From a friend – she sent it to me in the post. She *is* just a friend at the minute. Been chatting for a few months on socials. Friend of my cousin's. Lives in Scotland, plays hockey for *her* school team. But, yeah, I think we sort of . . . fancy each other? I dunno.'

'Well,' I say, pulling the necklace out of her jumper, so it's proudly on show. 'Whatever you decide, we're here for you. You've got us. For anything you need.'

'Well, it's because we're The Beehive...' she begins.

'...to be in The Beehive is to <u>be</u> in The Beehive...' Grace continues.

'...you won't get anywhere in life, without The Beehive,' I finish.

I look at their smiling faces and feel content for the first time in weeks. Turns out, we've all had our own stuff going on, behind the scenes.

'Is this the point in the movie where we put our hands in the middle and then shout, "Goooo, team!" because it feels like it should be,' Nisha says.

'Nah, let's not do that,' I reply.

'Agreed,' laughs Grace.

I grab their hands anyway and squeeze them hard.

Dear God, thank you for these girls. You totally delivered!

'Time's up,' calls Alan to me, scraping the scraps from the hot counter, not even looking over at me.

I feel a lump in my throat, tell the girls I'll catch them later, and sidle up to him.

'I'd really like my job back, Alan.'

'Well, I don't need the hassle, Indiana', he replies.

Wow, he's ANGRY.

'I know, I know you don't, Alan, but I'm SO sorry. I'm SO SO sorry. I was such a divhead that day. You see the thing is, Alan, I thought I'd fallen in love with this boy, and boys mess with your head and make you do crazy things, you know!'

Time to turn on the charm offensive.

'I mean, come on, Alan, I know you know what I'm talking about. I bet you made the ladies WILD back in the day, eh? The good ol' bachelor days?'

Alan pauses from topping up the battered cod, to consider what I've just said. 'Well, yes, they did seem to fall quite hard for me. A lot of people said I looked like Engelbert Humperdinck back in the day, you see.'

I have no idea who Engelbert Humperdinck is so I just say:

'Well, you know what I'm saying then! I was blinded by love, Alan, it wasn't like me. I promise, if you let me come back, I'll be the best table-cleaner you've ever had, I swear, please,

please, please, please, please, please, please, please, please, please—'

'ALRIGHT! Alright, keep yer hairnet on. I'll put yer back on the schedule. But this is yer last chance, Indiana . . .'

'Thank you, thank you, thank you!' I scream, running around behind the counter and squeezing him around his middle. He taps me on the head, awkwardly.

CHAPTER 21

A TEENY WEENY INNOCENT LITTLE LIE

FRIDAY JULY 23rd
7.00 a.m.

The jingle-jangle of my phone alarm sounds. It's the final day of the school year. *MADE IT.*

'I MADE IT, GARY!'

'Ah, congratulations, dahling. I always said you would!'

'Erm, no, you didn't?'

'Didn't I? Oh. Well I thought it. In my gecko mind . . .'

I pause for a second to enjoy this feeling. I'd love to say the sun was beaming through my window and the birds were tweeting to mark this occasion, but instead it's a bit overcast and I can hear the traffic from the street below. But today feels like a huge achievement. I'm a fully fledged member of St Cath's and one, I'm happy to say, who has been keeping out of trouble.

7.11 a.m.

I stroll sleepy-eyed into the kitchen for breakfast but apparently today is not any old morning in the Raye household. For there is a man in my kitchen. A man in . . . silky animal pyjamas.

'Oh, hi,' I say, smirking.

'Good morning, Indiana, and how are you this bright Friday morning?' says Jonathan.

He's trying to make this look like a casual, *nothing-to-worry-about, keep-it-light* kinda situation, but you can tell HE'S BRICKIN' IT. Tubs shoots me a look from behind him at the sink which says, 'Don't you dare.' But, of course, I can't help myself.

'And what brings you into my home this morning? Little sleepover last night, was it? *A grown-ups' sleepover,* was it?'

He splutters into his coffee and Tubs goes bright red.

'Indi,' she hisses, trying not to pop off.

'Nice pyjamas, Jon! What are those, little parrots on the trousers?'

'Er, I think they're owls, actually.'

'Verrrrrry nice!' I say, winking. 'Anyway, I'm fine, thanks, Jonathan. How are you?'

'I'm good too. I, er, I actually wanted to ask you something, actually . . .'

'D'you want a cuppa, Ind?' asks Tubs, to which I nod.

'. . . I, well, me and your mum, we've been seeing each other for a little while now and what I was thinking is, I'm moving house. Over to a place in Trafford with a little garden and I was thinking . . . and you can say no, but I was thinking . . . maybe you and your mum would like to start coming round mine or somethin'? Just maybe a night here and there, you know, build it up and that. I'd be happy to have you and it's just a bit more space for you. And I'll be honest, I'm not happy they haven't sorted out the damp here as yet. Look, think about it, you don't have to give me an answer now—'

'That would be mint, Jonathan,' I reply. 'I get my own bedroom when I stay, though, right?'

'Yep.'

'And can I paint it?'

'Don't see why not.'

'What if I said I wanted to paint it black?'

'I'd say you were having a laugh, sunshine.'

'OK, fair enough.' I smile, grabbing my brew and a piece of toast. I head back to my bedroom to get changed – it's non-uniform for the last day of term – and I smile at Tubs as I leave. She looks equal parts over-the-moon and genuinely aghast at the outrageous levels of maturity I'm showing.

I've done a lot of growing up these past few weeks.

I've even grown breast-wise: my bra's fitting much better these days. I pull on my tartan pleated mini skirt and the jumper with the holes and dig around a pile of washing to find my beret from Reece. It'll look on point with this outfit. *Tres chic*.

12.46 p.m.

'I've seen a girl who delivers the local paper down our road. I think I'm in love.' Nisha whispers to us in the canteen.

'Er, what about your Scottish lover?'

'Too long distance, ennit,' she says.

'Hang on, rewind. You've fallen in love with your papergirl, Nish?' Grace asks. She's come wearing the smallest of crop tops today and looks stunnin'.

'Yeah. She looks like the one who plays Hermione in *Harry Potter*.'

'Bet she's more like Dobby the House Elf!' screams Grace.

'How DARE you talk about my future wife like that!' laughed Nisha, and we all pop off and fall about laughing and get told to pipe down by a passing dinner lady.

1.15 p.m.

Urgh, Josh Wood is approaching us in the playground. *What does he want . . .*

'Can I have a chat? Privately?'

I sigh heavily. Grace doesn't even look him in the eye.

'You don't have to, Indi,' whispers Nisha, glaring at him.

She's right, I don't have to. But I want to. I want to say my piece.

I wave the girls off, their faces concerned, and head towards the science block. Josh gestures at me to sit next to him on the steps. I lean back against the wall and cross my arms.

'I just wanted to say . . .' he grunts, eyes fixed on his shoes '. . . I dunno why I denied what happened with us at The Jolly Fryer.'

'Oh right,' I reply, stony-faced.

'Cause, like, you could see on the video an' that anyway.'

'Yep.'

My answers are short and clipped and I can feel him getting frustrated with me . . . but I still haven't heard the 'S' word.

I stand back up and tower over him. 'You made me look like I was sooooo despo. Which, by the way, I WASN'T.'

'Yeah, I know. I dunno why I said you were begging it.'

I think back to the cinema. 'Also it wasn't even a good date, and it DEFO wasn't good enough to lose my mates over . . .'

Josh gets up too. 'I know. I just, er, wanted to say . . . I'm sorry.'

Better late than never, I suppose.

'You're forgiven,' I say, sauntering off and looking back at him. 'But you better believe, you ain't never getting THIS honey AGAIN, Johnny Hotpants!'

God that sounded bloody ridiculous. But ohhhhhhh, guess what, I don't care anymore!

2.34 p.m.

Jenko has put *Avengers: Endgame* on the big screen in the assembly hall as an end-of-year treat but everyone has already seen it, so we all talk over it.

'Indi!' calls Alice. 'Who's more attractive? Harry Styles or Robert Pattinson?'

'Harry, defo,' I reply.

'Agreed!' says Alice.

'Wrong, Alice,' says Reece. 'It's Robert Pattinson. Come on, it's *Batman*!'

Alice grins and turns away.

'She's unreal,' says Reece under his breath.

'What?' I laugh, thinking I must have misheard.

'She's unreal. Alice. Proper unreal.'

I feel my stomach drop.

I don't know what to say. Reece has never talked to me about girls before.

NO, INDIANA RAYE, NO.

THIS IS NOT HAPPENING.

AFTER EVERYTHING THAT'S HAPPENED THIS YEAR . . . DO I LIKE REECE AFTER ALL???

3.16 p.m.

We get let out fifteen minutes early. Most of school heads down the park to hang out while the sunshine hangs in the air; an end-of-term tradition at St Cath's apparently, but Nisha, Grace and I decide to go for the last chippy debrief of the term.

'Six weeks' holiday is it then, girls?' says Alan, as we clang through the door. 'Fantastic, I've got fryers that need scrubbing, fridges that need washing out, fish that needs descaling . . .'

'Give us a cone of chips each, Al, and you've got a

deal,' says Nisha. 'I actually wouldn't mind getting a bit more money in over the hols . . .'

'Me too!' I say quickly.

Would make Tubs pleased if I took on a few more shifts while I can. And besides, turns out working at The Jolly Fryer has been the best thing that's ever happened to me.

3.35 p.m.

'OK, hopes and dreams for next year?' says Nisha, dunking her chips in mayonnaise. 'I'm gonna make St Cath's regional hockey champions. And I'm gonna go on a date, ennit. A proper date! I don't know where I'm gonna *find* a date, but mark my words, its gonna happen! Can you believe we'll be Year Ten?'

'I know, right!? Grace, how about you? Hopes and dreams?' I ask.

'Gonna become an influencer,' she said definitively.

'You can't just BECOME an influencer, Grace,' I laugh.

'I can try . . .' she says.

'Hmm, good luck with that one. I have NO hopes and dreams for next year,' I say.

'Yes, you do, Indi . . .' says Grace, mouthing 'Reece' to Nisha.

I feel myself blush. 'I don't! I just want a nice, quiet year . . .'

4.57 p.m.

There've been whispers of an end of year party later at Mason's house but Grace decides we should sack it off and go round hers instead for a movie night, which sounds like a good plan to me. I'm done with parties and drama for now. I head home to get changed and grab a toothbrush, with the sounds of Oasis in my ears.

I was lying about the old 'hopes and dreams' thing by the way.

But it was a teeny weeny INNOCENT little lie.

They were right; I do I want to spend more time with Reece. His dad has invited me over to their family BBQ in a few weeks' time and I can't wait.

I'd like to visit Dad in Paris, if he'll see me.

I'd like to work out what I'd like to do as a job one day.

Can you become a professional cartoon drawer? Is that a thing?

I want to be a bit nicer to Jonathan – he seems like a decent guy.

I want a boyfriend. I WANT A BOYFRIEND DESPO.

Oh, and I'd quite like to re-do my first neck on with someone. With someone nice.

Maybe even someone special.

AND I STILL WANT TO GO TO GLASTONBURY!

Whatever happens, I know I'll be able to face it all with the best friends a girl could ever have; girls I can truly be myself around. I don't have to be something I'm not any more.

I take my phone from my pocket and punch out a message I should have sent to Nisha and Grace months and months ago.

> hey do you guys wanna come over to mine tonight instead? meet gary? tubs has bought pizza! 🐝🐝🐝

Beehive forever.

ACKNOWLEDGEMENTS

Hello! Thank you for reading *Indi Raye Is Totally Faking It*. I must be honest, I've been faking it too. Because I am not a writer. Or I wasn't . . . until I met my agent.

I'll never forget the day my agent, Chloe Seager at Madeleine Milburn Literary Agency, said: 'OK SO . . . instead of the self-help book (I had pitched), how about a fully-fledged novel?'

Now, Chloe didn't know what she was getting herself into. I had never written a novel. I'd never written fiction. I wrote most of my 6,000-word university dissertation two nights before it was due, tanked up to my eyeballs on Red Bull and Haribo, and now my agent was after a novel containing 60,000 words? Impossible!

But, with Chloe's help, we got there. Thank you, Chloe, for being the most supportive angel, always telling me the bits you found funny and for having sympathy for me that time I managed to delete A THIRD of my book off my laptop . . .

Next up, to Polly Lyall Grant and the Hachette Children's Group team. Oh my god. I can't believe I'm publishing a book with such a literary giant! I am so lucky.

Polly, you have read this book so many times and I have asked you so many stupid questions. Stuff like 'Should this be past tense?' or 'What's a verb again?' Y'know, stuff you learn in Year 3 English. You've been amazing, the best sounding board and you've also helped me immensely by removing jokes and anecdotes that might get me cancelled, so thank you.

Thank you to the wider Hachette Children's Group team: Lucy Clayton, Bec Gillies, Katherine Fox, Laura Pritchard. Thank you to Lizzie Clifford for the copyedits.

Thank you to Jen Alliston for the cover design and Luna Valentine for the cover art.

Writing a book pulled me away from being a TV & Radio presenter (my 'normal job') so thanks to my broadcasting agents, Money Management, who demonstrated patience when I flew into their office and screamed, 'I CAN'T DO IT, I CAN'T WRITE THIS BOOK!' and who replied, 'Lauren, you're a procrastinator. Just FINISH IT FOR GOD'S SAKE.' Thank you for your important and ongoing honesty.

To my husband Luke, who, as the funny one in the marriage, had to endlessly endure me sneaking into the kitchen asking, 'Luke, Luke . . . is this joke funny? Luke, what do you reckon to this gag?' I was like a bad stand-up comedian he couldn't get rid of, but hey . . . you chose to marry this, so . . . suck it. Thank you for making me funnier.

Cheers TikTok, for helping me keep up to date with ever-changing Gen Z trends and slang. And for the funny dog videos.

And the biggest thanks, of course, goes to my school friends, my best friends. Their sheer stupidity (seriously, they are idiots), the amount of adventures we had, the buckets and buckets of hilarious memories are the reason this book exists. There's nothing as glorious as female friendship; the type that makes you snort with laughter, or pee your pants a bit, or like me, need a puff on your asthma inhaler because you can't breathe, and I'm so thankful we're still making each other laugh after all these years. Can't wait 'til our husbands die and we can all go live in a care home together!

© davidreissphotography

Lauren Layfield is a TV and radio presenter, hosting Capital's *Early Breakfast Show*, regularly reporting for BBC's *The One Show* and presenting the BBC coverage of *Eurovision*. Her career started at CBBC HQ where she also hosted some of their biggest entertainment shows including *The Dengineers*, *The Playlist* and *The Dog Ate My Homework*. She's fronted ground-breaking documentaries *Let's Talk About Periods* and *Let's Talk About Sexism* and is an ambassador for the charities Young Minds and Bloody Good Period.